Pick Your
Poison

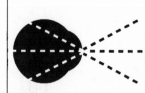

This Large Print Book carries the
Seal of Approval of N.A.V.H.

Pick Your Poison

A YELLOW ROSE MYSTERY

Leann Sweeney

Thorndike Press • Waterville, Maine

Published in 2004 by arrangement with NAL Signet, a member of Penguin Group (USA) Inc.

Thorndike Press® Large Print Mystery.

The tree indicium is a trademark of Thorndike Press.

The text of this Large Print edition is unabridged. Other aspects of the book may vary from the original edition.

Set in 16 pt. Plantin by Al Chase.

Printed in the United States on permanent paper.

Library of Congress Control Number: 2004109565
ISBN 0-7862-6817-4 (lg. print : hc : alk. paper)

For Candy, my sister, best friend,
and ally against the odds.

As the Founder/CEO of NAVH, the only national health agency solely devoted to those who, although not totally blind, have an eye disease which could lead to serious visual impairment, I am pleased to recognize Thorndike Press* as one of the leading publishers in the large print field.

Founded in 1954 in San Francisco to prepare large print textbooks for partially seeing children, NAVH became the pioneer and standard setting agency in the preparation of large type.

Today, those publishers who meet our standards carry the prestigious "Seal of Approval" indicating high quality large print. We are delighted that Thorndike Press is one of the publishers whose titles meet these standards. We are also pleased to recognize the significant contribution Thorndike Press is making in this important and growing field.

Lorraine H. Marchi, L.H.D.
Founder/CEO
NAVH

* Thorndike Press encompasses the following imprints: Thorndike, Wheeler, Walker and Large Print Press.

1

The sun could have melted diamonds that day, and I spent the afternoon poolside, wasting away in Liptonville for the thirtieth time in a month. I'd just come out of the water and was slopping on more sunscreen when I noticed Ben hovering by the gate to the pool.

Ben never hovers. As the hardest-working yardman in the kingdom of River Oaks — the overindulged and overendowed section of Houston — he stays far too busy to hover. His daily challenge is to keep the property that my twin sister and I own from turning into something reminiscent of a tropical rain forest.

He held a rake, and wore his regular white cotton shirt and gray khaki work pants. A wide-brimmed canvas hat shaded his face.

"You need something, Ben?" I asked.

"If you've got a moment, Miss Abby."

"A moment? I stay about as busy as a ghost-town undertaker, so I can offer you endless moments. Come on over here."

He rested the rake against the wrought-iron fence, dragged a chair from the patio table, and sat next to me. His lined face was tense with concern and he stared down at the pebbled deck. "Will your sister be home at the regular time?"

I set down my bottle of SPF 45. "I think so. Is something wrong?"

"Not wrong, exactly. Sorry . . . yes, maybe wrong — but nothing that's your fault, or Miss Kate's fault." He took off his hat and wiped a forearm across his sweat-beaded forehead. "Didn't think this would be so hard."

"You're not quitting, are you? Because if you need more money or —"

"I don't need your money, miss."

"Okay. So what is it? You seem upset."

"You and Miss Kate . . . well, I know you've been grieving. Trying to get over losing your daddy so sudden and all. I've been waiting for the right time to say what needs saying."

I'd never seen him so nervous. "I'm listening, Ben."

He hesitated. "See, that's why I was asking about Miss Kate. I don't think I can say this more than once, and you both need to hear. I was hoping I could come up to the house when she gets home from the university."

"Sure, but —"

"About six o'clock, then. Got work to do, miss. Lawn by the front drive needs edging." And with that, he practically ran back to his rake and retreated across the yard.

"Wait!" I called. "Can't you give me a hint what this is all about?" Secrets — and this sure sounded secret — are something you tell only one person at a time, and he needed to tell me *first*.

But he was hurrying toward the shed where we keep the lawn mowers, and if he heard me, it was ignored.

He'd left the gate ajar, and Webster, Kate's Border collie, took this as an invitation to join me. Since he couldn't fit beneath my low-to-the-ground chaise, he sought shade under the chair Ben had abandoned. After stretching out, I reached over to scratch his head.

"What do you think that was all about, Webster?" I said.

But he ignored me too, and soon I dozed off, still wondering what quiet, unobtrusive Ben might find too difficult to say more than once.

I'm not sure how much time passed, but the monstrous brick house Daddy willed to Kate and me was beginning to cast its shadow over the pool when Webster started all the commotion. At first I was grateful his barking woke me, because I'd slipped into this mini nightmare where I found myself at the altar dressed in white tulle and red cowboy boots, prepared to remarry my ex-husband. Seems I'd spent so much time on the deck this summer, I'd sizzled my brain cells along with the rest of me.

I slipped into the tepid water and swam a few laps, hoping to rid myself of the dream, but now that Steven had presented himself, the memories wouldn't leave me alone. When he was sober, the man could charm the gloss off a photograph, and he'd been sober for months, a fact he wasn't letting me forget.

But if I went soft on him, I'd be watching him hug another commode or be bailing him out of jail on a drunk-and-disorderly charge again. I could resist. I could be strong. Besides, I missed Daddy, not Steven. The "Ex Man" just happened to show up in a stupid dream.

Meanwhile, Webster hadn't let up with the barking. I returned to my chair and flopped onto my belly, palms pressed against my ears. But I couldn't drown him out, and since thinking about divorces and drunken encounters had primed my stinger, poor Webster was about to experience the full brunt of my irritation.

I raised up and shouted, "Don't you know it's hot enough to boil mercury, animal?" This had no impact, so I flipped over and sat on the edge of the chair. "You're gonna collapse in an overheated heap, you keep that up!"

He yapped louder.

Now, Webster's vocabulary is limited to about twenty words, most of them related to food and bodily functions. No surprise the word *overheated* didn't register. He kept on barking, transforming my aggravation into a full-fledged death wish.

I stood, took a generous gulp of watered-down tea from my ever-present thermos, and marched on him like Sherman through Atlanta.

The dog's frenzy, I soon discovered, was focused on the greenhouse door, but where he'd found the energy to pull off this canine rendition of a nervous breakdown I'll never know. See, Webster manages to squeeze in his twenty-three-and-a-half hours of sleep per day, come hell or high water. He is *not* your garden-variety Border collie. More like a basset hound in disguise.

When I reached the greenhouse, a little Plexiglas building beyond the rose garden and fig trees on the east side of the property, I stood menacingly above the dog, hoping body language would have a silencing effect. This seemed to work, because he did shut up.

"Guess you wore yourself out," I said, sounding smug.

Webster fixed his worried brown eyes on my face and sat down with a whimper.

Hmm. Maybe smug wasn't the appropriate emotion. Maybe I should be worried, too.

Nah. Probably just an armadillo or a possum. Either that, or a water moccasin slithered in there from the nearby bayou.

I reached over the dog for the door handle, ready to chase away whatever creature had him all riled up, but before I could say *woof,* Webster scampered between my legs like I was up on jacks in the garage and raced toward the house.

"What's got into you?" I mumbled, pushing my sunglasses to the top of my head. I pressed my nose against the screen to peer inside.

What I saw made me yank open that door, but then I clung to the frame, paralyzed by the scene before me.

Ben lay spread-eagled on the dirt floor between gallon pails of antique roses, and one look at his face told me I couldn't help him. His eyes were wide, his lips were blue, and his face was scarlet.

The tea I'd drunk threatened to erupt, but I swallowed hard and forced myself to take those few short steps to kneel beside him. A plastic watering can had tipped over — probably dropped it when he collapsed — and his right hand rested in a wide, wet circle. I checked his neck for a pulse, and though his skin felt warm, he was definitely dead.

I gripped his shoulder, my head bent. "Oh, my God, Ben, I am so sorry. So very sorry."

The small building seemed to close in on me then, the smell of roses, pine-bark mulch, and lemon thyme all mixing together with another odor, something familiar but one I couldn't identify.

I grasped the edge of the nearby potting table for support, then stumbled outside. The flimsy door shut with a *thwack*, and I stood for a second, my pulse roaring in my ears.

I had to call someone. The police? Yes . . . No . . . God! Why couldn't I string two coherent thoughts together? Maybe because I'd discovered two dead people in a few short months, first my daddy and now Ben.

I looked toward the house. *Yes. Call. Tell someone.*

I made myself move, slowly at first on those shaky legs, then faster and faster. But if I thought running like a scorched cat would make the horrible images of death disappear, I was wrong. Ben's wide eyes still seemed to be boring into me even after I reached the phone in the kitchen. Drenched with sweat by then, I dialed those three numbers you never want to use, tasting the salt on my lips, grateful for that tiny affirmation of life.

An hour had passed since I called 911. An ambulance and a swarm of police had crowded onto my lawn ten minutes after I phoned. But even though I'd clearly told the dispatcher Ben was dead, the paramedics showed up anyway. How I wished they could have Heimliched or resuscitated him back to life. Six patrol cars were parked at awkward angles on the curving drive, doors ajar, their whirling lights calling the neighbors to assemble outside the fence and gawk.

I'd been told to stay put after I led the first officers to the body, and so I sat twenty feet from the greenhouse door under the shade of a crape myrtle. People with shiny gloved hands were rushing around carrying plastic

14

bags, while other officers wrote in note-books, used cell phones, or spoke into walkie-talkies. They had propped open the screen door, and my gaze kept wandering back to Ben's body. He still lay between the roses, and I wondered why they didn't cover him up with one of those white sheets I always saw on the six-o'clock news.

"You the homeowner?" came a voice from the vicinity of my right shoulder.

I looked up. A man, maybe late thirties, his short blond hair darkened by sweat, stood to my right. He looked maybe six feet, one-eighty, wearing a button-down off-white shirt, mocha tie, and a "Don't Mess with Texas" expression. I got to my feet, brushing grass off the back of my legs. His police shield, attached to the chest pocket of his shirt, glinted in the late-afternoon sun, and from those shadows under his tired eyes, I pegged him as the president-elect of the Burned-out Cop Society.

I held out my hand. "Abby Rose, and yes, I'm the owner."

He ignored my gesture of greeting and said, "I see a compressor over by that cabana. Place air-conditioned?"

"Yes, sir," I answered, feeling like maybe I should salute with my useless, "out there" appendage.

15

"Good." He was already on his way before I could blink.

Bet that man struts even when he's sitting down, I thought, following on his heels.

He asked one of the uniformed officers if the cabana had been searched and dusted for prints, and was told the place was clean. We went inside.

I was scared, hot, and still in shock over my discovery, and the bathhouse-slash-refreshment center, with its cushioned wicker chairs and pastel walls, provided a cool, familiar atmosphere that calmed me almost immediately.

I grabbed a robe from one of the dressing rooms and a bottled water from the fridge behind the small bar, offering water to the policeman as well. He declined and took a pack of Big Red gum from his shirt pocket.

"My name is Sergeant Kline and I'm with Homicide," he said. "Have a seat."

Guzzling down half the water before I took a breath, I sat opposite him at the table in the center of the room.

He checked a palm-size notebook. "Ms. Rose, is it?"

"Yes. Abby Rose. But did you say Homicide? Because Ben looked like maybe he'd had a stroke or choked to death or —"

"We aren't certain how he died. But

there're enough questions concerning the physical evidence in the greenhouse that —"

"What evidence?"

Sergeant Kline chewed his gum, tapping his pen on the glass tabletop. "Ms. Rose, let me ask the questions."

He sounded irritated, just like those probate lawyers had when we went over Daddy's will and I kept interrupting their droning legalese for clarification.

"Okay. Ask away." I swigged down the rest of the water, thinking I might get frostbite if I took this guy's pulse.

"You told the first policeman on the scene that you heard nothing in the greenhouse prior to investigating the barking dog?"

"I was asleep. The dog woke me."

"And you live here with your sister, is that correct?"

"Yes, sir."

"But you indicated she was not at home today? That you and Mr. Garrison were alone?"

"Mr. Garrison?" I said, confused. "Oh — you mean Ben. Sorry, yes. We were alone." Shame heated my face. I didn't even remember Ben's last name. What the hell kind of employer was I?

Kline said, "We couldn't locate a driver's license or address book in Garrison's garage apartment here on the property. The medical examiner's officer found no ID in his pockets. No credit cards either. Were his quarters temporary? And if so, do you have a permanent address where we could find information to notify family?"

"The apartment wasn't temporary. He lived there all the time. His days off were Sunday and Monday and —"

"Do you have an employment application? Something with a former address? Relatives hearing through the media about a loved one's death . . . Well, we don't like that."

Did he think *I'd* get a rip-roaring kick out of such an awful thing happening? After taking a deep breath to keep myself from spouting off, I said, "My father hired Ben, and Daddy would have scanned the application, if there was one, then filed it on his computer. I'm sure if you give me time I could find —"

"So where's your father?"

"He . . . passed on," I answered.

Kline sighed, the release laden with fatigue. "Sorry to hear that. So how long did the victim work here? You know that much, right?"

"Maybe three months?"

The detective removed his pack of gum

and folded another stick into his mouth. He tossed the balled-up wrapper into the wastebasket adjacent to the bar, and chewed for a second before continuing. "Tell me about today. I assume you spoke with the victim?"

"Yes, I did."

"I know you went over this with the responding officer, but I'd like you to repeat everything you remember about today."

What I recalled most was Ben's odd behavior this afternoon by the pool. He'd never approached me like that before. But I hadn't mentioned this to the other policeman, maybe because Homicide wasn't part of his job description and it had never crossed my mind that Ben died from anything but natural causes.

But now, with this intense man whose rigid blue stare could knock a tank off course, the earlier conversation took on added significance. So after filling Kline in on my otherwise boring day, I said, "Out by the pool, Ben asked to talk to me about something, but wanted my sister present."

"What something?"

I hesitated, and the room seemed so quiet I swore I could hear my hair growing. "I — I don't know what something. He wouldn't say."

"Repeat his words as best you recall." He had his pen poised over the notebook, and his jaw was working the Big Red hard.

But the details seemed to have left my brain like powdered sugar through a sifter. "I can't remember. The feeling I got was that he was troubled."

Kline said, "Troubled? That's it?"

"Yes, sir."

"And this was the first time he'd ever seemed troubled?"

"Well . . . maybe I just didn't notice before today."

Another huge sigh. "Yeah, okay. What about access to the property? Any recent history of strangers hanging around? Or break-ins? Anything unusual?"

"No."

He wrote this down, as if somehow my complete lack of knowledge was worth saving for posterity. If Ben *had* been murdered, I couldn't offer a clue to help find his killer. And unless I turned up information in Daddy's files, I couldn't help find his relatives, either. I was beginning to feel about as useful as an outhouse on a submarine.

Someone knocked on the door — a welcome interruption.

An officer stuck his head inside and said, "The other Rose woman is here. And this one's lawyer." He nodded my way, his expression looking as if he'd just picked something green out of his teeth.

Kline flushed, his hard stare turned back on me. "You called a lawyer?"

"I didn't call a lawyer," I snapped back. I could do surly, too.

Kate squeezed past the policeman into the cabana and rushed over to me. "Thank God you're all right! You *are* all right, Abby?"

I nodded. "I'm fine."

She fixed a strand of humidity-damp chocolate-brown hair behind her ear. "When I saw those police cars, I — I didn't know what to think. But the policewoman at the gate said it was Ben. She said he collapsed."

"He's dead, Kate," I said quietly.

"Dead?" She looked at Kline and then at me. "Oh, my gosh! Did he fall? Get cut with the lawn mower? Bleed to death? And do this many police always respond to accidents?"

Kline addressed Kate. "Ms. Rose? Can I ask you to step outside for one second?"

"Why?" She looked down at me again. "Abby? What's going on?"

"No problem, just routine," Kline answered for me, sounding a whole lot gentler than I would have thought him capable of.

"What about the lawyer?" the cop at the door said. "You want him in here, Sergeant?"

"It's just Willis," Kate said.

"Oh. Willis," I replied. "Please keep him outside." How the heck had he found out about Ben? Had Kate called him? Or was this just one of his routine drive-bys so he could offer to run my life?

The uniformed officer took Kate by the elbow and they left.

"If you didn't phone the lawyer, what's he doing here?" Kline asked.

"He shows up unannounced on a regular basis. More friend of the family than attorney," I said.

"But you have a gate and a security system, right? I mean, that's standard equipment in this neighborhood," Kline said.

"With all the rent-a-cops hanging around, I rarely activate the alarm," I said, trying to slip this past him like it made perfect sense.

"So no alarm, and the gate was unlocked today, is that right?"

"Right." This guy probably thought I was born dumb and went downhill from there.

"One more question. Did you notice the burn on Mr. Garrison's hand during your last conversation with him?"

"The burn?"

"A large burn on the side of his right hand, from his small finger down to the wrist." He demonstrated the spot.

"I never saw any burn."

His lips tightened and he started writing more notes in his book. "Thank you, Ms. Rose. I would appreciate it if you keep today's conversation with the victim to yourself until I've had a chance to finish my interviews. That's all."

"That's all?"

He didn't look up. "You have something important to tell me, ma'am?"

"Well, no, but —"

"Then that's all."

Maybe in his mind. But that wasn't all. Not by a long shot. And you could write that on the wall in ink.

2

After I left the cabana, Kate and I exchanged a hug, and she went in for her little chat with the curdled detective. Meanwhile, Willis Hatch stood behind the crime-scene tape strung between the oaks lining the driveway. He waved for me to join him.

The uniformed cop at the cabana door apparently noted my hesitation to acknowledge Willis's presence, because he said, "Want me to get rid of him? I'd like to tell a lawyer where to go."

I sighed. "No, I'll talk to him. Are we allowed in the house?"

"Far as I know."

A short man with graying hair and glasses, Willis wasn't looking too lawyerlike this afternoon. He wore a T-shirt, gym shorts, and tennis shoes. Must have come straight from the health club. Though in his sixties, he's in better shape than I am.

"What are you doing here?" I said, ducking under the tape.

"I'm minding my business on the treadmill thirty minutes ago, and what do I see on the television above me? A news-chopper shot of your house, the lawn full of patrol cars. Your house, Abby. Does that answer your question?"

Oh, yes. Question answered. I'd have to send a thank-you card to Channel Five. "Let's go inside, Willis. The mosquitoes are preparing for their evening feast and I don't want to be on the menu."

He followed me up the driveway and along the winding brick path to the front door, jabbering about the outrage of the police invading Daddy's property and how Charlie wouldn't have let them run rough-shod over the place if he were still alive.

The policewoman previously stationed at the entrance earlier was gone, and we went inside.

"Why didn't you phone me right after you called the police?" Willis asked.

"Because I didn't need to call you."

I crossed the marble foyer — you could hold a political convention in the entry alone — and went into the study. Daddy had done all the household business in this room.

The heavy forest-green drapes were drawn, and the small study — small by the standards of the rest of the castle — still smelled like Old Spice and cigars. Since his death, I'd come in here just to sit where

Daddy had spent so much time. With his scent still so strong and his stacks of books, computer CDs, and disks piled in the barrister shelves, I could feel his presence, catch in my mind's eye a glimpse of his wide, free smile.

Today, however, I went straight to the giant mahogany computer desk, plopped down in the red leather chair, and booted up the machine. I'd done this only one other time since his death. It had felt then like an invasion of his privacy, and today was no different.

"What in God's universe are you doing?" Willis said.

"Helping the police locate Ben's family, or at least I hope so."

"On Charlie's computer?"

I typed Daddy's log-in password, and the icons on his desktop started to pop up.

"At least he told you his password," Willis said, pulling up an upholstered side chair. "I planned to ask you about that — see if you wanted me to clear out anything I have duplicated in my office files."

"He never told me the password. Took me the better part of an afternoon to figure it out. He's challenging me even after he's gone. So typical, huh, Willis?"

His gaze glued to the screen, he said,

"Indeed. But I still don't understand how his computer will help you locate Ben's family."

I explained about Ben's lack of identification and said, "I'm hoping Daddy scanned in the job application showing a previous address."

"Knowing Charlie, I doubt if an application exists."

"Daddy may have been disorganized — I mean, look at those shelves." I gestured at the far wall. "But you know how well he documented his business and his personal life."

"This is different. Charlie hired that man on impulse, and if he'd heeded my warnings about checking references before taking on these drifters, today's horrible events might not have occurred."

"Ben? A drifter? He seemed like a pretty stable, commonsense guy to me."

Using the search feature on the start menu, I typed in Ben's name. No files appeared in the window. When I replaced the entry with "employment applications," plenty of document names appeared, but the most recent was dated more than a year ago. I then expanded the files on the C drive, but saw nothing that even looked like a file related to Ben, just household budgeting, tax files, and copies of programs Daddy created early in his career as a software developer.

"Maybe you misjudged Mr. Garrison," Willis said. "*Likable* doesn't translate to upstanding citizen."

I turned to Willis. "Why are you so down on him? He's been murdered, for God's sake."

"Maybe my attitude isn't related to Ben. Maybe I'm still angry with Charlie for dying on me. One of our last disagreements involved Ben — how Charlie gave him the job without consulting me. He usually always asked my advice."

I sat back, understanding now. I was still pissed off at Daddy myself for making such an abrupt exit. "So Daddy consulted you about more than CompuCan business, then?"

I currently pretend to run CompuCan, the company Daddy left behind, seeing as how I'm the daughter with the computer science degree. But about five years ago Daddy phased out the software side, and now CompuCan vies for its share of the "you want it, we'll build it" desktop-laptop business. Since it's well managed by others with far more expertise in sales and marketing than I possess, I pretty much keep my distance.

Willis said, "To answer your question, Charlie was my best friend first, my client second, and we talked about everything. But he hired Ben without my input, and now that choice seems to have landed you smack in the center of a scandal."

"Have you forgotten we have a victim at the center of this so-called scandal, Willis?"

He hesitated, his cheeks infusing with color. "I-I guess I was sounding pretty callous. But my main concern is for you, Abby. If Ben was murdered, a killer sneaked onto your property while you were nearby."

"I-I never thought of that." And this realization jolted me. But not because I was worried about myself. No, the fact that Ben might have angered someone so much that they wanted him dead was what really bothered me. And the killer probably walked right past my sleeping body to do him harm. I'd heard nothing, and I should have.

"I'm going back to the club," Willis said. "I dropped everything when I heard the news. Left my clothes in my locker. You need anything, you call me, understand?"

"Sure," I replied, distracted. Why hadn't I heard anything this afternoon? Could I have saved Ben's life if I hadn't fallen

29

asleep? Or if I'd locked the gate? Or turned on the alarm? And how could I live with myself if I could have prevented Ben's death?

Kate returned to the house about fifteen minutes later. She too couldn't offer Sergeant Kline any information about Ben's family. Together we searched the study for any documents Daddy might have saved concerning Ben, but came up with nothing. Within the hour we were back outside, watching them load Ben into the medical examiner's van.

The setting sun created an apricot-and-red backdrop to this macabre scene — perfect colors for what was a far more emotional moment than I would have imagined. Tears slid down my cheeks and onto the front of the tank top I'd changed into. A hardworking man had been murdered while I slept by my fancy pool alongside my lavish home in my ritzy neighborhood. And wasn't I proud?

The number of police on the property had dwindled to one: Sergeant Kline. He stood somberly by as the stretcher was hoisted into the van. Without acknowledging Kate's or my presence, he then strode toward a white Crown Victoria.

I caught up to him as he was about to pull off the lawn.

He rolled down his window when I tapped on the glass.

"You remember something about that conversation with the victim?" he asked.

"No. Sorry. But I did check for the application we talked about."

"And?"

"I couldn't find one. But we own an old house in Galveston that Daddy used as a mini-warehouse for his document collection. He saved every scrap of paper he ever touched, so he could have stored —"

"Thanks, Ms. Rose. Let me know what you turn up." And with that, the window whirred back up.

I stepped away from the car and he drove off.

Sheesh, I thought, rejoining Kate. *That man's mother probably had to feed him with a slingshot.*

She and I walked back toward the house arm in arm, Kate's head on my shoulder. Though I felt a powerful sadness at what had happened here, guilt grabbed at me the most. I knew nothing about a man who had lived right next to me for months. Nothing except his name. What were his dreams? Who had he shared them with?

Where did he come from?

I kept imagining his family somewhere, maybe watching TV or reading books or taking a walk, completely unaware they had lost someone they loved. And so, before I fell asleep that night, I promised myself I would find out if Ben had a wife . . . children . . . or even aging parents. And I would speak with his family, offer them my sympathy. As Daddy always said, conscience is like a baby. It has to go to sleep before you do.

3

The next morning I lay curled under the quilt with Diva asleep on my hip. She's a calico with plenty of attitude, and my best friend, next to Kate.

White morning light sneaked between the slats in the blinds, and the central air-conditioning hummed its reminder that this would be another scorching day in the Bayou City. But there would be no languishing by the pool. I was committed to tracking down Ben's family.

I stroked Diva's back, then eased her off me. She settled into the quilt folds and closed her eyes while I sat on the edge of the bed and stretched, ready to head for the shower.

The nightstand phone rang before I put a foot on the floor. I picked up.

"Abby?" snapped a female voice I recognized as belonging to my aunt Caroline Lemoyne. She comes on about as gentle as a mouthful of spicy gumbo, and even though she'd uttered only a single word, I knew she was hot.

"Hi, Aunt Caroline," I replied, trying for nonchalant.

"Tell me what happened. Every detail. And I especially would like to know why I had to read about this murder in the *Chronicle*."

"I didn't have much chance to —"

"Very unflattering picture of you and your sister, by the way. The newspaper used that awful shot from the Ackerman Charity Ball. The one with you in that red dress that makes you look so . . . plump."

Oh, brother. That "unflattering" picture in the hands of reporters? A true social emergency.

"The *Chronicle* said it was a murder, then?" I said, focusing on the one interesting thing she'd managed to say. "Because the police wouldn't confirm that yesterday."

"I'm not sure it's confirmed even today. You know how vague newspaper reporters get when they don't possess all the facts. And who died, may I ask? Because apparently his identity is being withheld."

"Remember the yardman, Ben Garrison?"

"Oh. Him. Well, then this murder theory makes no sense. Gardeners work with poisons all the time. Do you have a rodent problem? Is that how this cyanide affair played out?"

Cyanide? Yes! That's what I'd smelled in the greenhouse. Almonds. "I didn't even know about the cyanide. Did the article say anything else of interest?"

"Are you saying a man dies violently on your property and you know nothing? *And* you don't bother to call me?"

"We were kind of overwhelmed by all the police searching the place, collecting evidence, asking questions. Then a slew of reporters hung around outside the gate even after the police left. You'll be pleased to know we didn't talk to them, by the way."

"At least you have *some* sense left, but you still should have contacted me. We may not be blood relatives, but I have cared for you all your life, and with Charlie gone, I'm the only person you girls have left in this world."

I bit my lip to keep from saying something I might regret. Would a day go by when she would not remind me that Kate and I were adopted?

"You're right," I said. "I should have filled you in."

"Yes, you should have. Have you brought Willis in on this?"

"He came by yesterday."

"And you have an alibi, I take it?"

"You think I need an alibi?"

35

"Abigail, your temper has caused you plenty of problems in the past."

"Oh. So you think Ben didn't prune the wax ligustrums to my liking, so I cooked him up a pot of cyanide soup?"

"No need for sarcasm. You have my unwavering support no matter what the outcome of this sordid affair."

I had to change the subject — either that or slam the receiver down in her ear. In my best fake-sweet voice I said, "By chance did Daddy talk to you before he hired Ben? Say anything about him? Like where he came from, maybe?"

"No, Charlie didn't share anything with me. Why should he? I must say, I found Ben to be an impertinent sort. Probably upset the wrong person and got himself killed."

"Impertinent? With you?"

"Not with me. I hardly knew the man," she said quickly. "But he always seemed to be lingering around the windows when I would drop by, or I'd see him hanging about where Charlie or Willis or other visitors were gathered. Not exactly a trait you like in your hired help."

I thought the "hired help" was supposed to do exactly that — hang around and do their jobs. Time to move on again. "Aunt Caroline, since you've had some experience

36

with divorce, I was wondering if you ever used a private detective."

"A private detective? Why?"

Her lack of a yes or no told me she probably had used one during the course of her three divorces. "I'm asking because I owe Ben's family an expression of sympathy. The man died in our greenhouse, working for me, and if I hire a detective, maybe I can locate his kin and somehow explain what happened here."

"Isn't that the responsibility of the police? I mean, you pay plenty of taxes. Seems ridiculous to waste your money on a private investigator."

"Just considering my options. Listen, I desperately need a shower. We'll talk later, okay?"

She said good-bye and I hung up, concluding she was right about one thing: I didn't need to pay a detective for a job I really would rather do myself.

Half an hour later, I padded into the combination kitchen-family room with Diva close at my heels. Once my favorite spot, this section of the house held unpleasant reminders of my marriage to Steven. Almost every quarrel had ended here, with him running out the back door to drink away his anger. My bitterness had stayed trapped inside me since we split, ticking away. Always ticking.

But this morning the breakfast alcove, the fireplace yawning back at the chintz-covered easy chairs, and the long row of luminous oak cabinets welcomed me like a returning friend. For the first time in months, I felt as if I had a purpose.

Sections of the morning paper littered the kitchen table, which meant Kate must be awake. As if on cue, the back door opened.

"Hi, kiddo," she said in her smiley morning voice. Webster ambled in behind her. She was dressed for her intern sessions at the university, wearing a crisp white blouse and tailored beige slacks.

"Did I ever mention you're too damn cheerful to be related to me?" I said.

"You have," she answered. "Always in the morning, before coffee."

Though Kate and I are twins, no one ever guesses. We both have brown eyes, but Kate stands two inches taller and has lustrous dark tresses, while I doctor my own short brown hair to what those creative geniuses at Clairol call Evening Claret.

I dumped tuna onto a saucer and Diva purred her appreciation when I set the dish in front of her. She swiped at Webster's inquiring muzzle before starting in, and he whimpered and sat down. Always the optimist, he was sure one day she'd share. *Never happen*, I wanted to tell him. *Not in any of her nine lives.*

Kate took a container of yogurt from the refrigerator. "That policeman called while you were in the shower. He's coming over." She glanced at her watch. "In fact, any minute. He said you were the one he wanted to talk to, but I could stay if you need support."

I opened the tall pantry next to the refrigerator. "I can handle him. Working on your D.D. takes priority." Kate is almost a clinical psychologist, and D.D. stands for Damned Dissertation. We never say those words aloud.

"Call if you need me," she said. "If I'm not in session, you know which corner of the library I occupy. Probably for the remainder of my natural life."

When I was sure Kate was gone, I replaced the bran flakes I'd been holding for her benefit and traded them for the brown-sugar Pop-Tarts stashed behind the raisins. Kate's "healthy choices," as she likes to call them, would gag a sword swallower. I'd just finished popping my tarts into my mouth when Sergeant Kline arrived.

I led him back to the kitchen and we sat at the table.

He folded several sticks of gum into his mouth, stuffing the wrappers in his pocket. "I'll get right to the point. After we ran your gardener's prints last night, we learned he supposedly offed his wife fifteen years ago. He ever mention that little detail?"

I leaned back in my chair, stunned. "You're saying a man who thought AMDRO was too harsh on the fire ants killed a woman?"

"You sure do shoot from the lips," Kline said, pulling out his notebook. "So tell me about the guy's routine. He took care of those roses in the greenhouse, right?"

"Of course. He cared for all the plants. That's what gardeners do."

"Anyone else ever dabble around in there? Maybe feed those roses?"

"Not me. I wouldn't know rose food from rose hips."

He gave me one of those "that figures" looks. "So what about your sister? She have a green thumb?"

"What does this have to do with anything? I understand Ben may have died from cyanide poisoning, so why are you focusing on the roses?"

"You've been reading the newspaper, I

40

see." He sighed. He seemed to have an un-limited supply of sighs. "Since the local TV stations will be running the story this after-noon, I can confirm this *was* a cyanide poi-soning — and not accidental. Now back to my question. You know anything about the yardman's routine as far as those green-house plants were concerned?"

"When I think about cyanide, I think of gold mining and rodent extermination rather than plants, so —"

"Ms. Rose, I don't have all day. Just answer the question."

"Sorry, yes, Ben took a special interest in those roses. He cut the most beautiful stems for the house, and we've had vases and vases in every room all summer."

He leveled a "lady, you have the IQ of a cactus" stare my way and said, "That tells me nothing about his routine. Who knew what he did out there?"

"Well . . . I guess anyone who's been around on a regular basis."

"Like who? How many people had access to your property?"

"Since you've already established I'm not too efficient about securing the grounds, I guess just about anyone."

He nodded. "That's what I thought."

"Of course, I could give you a complete

list of everyone I know, but . . . you don't have all day."

He chewed his gum for a few seconds, never taking his eyes off me. "Keep up the jokes if this situation amuses you. But I intend to find out what happened here. There is nothing funny about someone sniffing enough cyanide gas to make him look like a bowl of boiled crawfish."

I blinked, genuinely sorry for my smart-ass attitude, but before I could apologize, he leaned toward me.

"Maybe I need to point out that *you* had the most access to those roses and plant food around the time of the murder."

He smelled like cinnamon, and I might have liked his fine-looking face six inches from mine if I hadn't just discovered he considered me capable of murder.

The sound of his ringing cell phone interrupted the unsettling silence that filled the kitchen.

"Excuse me." He stood and unclipped the phone from his belt, then turned away. He'd left his little notebook on the table, so I furtively turned it toward me, trying to peek at what was written there.

But before I could read two words he whirled and snatched the notebook up. After offering single-syllable responses to whoever was on the other end of the conversation, he hung up.

"Do you seriously believe I could have hurt Ben?" I asked.

"We'll pick this up another time, Ms. Rose." He started for the back door.

"But what about Ben?" I called after him.

He stopped and faced me. "What about him?"

"Have you located his family?"

"That's no concern of yours."

"I think it is. Has someone claimed his body?"

"Maybe no one cares enough to claim the body of an accused killer. You see, Ms. Rose, this job reminds me every day that what goes around comes around."

He scanned the room, pausing at the late-model refrigerator with the see-through door, moving on to the grill in the island and taking in the antique trunk and Oriental rug in front of the fireplace before his gaze returned to me. "You were acquainted with the dead man, and by all appearances you and your sister can afford a casket — and maybe even a little prayer for the victim."

I felt my face redden, a mix of embarrassment and anger replacing my earlier irritation. "It doesn't take a NASA engineer to see we have money, but that's not the point.

Even though I didn't know Ben Garrison all that well, I cared about him, and I'm certain he had someone who cared a whole lot more than I do."

"If it's that important, go find his people yourself. Just make sure your bleeding heart doesn't ruin your fine foreign carpet when you head out the door." His faded-denim eyes held mine for an instant before he whirled and strode the length of the kitchen.

He paused, hand on the door, and said over his shoulder, "And by the way, if you plan to find his family, you might want to know his name wasn't Garrison."

4

Although Sergeant Kline had told me Ben's last name wasn't Garrison, I still had no idea what his real name was, and I would need that information to locate the family. Since Kate's longtime boyfriend, psychologist Dr. Terry Armstrong, consults for HPD on occasion, I thought maybe he could help me out.

So right after Kline left my house, I paged Terry. Though hesitant, he finally agreed to meet me at the office he sometimes uses at HPD headquarters. But when I arrived and went up to his floor, I saw him at the end of the hallway walking toward me, briefcase in hand.

When we met halfway down the corridor, he said, "After I showed up here, I bumped into a cop who wants me to consult on a case, so I need to get downstairs for a prisoner interview."

"Did you find out anything about Ben?" I asked, matching Terry's long strides as we headed back to the elevators. The man's so tall, I practically need a stepladder to look him in the eye.

"Same thing you could have learned if

you'd waited for the five-o'clock news. I tried to call you, but you didn't have your cell turned on. Ben's real last name was Grayson."

"And he was *Ben* Grayson, then?"

Terry nodded, stabbing the down button.

"I was hoping you might help me with more than his name. See, Ben apparently had a criminal history."

Terry looked down at me, his usual bland expression replaced by concern. "And he was living right there with you and Kate?"

"Both of us thought he was a genuinely nice guy, Terry. Sweet and gentle. I'd like to know more about that old murder charge, because I can't believe we misjudged him that badly. Think you could find out for me?"

"A murder charge? Uh, Abby, I'm not sure that's a good idea."

"You have access to an HPD database, right?"

"Limited access. I'm betting those Homicide dicks — pretty intense crowd, those guys — don't want me messing around in this."

"All I need is Ben's former address, maybe a little background information on the charges against him."

Terry looked down at me, still not convinced. "What does Kate think about your coming down here?"

"She's the one who sent me. One of your 'intense' Homicide guys practically accused us of murder." Okay, so maybe I was manipulating the facts a little, but Terry adored Kate. He'd be more inclined to help if he thought she'd sent me here.

The ploy worked. A minute later we were in Terry's cramped little office, and he was typing commands on his computer while I looked over his shoulder. But after he hit a few keys, the dreaded window demanding another password appeared.

Terry swiveled in the chair and looked up at me. "I don't think I'd better press my luck. I doubt the lead detective — Sergeant Kline, right? — would offer me access unless I was officially on the case."

"Can't one of your cop friends lend you their password?"

"If I want to keep a nice hunk of city change coming my way for consultations, don't you think I'd better respect my limits?"

I picked up Terry's phone and held it under his nose. "Would you call Homicide for information, then? Kline won't tell me anything."

Terry gently took the phone and replaced

the receiver. "HPD has plenty to do without being hounded with requests from the curious public."

"I am not the curious public! We're talking about locating a dead man's family. That old murder file would give me names and addresses of people who should be informed about Ben's death."

"Abby, leave this alone. Just because HPD isn't doling out information doesn't mean Kline hasn't notified Ben's family." Terry backed out of the program and turned off the computer. "I may have to work with the guy on a case sometime, so I don't want to get on his bad side."

"Oh, I can understand not wanting to get on his bad side. But back to Ben. Aren't you wondering why he was using an alias?"

"Maybe Ben thought your father wouldn't hire him if he had a shady past."

"Okay. But aren't you rankled the police think I might have killed Ben? Or that Kate might be involved?"

He smiled. "Now you're exaggerating. What possible motive could either of you have to kill Ben?"

I opened my arms. "See? That's what I mean."

Terry stood, gripped my shoulder, and squeezed. "Be patient, Abby. From what

I've heard, Kline has a reputation as a smart cop. He'll solve this. Meanwhile, I have a job to do. A man claiming to be General Patton strolled around a local elementary school with a loaded gun yesterday, and he needs to prove exactly how crazy he is if he wants to avoid that big, bad jail up in Huntsville."

I stepped back, feeling like I'd been trying to eat soup with chopsticks for the last ten minutes. "So all I get for my trip down here is this touchy-feely apology?"

He laughed. "Here's a better apology. Give me twenty minutes for this observation; then we'll pick up Kate and I'll buy you two lunch at Houston's restaurant. I could go for one of those giant Caesar salads . . . or maybe I'll have that prime-rib sandwich I love so much."

His eyes reflected that love. How a man like Terry, who was as thin as a broom handle, could eat like a hog on a holiday and never gain an ounce was beyond me. "As long as you don't bring General Patton along to share our meal, lunch sounds great." With effort, I smiled, thinking that the next time I needed help, I should ply him with Hershey's Kisses.

He grabbed his briefcase and I watched him walk to the elevators. Terry may be kind, intelligent, and good-looking, but he had a lot to learn about me before we penned his name into a slot on the family tree. I knew plenty of password tricks, and I couldn't think of a better way to use them.

As soon as Terry disappeared into the elevator, I turned the computer back on. I'd already memorized his Windows log-on and the first password — he hadn't really tried to hide them from me — and when the access-denied screen popped up, I sat back in the chair. Daddy's password had been tough to crack. Were the police as smart as a lifelong computer nerd? I was about to find out.

When the first hacker code didn't work, I prayed I wouldn't have to go the alpha-numeric route. That might take days. But most programmers build in an override feature, and I had a method or two more to get me past this barrier. With persistence, all things are possible.

Sure enough, after five minutes of creative finagling, I pulled up Ben Grayson's file. I was so engrossed, I didn't realize Terry was standing in the doorway until he said, "What in hell do you think you're doing, Abby?"

I jerked around and glanced at my watch. "Gosh. If it only takes you a few minutes, I hope you're never called upon to judge my sanity." I stood, flipped off the monitor, and faced him, hoping my cheeks weren't as crimson as they felt.

He stared at me, unsmiling.

"Can't seem to keep my hands off a computer when I'm around one."

"Right," he said. "What'd you find out?"

"Quite a bit, actually."

"Good. Glad to accommodate my future sister-in-law," he said sarcastically. "You didn't hear anything about Grayson from me, understand?"

I nodded vigorously. "Sure. No one will ever know."

"Let's get out of here. I need lunch."

"Good idea, and I think salad will work for me. I ate a platter of nachos last night like I was skinny, so it's time to atone."

I steered away from any discussion of Ben during lunch, but once Kate and I were home, I filled her in on the little bit I'd learned about Ben, how his wife had been murdered and how he had been the one and only suspect, but was never tried, much less convicted. "And remember when I went to the rest room at the restaurant? Well, I called the sheriff of that small town where Ben lived . . . where he supposedly committed this murder."

"And?" Kate was sitting near the fireplace brushing Webster while I hunted through the kitchen desk looking for the Texas map.

"Nothing — yet. He said he could see me today, and I agreed to drive up there."

She stopped brushing and Webster scrambled to his feet and escaped, settling a safe ten feet away from her. "Terry thinks you should stay out of this, Abby. And I tend to agree."

"Ah. Found it." I took the map to the kitchen table. "I need to understand what happened in Ben's past, and maybe then I'll know why someone wanted him dead."

Kate marched over to the pantry and began searching the shelves.

"What are you looking for?" I said. "We just ate."

She turned and held up a canister. "Sounds to me like you need a good detoxification. This tea from Africa will —"

"The red stuff that makes my lips swell?" I asked. "That tea is scary."

"No. Something different." She filled a mug with water and set it in the microwave. "Trust me. This will clear your head."

Webster sauntered to Kate's side and sniffed the air when she removed a tea bag from the canister. If a dog could look disgusted, Webster looked disgusted. He made a beeline for his lamb's-wool rug by the back door and feigned sleep.

"Kate, did you hear me say our police expert, Sergeant Kline, failed to mention Ben was never indicted for that murder he supposedly committed?"

"I heard."

"That's an omission that kind of ticks me off. What about 'innocent until proven guilty' and all that founding-father stuff?"

"If the police think Ben was guilty of his wife's murder, I'm betting they had good reason to suspect him."

"There has to be more to the story. You knew Ben, how kind he seemed. I need to hear what happened, judge for myself." I unfolded the map on the kitchen table and found the town of Shade, situated sixty miles north of Houston.

The microwave dinged and Kate took the steaming mug and dunked the tea bag in the water several times. "Okay. Let me go with you. Not today, since I have a client later this afternoon, but —"

"The sheriff said he could spare a few minutes this afternoon; otherwise, I'd have to wait until next week. It's not my fault you have a life that actually requires a Franklin Planner. I'm doing this."

"Like Daddy used to say," Kate said,

"trying to talk you out of something you've set your mind to is like trying to take dew off the grass. But when you get back, I want to put all this aside. We have unfinished business."

"You're talking about the house, I take it?"

She nodded. "I know you don't want to live here alone once I move out, so we have decisions to make. Big decisions."

"You're moving in with Terry for sure, then?"

"I need to live with him before jumping into marriage. I don't want us to end up like you and Steven. Watching what you went through with him has spooked me, I guess."

"Spooked you? Come on, Kate. I found it entertaining — kind of like a circus, really. Steven the juggler, balancing two and three women at once. Steven the magician, disappearing for days on end. Steven the lion tamer, handling Abby's temper with deft and evasive —"

"Abby!" Kate cut in. "Did you forget I had a front-row seat for your so-called circus?"

"Well, I'm a born-again virgin . . . not even angry with Steven anymore. He and I do much better as friends." I foraged around in the depths of my purse for the ever-elusive keys, avoiding eye contact.

"You still care about him."

"We had chemistry. Strong stuff. But it's fading." I waved a hand in dismissal. "Believe me, I can control my feelings."

Kate filled a travel tumbler with ice, poured the tea in, and brought the cup to me. "Drink this on the way. Obviously you need a good detox."

Once out the back door, I lifted the plastic tumbler to my nose. Even with the lid on, I could smell something herbal enough to drive buzzards off roadkill. Some things I would miss about Kate when she moved out; some I would not.

I poured the tea out the window at the first stoplight I came to.

Heat radiated off the blacktop as I drove away from Houston. We needed rain. Thanks to a late-summer drought, the usually vibrant green medians were parched brown stripes stretching into the horizon. As I sped farther from the city, the traffic thinned and I savored the expansive landscape still undefiled by strip malls and Wal-Marts. With the cruise control set at seventy, I considered what I'd learned from hacking into Terry's computer. Seems Ben had been the chief suspect in the death of his wife. She'd died at home fifteen years ago, after swallowing a cold medicine laced with cyanide. Was it coincidence husband and wife died from the same poison? I didn't think so, and I had no doubt Sergeant Kline would agree with me — if he had an agreeable bone in his body.

The Shade police had taken Ben into custody right after Cloris's death, but he'd been released the same day. Seems no direct evidence connected him to her murder. He was questioned several times in the months that followed, and from what I could discern from the brief reports I'd read, he was their only suspect, his apparent motive being a large insurance policy taken out on Cloris the year before.

But even though I'd learned where Ben lived before working for us and heard about his troubled past, I still had no idea if he left any family behind. But I intended to meet them and offer them any help they might require if, in fact, they existed. As I drove deeper into rural America, I thoroughly convinced myself I was doing what Daddy would have done by paying my respects to an employee's family. You'd have thought I'd never heard a word about the road to hell.

An hour later I sat across from Sheriff Stanley Nemec, his battered wormwood desk between us. The ceiling fan churned above, crying out for WD-40 every few seconds. A chaw of tobacco bulged in the man's left cheek, and his gray-streaked mustache gave way to a quarter-inch stubble on his cheeks and chin.

After pressing his tobacco lower between his cheek and gum with a fat finger, Nemec said, "Died a complicated death, Mrs. Cloris Grayson did. Someone went to plenty of trouble."

"And you're certain Ben killed her?" I said.

"A lead-pipe cinch. He had plenty of time and plenty of reason to do the deed. What chaps my hide is that if you're persuaded to kill someone, you shoot 'em and get it over with. Nail them in the back, if you can't look 'em in the eye. Only a coward slips poison in stuff that's supposed to make you feel better."

"Could she have committed suicide?" I asked.

"I considered the possibility and rejected the notion ten seconds later. Why go to all the trouble of taking cold capsules apart and packing them with cyanide? Hell, she coulda just swallowed the stuff." Nemec leaned forward and spit in the paper cup he held.

"I see your point. But could anyone besides Ben have tampered with the medicine?"

"I suppose, but no one had a motive 'cept for him. Course, he had himself a convenient alibi. Doing carpenter work up on Ridge Road in front of six men the day she died. But I always said he coulda snuck that poison in anytime."

"There was no real proof he murdered her, though?"

"No signed confession. No fingerprints on the medicine bottle. No cyanide in the shed. None of that. So, much as I tried, I couldn't pin anything on him."

"But you still think he killed her?"

"Sure as hell's hot."

"Did Ben have any relatives besides Cloris?"

"They had no kids, and he had no other kin I know about, but he remarried not long ago. Local widow named Ruth Sawyer. Fine person, too. What she saw in him is the real mystery here."

"He had a wife?"

"Yeah. They was *newlyweds*." He said this last word with undisguised contempt.

"You disliked Ben?" I said, thinking it odd that a newly married man would work so far from home. Had he come back here on his days off?

"Disliked Ben?" the sheriff was saying. "Nah, I hated him. Made his life hell after he murdered Cloris. Figured if I couldn't stick him in jail, I'd make him feel like a cell might not be such a bad idea. Better than livin' with me hounding him day and night. To this very day, I don't understand why he stayed in this town."

"Did he ever offer an explanation?"

Nemec nodded and spit again. "Oh, sure. Told me every chance he got how he'd never leave until he proved me wrong. Then he goes and marries the widow of the guy who sold him all that insurance on Cloris. I considered that more than a little fishy."

"But his wife's death was years ago. Did Ben even know Ruth Sawyer then?"

"Course. Everyone knows everyone here in Shade."

I'm sure they did. "Seems Ben's wife is the person I came here to find. Could you tell me where she lives?"

"I already broke the news to her after HPD faxed the first report yesterday. She's pretty tore up, so you best leave her alone." He leaned back in the chair, his gut hanging over his belt. Rusty-brown tobacco stains dotted his dingy shirt, along with whatever he'd had for lunch. Something with mustard, I decided.

"I want to speak to her, so if you don't mind —"

"I do mind. I don't want you bothering the woman. She's been widowed twice now."

I rose. "Since everyone knows everyone here, I suppose plenty of other folks in Shade could point me in the right direction."

Nemec stood and placed his chunky hands on the desk, his jowled face dark with anger. "Don't go bringing up that murdering no-good's name around my town. Just go back to Houston and leave us be."

"I wouldn't have to bring up his name if you'd simply help me out," I replied sweetly, countering his agitation with a calmness that surprised me. For some reason, I had gained an advantage with this man, though I wasn't sure why.

He stared at me for a second, his lips pursed, eyes narrowed. "Okay. I'll tell you where Ruth lives if you have to know. But you'll need to answer me one thing first. The fax from HPD said Ben was poisoned, nothing else. Exactly how did that son of a bitch get his?"

"Cyanide," I answered quietly.

His mouth spread in an unpleasant smile, revealing stained, uneven teeth. "Finally got a taste of his own medicine, huh?"

Not long after I left the sheriff's office, I sat down with Ruth Grayson in the small front room of her one-story wood-frame home. Our comfortable twin chairs with their worn upholstery offered a view out a large picture window. A round oak table covered with lace doilies sat between us.

After I'd offered my condolences and told Mrs. Grayson what I could remember of Ben's last day on earth — which was precious little, unfortunately — she wanted to fix me tea, even offered to cook me an early supper, but I persuaded her I needed nothing more than time to talk about Ben.

Twisting a blue tissue with arthritic fingers, she said, "I still can't believe he's gone."

"I know this is difficult," I said, "but I visited the sheriff first and he was telling me that —"

"Oh, I know what he said, that my Ben was a killer. That he murdered Cloris. Isn't that right, miss?"

"Well . . . yes."

"Let me set you straight, then. Ben loved

61

Cloris with all his heart. That's one reason I didn't marry him when he first asked me. Her ghost was still perched on his shoulder. The man missed her something awful."

"And this is the woman he was accused of killing?"

"Don't make sense, do it? But Miss Rose, I'm not sure Ben would be happy with me talking about Cloris. That was his business, like he always told me."

"Okay, let's talk about Ben, then. Why are you so certain he was innocent?"

"You married, Miss Rose?"

"I have been, yes."

"Because if you've been married, then you know that if you live with a man, see how he does you day in and day out, how he handles what the Lord sends him, well . . . you know if he's a liar. Ain't that true, miss?"

"Yes," I said, silently adding, *though sometimes not right away.* "But why didn't Ben leave Shade? He could have started over in a new town."

"He feared the insurance company would think he was guilty if he ran off. You see, they tried to wangle out of paying after Cloris's death, seein' as how he was a suspect and all."

"Sheriff Nemec mentioned an insurance policy," I said.

The weather-worn skin over her prominent cheekbones took on color. "He told you about that, did he? Bet he didn't mention how Ben only bought that insurance to help my first husband out. We were losing our shirt with the farm and started selling policies on the side. So Ben — and plenty of others, I might add — bought insurance he didn't even need. And *that* was the Ben Grayson I knew." She nodded, her mouth drawn into a stubborn pucker. "He was never no wife killer. Not never." Her chin quivered and she fought back tears, then said, "It's okay, Miss Rose. Don't look so worried. I'm all right."

"Please, call me Abby." I reached across and touched one thin arm. "I didn't come here to upset you. I want to help. How can I do that?"

"You could help me bring him home so I can put him to rest. I never been to Houston. Wouldn't know where to start if I had to go there and . . . find him."

"I'll arrange everything. You won't have to leave your home."

"You'd do that for a stranger?"

"It's the least I can do."

She studied my face, then said, "You're one fine lady, Miss Abby. Even if you do come from the city."

63

I smiled. "I take that as a high compliment. I have one more question. Ben was using the name Garrison while he worked for me. Why did he change his name?"

She blinked her red-rimmed eyes several times, looking as if she'd put a bucket down a well and brought up Coke instead of water. "He was using some other name? He never said a word about that."

"When did you speak to him last?"

"About a week ago. He called, said he was making progress. Sounded happier than I think I can ever remember."

"Making progress? On what?"

"Well, I assumed on finding out who killed Cloris. That's why he went to Houston in the first place. He's been trying to find the person who killed her ever since she died. Sometimes he'd follow a lead for weeks and come back with nothing. But this last time was different. He's been gone long on three months."

I leaned back in the chair, questions flying through my brain like gnats. "I-I guess I assumed Ben came to Houston to find work."

"Oh, no, Miss Abby. We had plenty of money since the insurance finally paid him what they owed — with interest, I might add."

So Ben had ended up at *my* house to

search for the truth about his wife's murder. What clue had led him to us? Had he found the proof to clear his name? And was he killed because of what he'd learned?

I stood. "You've been so helpful, Mrs. Grayson. I won't keep you any longer."

"You've gone white as flour, miss. You sure you're all right?"

"Well, I'm not sure I understand why he ended up working for my sister and me, that's all."

"Could be a simple explanation, Miss Abby. Ben's been a workingman all his life. Could hardly think straight if he wasn't using his hands. Can't see him holin' up in some hotel while he was in the city. That woulda never suited him. Carpentry was his first love, but he liked working with the earth, too. My guess is he took the job to keep busy while he looked for the killer."

"Maybe," I said, not sure I bought this explanation.

Ruth Grayson and I exchanged phone numbers, and I promised again that I'd move Ben's body back to Shade for burial as soon as the police gave me the okay.

After we said our good-byes, I walked out into the late-afternoon heat, slid behind the wheel of my Camry, and pulled onto the dirt drive that led to the main road.

A cloud of dust signaled the approach of another vehicle, and with the road barely wide enough for my car, I wasn't sure I could squeeze over without sideswiping the rail fence. I started to back up, but then recognized the car and braked.

Willis's Mercedes lurched to a halt beside me, and he rolled down his window.

I did the same and tried to sound pleasant despite my irritation. "Hi, there, Willis."

"What in hell do you think you're doing?" he asked.

"Long way from home, aren't you?" I forced a smile. I was not in the market for a surrogate father, even if he'd driven sixty miles to apply for the job.

"I asked you why you're here." His nose wrinkled and the sunglasses on the bridge of his nose edged closer to his eyes.

"Paying my respects to Ben's widow."

"Kate tells me you found things out about Ben. Unpleasant things." He blotted his wet forehead with a handkerchief.

"Depends on whose version you listen to. And exactly why are you here?" Heat poured in through the open window, and I could feel sweat erupting on my hairline.

"Charlie expected me to look out for his girls after he died, so when Kate told me what you were up to, I thought I should help. The sheriff sent me this way."

"You may be surprised to learn that I go to bed after *Letterman,* so I qualify as an adult. I can handle my own affairs."

I pressed the window control and stomped on the gas, leaving him behind in a whirl of red dust.

5

Willis followed me home from Shade, coming in on my heels through the back door when we arrived. To my dismay, Kate immediately invited him to dinner.

She had prepared an organic vegetable ragout, and we ate in the kitchen, probably because any concoction containing rutabagas was never meant to be eaten in a dining room the size of a football field. No, I consider rutabagas, turnips, and collard greens to be kitchen food, the kind of stuff you feed the dog when no one's looking.

Willis seemed completely unruffled by our previous testy encounter, so after we finished eating, I reminded him about his offer of assistance when he'd come over yesterday. "I think that's why you drove all the way to Shade today, right? To help me out?"

"That's right." Willis wiped a zucchini seed off his chin with his napkin.

"Then help me arrange for Ben to be moved north to Shade for burial as soon as the medical examiner releases his body."

"What?" he said.

"I promised Ruth Grayson her husband

could be buried back home, and I'm not sure how to start the ball rolling. Since you seem so all-fired anxious to be involved, maybe this assignment will satisfy your need."

Willis turned to Kate. "Can't you talk some sense into your sister?"

"I avoid telling Abby what to do," Kate replied. "Makes it much easier to live with her that way."

"You think it's easy living with someone who thinks tofu is actually edible?" I shot back.

She just smiled.

"Anyway," I went on, getting back to Willis. "I promised Ben's widow, so please make the arrangements. Bill me at double your hourly rate, if that makes you feel better."

"Hourly rate will suffice," he replied tersely.

Kate broke the uncomfortable silence that followed. "One problem solved. Now for the other issue. Selling this house. Helping us with the legalities might be more up your alley, Willis."

He flushed so deeply I feared his blood pressure might shoot off the charts. "The dirt hasn't settled on Charlie's grave and you're selling his house?" He pushed away from the kitchen table, a jagged vein in his temple pulsing. He stomped over to the sink with his plate.

"This isn't about Daddy, Willis," I said. "Kate's moving in with Terry, and the idea of living alone in an airplane hangar disguised as a house does not appeal to me. I need a smaller place."

Willis turned and stared at me for a second, then closed his eyes and took a deep breath. Sounding calmer, he said, "What does Caroline think about this idea?"

"She doesn't know yet," I said.

"Really?" Willis said. "I suggest you inform her before the For Sale sign goes up. And now I'd better leave before you two spring something else on me."

I walked him down the hall and across the foyer, surprised to see we had another visitor when I opened the door. Steven Bradley, my ex-husband, stood on the front porch, his finger ready to press the bell.

"Hi there," he said.

New contact lenses, I noted. This time he'd chosen an intriguing sea green. I had to admit a little ocean in his eyes looked pretty darn good.

"I'll be running along," Willis said uneasily, glancing back and forth between us as he slipped past to the walkway.

Steven stepped inside. "I see my favorite girl has gotten her name into the newspaper — nice picture, by the way. So tell me, what's been going on here, babe?"

"I am neither your *babe* nor your *girl,* a difference of opinion that probably explains why we're divorced."

He grinned wider. "I knew that. Sorry. How's about you tell me the straight story? Because I'm not sure I can believe what I read in the *Chronicle*."

"If you promise not to address me with any word synonymous with *child,*" I said.

He held up a hand. "Promise."

We walked into the game room, his favorite spot when we lived here together — maybe because he'd purchased the big-screen TV, the DVD, stereo, and home-theater equipment himself. Steven sat down on the butter-colored leather sectional and stretched out his legs.

I sat next to him and started at the beginning, when I first discovered Ben in the greenhouse. By the time I finished, Steven was shaking his head in disbelief.

"And you're doing a funeral for this Ruth person? Then what, Mother Teresa?"

"Save the sarcasm, Steven."

"If I know you, Abby — and I do believe I'm familiar with every square inch of skin and strand of hair — you're more than a little interested in why Ben got himself killed. Does your curiosity have anything to do with this charity project?"

"I would have helped Ruth Grayson no matter what. After finding Ben like that, I feel so . . . so . . . responsible."

"Responsible? Some nutcase kills a guy and you feel responsible? I don't get it."

"I never took the time to get to know Ben, to really talk to him — and I should have."

Steven reached over and took my hand. "You've had a rough few months since losing Charlie. Cut yourself some slack."

"But why do I feel so guilty?"

"You got me." He slid over and fingered a wisp of hair near my temple. "I like your hair short, by the way. Like the color, too. Red suits you."

I could smell his soap, the hint of an unfamiliar cologne, and I was tempted. But I refused to give in, even though lust was powerful enough to transcend insight and obliterate a long list of unpleasant memories, at least temporarily.

I pushed his shoulder. "Stop it. And move back over there where you came from."

He laughed. "Sure. Whatever you say." He migrated about six inches away and intertwined his fingers behind his head. "Now

72

tell me how you plan to solve Ben's murder, 'cause I know you've been thinking about exactly that."

"I'm not planning to solve anything. I might check a few facts concerning the old murder case, though."

"And how will you do that?"

"Talk to people, maybe dig up old newspaper articles, search Ben's room."

"All the things police do, right?"

"Well, yes, but maybe they've overlooked something."

"And where will all this snooping around lead you?"

"I have no idea, but Ben came here for a reason. I want to know why."

"Even a horse with blinders on can see what's up ahead, Abby. This could get you in big trouble."

I drew up my legs and hugged them to my chest. "That idiot cop already thinks Kate or I had something to do with Ben's death, so what have I got to lose?"

He grinned and nodded. "I like that."

"What do you like?"

"The fact that someone else besides me has gotten under your skin."

"Not funny, Steven. Let me remind you that no one, and I mean no one, ever pissed me off more than you did with all your drunken craziness."

"Hey. We're supposed to put the past behind us — at least that's what you told me the last time we talked. I haven't had a drink in one hundred and forty days, so I'm doing my part."

"That's what you keep saying."

"It's the truth."

"Sorry. Guess you have been trying," I muttered. But why in hell should I be sorry about anything? He was the one who owed the apologies.

I decided to retreat from this precarious ground by changing the subject. "By the way, Kate and I have decided to sell the house. She's moving in with Terry, and I'm not sure I want to live here alone."

"Don't, then," he said quickly. "Let me move back in."

"No way. We failed miserably and completely as a couple, and I like to think I learn from my mistakes."

"One of these days I'll convince you I'm a changed man and you'll reconsider."

What he didn't know was that I had reconsidered, and then reconsidered the reconsideration. Despite all our fights, despite the long nights when he left here and I didn't know where he was, despite words that hung like a venomous cloud long after

74

they were spoken, I still wanted Steven. But wanting someone and loving someone are very different.

"Listen," I said, hoping to ease the tension between us. "I need some work done on the house in Galveston before we get any further into the hurricane season."

"No kidding. I helped your daddy cart some boxes over there a few months before he died and told him as much."

"Daddy actually let you help him with something?"

"You know something, Abby? He and I got along a whole lot better after you and I divorced. Guess he figured he had you back where he wanted you."

"Point to Steven," I replied, trying to sound like his jab didn't bother me. "Do you have any big jobs pending?"

"I'm building one house, got appointments to talk with a few people about contracts. Nothing too time-consuming."

"So you could look the place over, see what needs fixing?"

"I don't know. I might brush up against you, or touch your hair, or smile at you too much if we work together. Get you all pissed off."

"Quit it, Steven. We can be friends."

"Sure. Friends," he said, unsmiling.

After I gave him a key to the Galveston property, he left, still moping, and as I went upstairs to wash the Shade dust from my hair, I told myself I'd made a mistake asking him for help. But like Daddy used to say, it's always easier to borrow trouble than give it away.

6

The next morning Kate and I decided to take Willis's advice and inform Aunt Caroline about our plans to sell the house. She arrived an hour after we called her, and the three of us gathered in the formal living room — or the "parlor," as Aunt Caroline liked to call it. Filled with antique end tables, a brocade love seat, tapestry chairs, and a grand piano, the room seemed old-fashioned and pretentious to me, and I hardly ever spent time there. Knowing this conversation would be difficult didn't make me feel any more comfortable.

Aunt Caroline's white hair framed her small, pointy face, and I wondered if she'd fit in another face-lift since I last saw her. Pretty soon she was going to run out of skin to tuck behind her ears.

Kate broke the news about our decision, and Aunt Caroline's reaction was swift and strong.

"You have to be joking," she said. "This is outrageous."

"Now that Daddy's gone, we have to get on with our lives," I said. "Kate has plans, and so do I."

"Your father would consider this a betrayal. He came to this city dirt-poor, with nothing but the clothes on his back. When he finally earned enough to build in River Oaks, he felt like he'd accomplished something important."

"I'm sorry you disagree with us," I said. "But this house is too big for me to handle alone, and Kate —"

"I could move in with you, then." She followed this ghastly suggestion with a sigh. "From a business standpoint, selling my house makes far more sense. After that horrible incident in your greenhouse, the property value has probably hit rock bottom."

I glanced at Kate from the corner of my eye. The thought of Aunt Caroline living with me . . . Well, let's say I felt a need to pray to the porcelain god.

"Abby and I are selling," Kate said firmly. "But Daddy left us so many paintings, antiques, and other artwork, maybe you could take a few things for yourself before we start packing up."

I nodded my agreement, liking this bribery idea. "I don't know where I'll be living, but I certainly won't have room for all this furniture."

Her expression reminded me of the Wicked Witch meeting up with those flying monkeys in *The Wizard of Oz*. I half expected her to rub her hands together with glee. "How generous and thoughtful of you both. A number of objets d'art your father acquired in Europe mean a great deal to me." She smoothed a few wrinkles on her turquoise silk slacks.

I'd be willing to bet every single item she wanted to cart away from here carried a four-digit price tag. Money was all she cared about. I could move to Russia and it would be fine by her as long as I left the house, the business, and the bank account here.

"I'm glad we settled this so amicably," said Aunt Caroline, now nauseatingly chipper. "Now, tell me about this dreadful man who got himself murdered. Was he a drug dealer? Is that why he was killed?"

"Ben was no drug dealer," I answered. "And refresh my memory on the current 'dreadful' criteria, Aunt Caroline?"

"No need to get testy, Abigail. I like to be informed, that's all. I mean, what if this killer had poisoned you, too?"

"Who would want me dead?" *Besides you?* I wanted to add.

Kate said, "Don't you think Aunt Caroline has a point?"

Great. Two against one. "Not since I'm very much alive and Ben's not. Did Daddy ever mention Ben to you, Aunt Caroline? Like why he hired him, for instance?"

"No," she said quickly. "Your father took care of his household business and I took care of mine. Seems he made a serious mistake about that particular gardener, though."

"Why?" I was sure she knew something about Ben, something she wasn't saying.

"Because the man went and got himself killed, that's why," she replied. "Can we change the subject, please?"

"What do you know, Aunt Caroline?" I persisted.

"Abby," Kate said, "what's wrong with you? I'm beginning to think you're the one who knows something."

"I discovered Ben came here looking for his wife's murderer. Came to our house," I said. "I was hoping Aunt Caroline might shed some light on that. Did Daddy tell you anything about Ben?"

"You think Charlie willingly shared information with me? Do you ever remember that happening, Abigail?"

Kate said, "Are you saying Ben came here for some reason other than a job?"

"I'm not sure, but I plan to find out," I answered. I went on to explain Ben's mission to find his wife's killer, then said, "I'm taking a trip down to the old Victorian in Galveston to check Daddy's files. Maybe he left some clue behind concerning his relationship with Ben."

"Good luck sorting through that mess," Aunt Caroline said. "I'm surprised the second story of that house hasn't collapsed from the pure weight of all the junk Charlie saved."

"I haven't been there in years," I said. "Time I went, wouldn't you say?"

After Aunt Caroline left, Kate and I headed for Galveston together. The island city of brick and stone, southeast down the interstate, stands in steadfast opposition to the smoked-glass glitz of Houston. As we sped over the causeway that spans the strip of sea separating Galveston from the rest of Texas, I rolled down the window to enjoy the ocean breeze.

Webster, who had been sitting at Kate's feet with his nose fixed reverently on the Camry's air-conditioning vent, stood up when the fresh air filled the car. His nose twitched and then he curled back down. Sniffing probably expended too much energy.

"Didn't Steven move his business down this way?" Kate asked.

"Yes, and he's agreed to assess the Victorian. See what needs repairing. I remember Daddy saying something about foundation and roof problems."

"Uh, Abby, was that a smart move? I mean, I know you say you're friends now, but —"

"If Steven stays sober, he'll do a great job. Despite his other flaws, his ability with a hammer and saw is unarguable," I said.

"Like his skill with other tools?"

I blushed. "He's always been handy. I won't deny that."

"Jokes aside, be careful," said Kate. "He's already hurt you plenty."

We turned onto P Street and stopped in front of the once-vibrant-blue Victorian, Charlie Rose's first real estate purchase decades ago. The siding was buckling and peeling, the house shamefully defaced by the constant assault from the gulf mists. Even the gingerbread trim had turned gray with mildew.

I parked on the street, slid from behind the wheel, and started for the front door, turning back when Kate didn't follow.

It seemed she couldn't convince Webster to join us. He sat at the end of the walkway like a statue. Usually he'd follow Kate to the ends of the earth, but the ends of the earth apparently didn't include this particular house.

"Come on," she begged, tugging on his collar.

Webster didn't budge, so she attached his leash and dragged him down the walkway and up the broken steps.

"I've never known him to be this stubborn," she said.

We walked up to the door and Kate's fingers flew to her mouth. "Oh, my gosh! Look."

A broken padlock dangled off the latch.

"Uh-oh," I said.

Kate took a step backward. "Whoever broke the lock might still be in there."

Webster lurched, freeing himself. He hightailed it off the porch, galloped to the car as fast as a hoop snake, and started clawing the car door. I was more convinced than ever that he had Cowardly Lion in his pedigree.

"Stop that animal from ruining my paint job, Kate."

She hurried after Webster, saying, "I'm calling nine-one-one," over her shoulder.

"Don't overreact. Let me check the place out first."

"You shouldn't do that," she yelled, cell phone in one hand, Webster's leash in the other.

I've always considered *shouldn't* a fighting word, so I pushed open the door and stuck my head inside. The rooms on either side of the foyer were as dark as the bottom of a well, probably because the windows had wooden shades that completely obliterated all daylight. Kept the place cool in the summer heat.

Once I propped open the front door with my purse, I had enough light to see the stairs directly in front of me. I tried the foyer light switch, knowing we kept the electricity turned on, but nothing happened. Might not even be a bulb in the socket.

I stepped all the way in and edged my way along the wall until I could feel the molding of a door frame. I inched farther down to the window, hunting with my fingers for the centerpiece that controlled the slats until I found it.

Daylight brightened the front living room, sending huge roaches scurrying in every direction. I shivered with disgust, thinking I should have anticipated their presence and brought a shotgun — I'm pretty good with a gun. Daddy raised real Texans, not Southern belles, thank you very much.

This room led to the dining area, and to the right of the dining room was the kitchen.

Straight past the stairs would get me to the kitchen as well, and there were four bedrooms and a couple bathrooms upstairs.

"Abby?" Kate whispered from the foyer.

"To your left."

Kate's silhouette was framed in the light of the door and she held Webster by the scruff, an umbrella poised in her other hand. "My phone wouldn't respond when I dialed nine-one-one, so a lady three doors down called the police."

"Between your umbrella and your dog, I'm sure we're as safe as squirrels up a tree until they get here."

"Very funny."

Then we both heard it.

A shuffle or a scrape. Coming from upstairs.

Kate gasped, her umbrella weapon clattering to the floor. She zipped to my side, dragging Webster with her. "Let's get out of here," she whispered, digging her fingers into my arm.

Webster started pedaling, his nails clicking on the wood floor.

"Calm down or you'll give the poor dog a heart attack. This is our house, and I'm finding out this minute what's going on. Who knows? Maybe there's a bird trapped upstairs — or even a possum." I sounded brave enough. But was I trying to convince Kate — or myself?

"Okay," she said. "But help me put Webster in the kitchen first. He'll never go up those stairs."

She was right. "Come on, you poor excuse for a dog," I said, pushing him from the rear.

Kate stuck with his front end, but when we reached the kitchen door, footsteps — running, pounding steps — echoed through what I thought had been a vacant house.

Someone was coming down the stairs.

Neither of us had time to move before we saw a gray blur race through the foyer and out the open front door.

Kate started screaming, "Oh, my God!" over and over, which sent Webster flying through the kitchen entry beyond us.

I almost went after whoever ran off, buoyed by the idea that the intruder felt compelled to escape. I've always preferred my criminal types on the spineless end of the bell curve. But I didn't think that would be too smart, so I said, "Pull yourself together, Kate. We'll corral Webster and wait in my car for the police."

I turned my attention to the kitchen, where sun persisted through the grime of curtainless windows, striping the room with dust-filled rays of light.

What I saw didn't register at first, considering I expected to see Webster cowering in the corner rather than where he was — sitting in the center of the room . . . next to the man lying in a pool of blood.

7

I hurried over and knelt next to the man, pressing my fingers to his throat to take yet another pulse in less than a week.

Kate flipped on the light and opened the blinds. That was when I realized whose pulse I was taking.

"You'd better not be dead," I said under my breath. "We've got too much unfinished business, buster."

But Steven's pulse was strong — racing, in fact. Blood still oozed from a gash at the base of his skull, and with nothing better available, I pressed the hem of my T-shirt against the wound.

"Is he . . . you know?" Kate stood above us, her mouth white-ringed with fear.

Steven answered the question himself by moaning and turning his head in my direction. "Abby? Is that you?"

"Yeah. I'm here."

His eyes opened wider and then his hand flew to the back of his head.

"Don't move," I said sharply.

But did he listen? Of course not. He sat bolt upright, like Dracula popping up from his casket.

"What in hell happened?" He surveyed the room, obviously disoriented.

Meanwhile, Webster plopped down in the corner.

Steven gingerly removed his pale yellow Polo and held the wadded shirt against the gash.

A siren whined from several blocks away. Our siren, I hoped.

"We called the police. I'm sure they'll call you an ambulance," I said.

"I don't need any ambulance. If I ever get my hands on the bastard who hit me, he'll be one sorry-ass cowboy." Steven slowly rose, but once upright, wavered on wobbly legs.

I supported him by cupping his elbow. "Why don't you humor me and sit still a minute longer?"

"Don't tell me what to do, okay?" He flushed with anger.

"Back to your old self in record time, I see. Fine. But the next time you need help, count me out."

"She's just glad you're okay, Steven," Kate said. "She gets a teensy bit irritable when she's scared."

"You don't need to explain my behavior to him, Kate. He's an ungrateful slob,

89

which, of course, is not a news flash."

"Me, ungrateful? I don't recall ever hearing you say kiss my foot, much less thank-you," he shot back. "I came here to help you, babe, if I remember right."

"Don't call me babe!"

When the police arrived a few minutes later, we were still arguing. From her expression, Kate was even more thankful than I was for the interruption.

They examined both doors, checked the windows, and started filling out reports. Policeman One convinced Steven that an emergency room visit might be a good idea, but agreed an ambulance wasn't necessary. Then Policeman Two added his two cents, saying he'd have to be dead or unconscious to ride in an ambulance, since every paramedic he knew drove like a New York cabbie. "Besides," he added, "everyone bleeds. Doesn't mean you're dying."

They all laughed.

I had to interrupt this conversation before I became seriously nauseated. "Could we delay this meeting of Extra Y Chromosomes Anonymous? A crime was committed here."

Cop One said, "You talking about the broken lock or the assault?"

"Both," I said.

"I guess you saw that the back lock was

broken, too," Steven said.

Policeman Two nodded. "I noticed. We've had a problem with homeless folks in the area wanting out of the sun. Might have been one of them." He looked at me. "You didn't secure the place very well, if you don't mind me saying. Padlocks aren't much use. Now, if you kept that dog around, he might work. Dogs are the best theft deterrent going."

"Thanks so much for providing my law-enforcement lesson of the day," I said.

Cop Two smiled. "Sorry, ma'am. Didn't mean to upset you. Our homeless in Galveston are pretty harmless for the most part, but if Mr. Bradley here caught one off guard, the guy might have freaked out."

"Whoever was responsible, I'd appreciate a thorough investigation," I said. "A man was murdered on my property this week, and this incident could be connected."

"Murdered? Here?" said Cop One, finally showing interest.

"No. In Houston."

He scratched his head. "Who killed him?"

"They haven't found out yet," said Kate.

"But you're not involved, right?" said Cop Two, eyeing me suspiciously.

"Of course she's not!" piped in Kate.

"Can't we focus on this crime?" I said.

"What about fingerprints? And interviewing the neighbors?"

"We'll do that, ma'am. But I hope you don't mind if we communicate with the boys at HPD while we're at it," said Cop One.

"Why? Because you think I'm a serial killer who flubbed the job on old Steven here?" I thumbed at my ex, then gave a disgusted wave of my hand. "Call whoever you have to."

I folded my arms and slumped against the nearest wall. When was the last time I'd been in such a foul mood? Probably when Steven and I were together. Most times I felt like the tail was wagging the dog back then, too.

When I realized Steven's truck had been parked out back by the garage all along, I felt like an idiot. If I'd bothered to go around to the back door, I would have seen the pickup and been better prepared for what Kate and I found inside.

Kate chauffeured Steven to the hospital in my car, despite his protests that he wanted to drive himself. The two of us had gone a round on that, but the wisdom of his new-found buddies on the police force prevailed, and he begrudgingly allowed Kate the honor. Meanwhile, I took the dog for a potty break.

While Webster took his time finding the perfect spot in the backyard, the forensic crew arrived. When I came back inside, I was relegated to the front room until they finished their job. Cop One had me sign the police report and told me he would let me know if they found the intruder. He and his partner left, and when the forensic crew came downstairs, one of them cheerfully informed me that the culprit had left "a hell of a mess upstairs."

And what, I wondered, was so darn delightful about that?

Webster, now Mr. Cooperative, had no problem following me, and as I went upstairs, I asked myself how much havoc could one little old vandal wreak in an empty house?

But within seconds I answered my own question.

"Plenty," I said aloud from my vantage point in the doorway of the bedroom. "Plenty indeed."

I was sitting cross-legged on the floor in the bedroom, papers scattered in every direction, when Kate and Steven returned from the hospital.

"Whoa, Abby! What happened here?" Kate said, handing me a sack from the local sub shop.

Steven followed her into the room, offering a jumbo iced tea, which I accepted gratefully.

"Welcome to Daddy's stockpile," I said. "I remember him saying, 'Why rent a warehouse when this place will serve the same purpose,' but I never realized his pack-rat mentality went as far as paper wads. Whoever was up here dumped all four of Daddy's filing cabinets."

"Looks like you've got your work cut out for you," said Steven.

I had nursed him through enough hangovers to recognize the strain in his tone. The man had a giant headache. "How's your head?" I asked.

"Five stitches, and my plot at the cemetery is still empty," he replied. "What's in all these files?"

"Documents from back when Daddy first started CompuCan. Certainly old tax files. I've seen plenty of those already. I've also run across Kate's and my report cards, twenty pounds of newspaper clippings, a dozen recipes for salsa, and napkins from every restaurant this side of the Mississippi."

"Why would anyone save this stuff?" He pushed sheets of paper around with his booted toe.

"Because Daddy saved everything," Kate and I said in unison.

"Either the guy who broke in wanted something real bad or he was plain ornery," Steven said.

"If there's a reason other than vandalism for this mess, I'd sure like to know," I said. "And I'm still wondering if this has something to do with Ben's murder."

"I'm more interested in who clubbed me. No one's gonna blindside me and get away with it." He rubbed his head near his recent reminder of the day's events.

"How did this person get the jump on you, by the way?" asked Kate.

"I came by to inspect the place, see what needed doing."

"Did you see this person? See anything?" I asked.

"Actually, my new contacts were bugging me, so I'd taken them out."

"Ah. So you were literally blindsided," I said.

"Why do you think I let Kate drive me to the hospital?" he said. "I sure as hell couldn't navigate with that skull crusher of a headache and my contacts out."

"If you knew you couldn't drive, why the hissy fit when I suggested Kate take you?" This I had to hear.

"Abby, there's a hell of a difference between you telling me anything and regular people telling me."

"Is that supposed to make sense?" I asked.

"Does to me," he answered.

"I forgot. You're different. Kate, would you help me make order out of this chaos?" I sat on the floor and gathered papers toward me, trying to ignore my anger. Just like the old days, I shoved my feelings down, and this led within minutes to a slow burn in my midsection. If only my familiarity with that sensation could have bred enough contempt for me to tell Steven to get lost — permanently.

Kate and I began our chore, while Steven, unable to remain still despite the head injury, stuck around and busied himself with his measuring tape, preparing for the job ahead.

An hour later, Kate and I had hardly made a wave in the paper ocean. I reached into my tea and removed the remnant of an ice cube, which I tossed to Webster. He crunched away, happy as a hog in a mud hole.

"Sorting through all this could take weeks," I said. "Why would someone do this?"

"Maybe one of those homeless people decided to make a paper mattress." Kate swiped a hand across her forehead. Despite the window air conditioner droning in the background — no central air in this old place — the room felt like a steam bath.

I held my cup against my temple and savored the chill. "Well, if the break-in is somehow connected to Ben, the intruder may have taken the evidence with him. All we've found are credit card bills dating back twenty years, canceled checks beginning in 1960, and bank statements galore. Vitally important, if you work for the IRS and need your daily fix of old financial records."

Kate said, "We should start packing boxes, get rid of some of this stuff. What about that pile?" Tight-lipped, she nodded at a stack of medical records from our mother's numerous hospitalizations.

I didn't want to deal with those, and I could tell Kate didn't either. Our mother, Elizabeth, had died from complications of cystic fibrosis when we were about three years old. Neither of us remembered her — she'd been too ill even to care for us — but Daddy spoke of her often, reminded us that she had loved us dearly and had been heart-broken when she became wheelchair-bound less than a year after our adoption. She'd died when we were three.

"I say we concentrate our efforts on anything that might be connected to Ben," I said, glancing around.

"There may be nothing here," Kate said. "This vandalism could be totally unrelated to his murder."

"I wouldn't place bets. Too coincidental."

Kate picked up a folder and fanned her face. "You still think Daddy had Ben's employment application? And why would you need that now? We know where he lived, know about his past."

"I'm interested to learn whether Daddy knew Ben's real identity. He could have been helping him find Cloris's killer. If we uncover something to prove —"

"I'm still not convinced Daddy was helping Ben. And do you really believe Daddy could have kept that big a secret from us?" Kate asked.

She had a point. But maybe someone in Daddy's past — an employee, perhaps — was somehow connected to Cloris Grayson's death. "If Daddy didn't share this secret with us," I said, "he had a damn good reason. A good-hearted reason. Agreed?"

"Agreed," she said.

"Okay. So our job is to find out why Ben was hunting for a killer at our house. What, if anything, did his presence have to do with Daddy?"

I was about to start sorting through more documents when I noticed something taped to the folder Kate was using as a fan. "What's that?"

She returned my puzzled expression. "You mean this?" She held up the manila folder.

"It's an envelope," I said, crawling over beside her.

Kate peeled off the tape that attached a small envelope to the back of the folder. Inside was a key.

"Looks like a safe-deposit box key," I said, searching for an identifying logo.

"I thought we emptied all the bank boxes after Daddy died," Kate said.

"Apparently not. So how do we find out where this one is located?"

"I have no idea," Kate said.

"Maybe this is the clue we need. By the way, Willis called me early this morning and said Ben's funeral is tomorrow. Can you drive to Shade with me?"

"Tomorrow? No way. I have marathon family therapy sessions."

"I guess it's me and Willis, then. How exciting." I rolled my eyes, thinking about riding up and back to Shade having to endure his company, listening as he carried on about how, if I'd only give him the chance, he could expertly run my life. For a small fee, of course.

8

As we drove the sixty miles to Shade in Willis's Mercedes the next day, the blended scents of leather and aftershave threatened to tranquilize me. I'd have preferred we travel in my car, rather than his bragging machine, since I've always had a problem with driving around in an automobile worth the price of a college education. But Willis wouldn't hear of making the trip in anything but his fully appointed Mercedes. I was certain that before we left Shade after the funeral, I'd hear some good old boy oohing and aahing over Willis's car, saying things like, "That dog'll hunt, and bring back the duck stuffed." Then Willis would beam with satisfaction. After all, that was what he paid a small fortune for — those Mercedes Moments.

The hearse carrying Ben's body stayed close behind us on the interstate. I'd had no problem forking over the money for Ben's transportation home. He deserved what little I could offer in that department.

As if reading my thoughts, Willis said, "I still don't understand why you're paying a fortune to bury this man, Abby."

"What do you mean?"

"Why foot the bill for his funeral? I say let the widow pay."

"Like I can't afford it." I pushed the scan button on the radio, wishing I could turn the conversation in a different direction. I sensed a lecture in my imminent future.

"If you want to run your father's business and make a profit, you'd best learn to thoroughly evaluate each charitable impulse. You can't pay through the nose for every employee who experiences a stroke of bad luck."

I looked at him, incredulous. "Is that what you call being murdered? A stroke of bad luck?"

The familiar strains of "Hotel California" filled the car, and I reclined the seat, closed my eyes, and hoped the conversation was over.

But no. He kept on talking. "Did you ever consider that the police might conclude you're trying to ease a guilty conscience by going to all this trouble today?"

"I *am* wrestling with my conscience, but not because I murdered anyone."

"But you don't have an alibi, do you?"

I glared over at him. If he wanted my attention, he had it now. "Like I told Aunt

Caroline, I don't need an alibi."

His heavy-lidded eyes held that legal glint I always saw when we're reviewing contracts at CompuCan. He said, "If you say you don't need an alibi, I believe you, Abby, but that doesn't mean the police will."

"I didn't have a reason to murder Ben. I don't have a reason to murder anyone." If he'd turned my way he would have been blinded by my stare.

"Perhaps you should concentrate your efforts on your cash flow. Bail for murder is usually high. And you should be prepared to tell the police exactly what you were doing on the afternoon in question, should they ask."

"They already asked and I already answered. If that detective has even half a brain, he'll realize Kate and I had nothing to do with Ben's death. Now could we please drop this? I'm sure I'll be called to testify before a grand jury, but I promise to let you know before I go to court. Does that make you happy?"

He nodded, pleased at this small compliance, then abruptly switched radio stations. Much to my dismay, Wynonna's contralto filled the car.

After the service at the First Baptist

Church, we drove to the cemetery. Willis and I joined those assembled for prayers at the grave site, and stood under the tent I'd arranged to shade us from the unbearable heat. Ben was being laid to rest next to his first wife.

Daddy had died in the spring, and the day we buried him had been clear and cool — nothing like this. It was hot enough to sunburn the birds.

I looked at Ruth, her head bent, her hands clutched tightly together at her waist. She was about the same age my mother would have been had she lived. Feeling a familiar ache in my gut, I whispered, "Was it this hot the day of Mom's funeral?"

Willis leaned toward me, looking confused. "What?"

"You were there, right?"

"Well . . . yes. But I don't remember what the weather was like."

"Daddy never talked about her . . . service."

"Her death was not something he wanted to remember. Never saw a man so miserable as when she finally died."

"And what about our real parents? If they were buried out in El Paso, where the plane crashed, it was probably even hotter than this." Kate and I were adopted after Jane and Morris Mitchell's private plane went down in the West Texas desert, leaving their twin daughters orphaned.

"Why are you bringing all this up now?" Willis whispered, sounding irritated.

"I guess funerals make you think about details, about a past you weren't a part of but that's still a part of you," I said.

Willis placed a hand on my shoulder. "Don't think you and Kate are alone, Abby. You have Caroline and me. We'll always be here for you."

The preacher began reciting the Lord's Prayer, so I shut up. But before I bowed my head, I spotted Sheriff Nemec, who'd stopped a good distance from the grave, out of Ruth's sight. Not that she would have said anything about his showing up for Ben's burial. She wasn't the type for confrontations. At least by hanging back beneath a live oak, Nemec showed her a measure of respect — which surprised me. After our last encounter, I wouldn't have pegged him as being even that sensitive.

From his passive face, bloated on one side from a chaw of tobacco, I couldn't imagine what he was feeling. Elation? Satisfaction? Or did I detect a hint of sadness because the pursuit had ended? Whatever was going through his mind, he stood quietly, hat in his hand, until they lowered Ben's casket into the ground. When the coffin disappeared completely, he put on the Stetson, wheeled on his booted heel, and returned to a pickup parked on the small rise beyond the tree.

I glanced back at Ruth, who had chosen off-white lace for the funeral. I wondered if that was the dress she'd been married in. In the circles Aunt Caroline and Willis traveled, people would have buzzed over a woman not choosing black, but here, with neighbors Ruth had known forever, no one would misunderstand or say anything unkind.

The small crowd dispersed, and Ruth remained still and tearless while two men shoveled spades of clumped red clay over the casket. The sickly-sweet scent of dying flowers drifted toward me on the hot breeze.

"Ready to head back to Houston?" whispered Willis, who'd been squirming next to me like a leech on a hook.

"First we're paying our respects at Ruth's place," I whispered back.

"You didn't tell me that." He focused on his Rolex. "I have to return to town. Considering this funeral cost you a tidy sum, I only came to keep an eye on how your money was spent today. I must say, they did a fine job on the flowers . . . and the service benefited from those lilies you insisted on. Surprises me they could find such lovely ones, seeing as how we're out here in —"

I elbowed him in the ribs. "Would you shut up? Ruth is still praying."

Willis hadn't even flinched when I hit him. It seemed his workouts were effective for more than networking with the "right people."

"Abby, I must leave. I have a client waiting," he said.

I pointed in the direction of the sleek black Lincoln parked on the grass about fifty yards away. "That hearse is headed back to Houston. Why not hitch a ride and I'll drive your car back to town later tonight?"

"You can't be serious," he replied.

"I'll be satisfied I've received the best service for my dollar with passengers in that contraption going in both directions. How's that for a sound business decision?"

"Um . . . maybe the hearse could wait for you and I'll drive back in my car now?" The sweat on his balding forehead drizzled past his temples.

"You're not squeamish, are you, Willis? Besides, another dead person back in Houston is patiently awaiting that hearse's return so they can experience city traffic one last time. Say, do you suppose the Six-ten Loop is actually purgatory? Miles and miles of endless, congested highways going around and around and —"

"Abby, I'm not —"

"Seriously, Willis. The hearse driver told me he has another funeral." I smiled, deciding I hadn't had this much fun in a long time.

He adjusted his sunglasses and cleared his throat. "If that's what you want, I'll happily accommodate you." With that, he turned stiffly and handed his car keys to me. "When can I tell Kate to expect you?"

"I'm not sure," I replied. "Tonight sometime. Borrow my car if you need one. Kate knows where I keep the spare key. And thanks for coming with me."

I felt a twinge of guilt at seeing his stricken face. He'd only sought to advise me in my best interests, and what did he get for his trouble? A long drive in a hearse, all the while praying none of the "right" people saw him.

That sense of culpability passed swiftly, however. Maybe this unusual trip home would teach Willis not to try to control me. I hated men trying to control me.

The finest meals in Texas are served after

funerals, and Ruth's kitchen table attested to that fact. I had loaded up with fried chicken, sour cream–dill potato salad, baked beans, and homemade pickles, and was balancing the plate in one hand while holding a glass of fresh lemonade in the other. I headed for the porch, where callers had gathered in the late-afternoon reprieve from the heat. When I passed Ruth on my way outside, she dropped a hot biscuit on top of my chicken.

"This looks wonderful," I said. "But aren't you eating?"

"I know I should partake of what these fine people have provided, but I haven't had much appetite since Ben died."

She followed me outside, where we joined the remaining mourners. An old gentleman rose and offered his rocker, then said his good-byes. The others soon followed his lead until only Ruth and I remained.

She rocked rhythmically, the setting sun highlighting the grief in her tired eyes. "I want to thank you again, Miss Abby, for your kindness and understanding, and for bringing Ben home. He would have been most grateful. Most grateful indeed. When they find who done this, he'll truly rest."

"Have the police contacted you?"

"Only Sheriff Nemec. Said the city police

sent him over to ask me questions."

"What kind of questions?"

"Oh, like, do I know anyone with a reason to harm Ben. I said, 'Besides you, Stanley?' He looked through Ben's belongings, and then after he left I spent money on a long-distance call to the city. I wanted to see what was bein' done about finding his killer, since I don't think Stanley will be breaking his back to find answers. Lady who I talked to says I got to have a case number. Says don't I know there's four million people in Houston? Says how's she supposed to tell one dead body from another without a case number? One thing's for sure, miss. That'll be the last time I call them folks for anything. Don't need to pay money on no phone bill to be talked to like that." She lifted her chin and her lower lip quivered.

"I'm so sorry." To myself I added, *Thank you, urban America.*

"It ain't your fault. Lady was probably right. He was nothin' to her."

"But he was everything to you." I laid my hand on hers. "I'll find out who killed him, Ruth. I promise."

"You don't need to on my account. This funeral today was more than I ever expected. I'll be grateful for the remainder of my days." She closed her eyes and rocked faster.

110

"I have another reason for wanting to know what happened to Ben. The police questioned me. Treated me like I might be involved."

Ruth stopped rocking. "They've got half the pickets missing from their fence if they think you coulda had anything to do with Ben's death."

"Thanks for the vote of confidence." I smiled.

She squeezed my hand.

"Did the sheriff take anything of Ben's?" I asked.

"Nope. Nothin' to take, that I know about."

"And what about Cloris? Did Ben save anything that belonged to her?"

"Plenty of stuff. But Stanley didn't even ask about her. He should have, though, shouldn't he? Course, with Ben dead, he probably thinks nothin' else matters."

"Would you be upset if I looked through Cloris's belongings?"

"Not at all, but since the trunks are stored overhead, I'll be needin' your help getting to them. Can't much navigate a ladder these days, what with the arthritis."

"You don't need to navigate anything. Is there a space in your overhead attic for me to sit?"

"Small spot. Ben laid some plywood up there."

I followed her inside to the hallway leading to the two back bedrooms. A cord hung from the ceiling, and I pulled down the attic ladder. Heat and dust whooshed out to greet me. Best time of day for this kind of work, I thought as I began the climb. The outside temperature had dropped below ninety.

"There's a ceiling bulb. Just pull the string. Cloris's trunks are black, if I remember right. While you start looking, I'll be fetching you some water. Hotter than Hades up there."

I turned on the light and found two footlockers within arm's length. I settled cross-legged on the small wood platform and pulled the closest one to me. I opened the lid, and the smell of mothballs escaped around me. Neatly folded dresses and underwear, circa 1970, were piled to the top of the trunk. I began searching through the clothing — Cloris was apparently a small woman — but found nothing of interest except two miniature teddy bears that looked like they had never been touched, much less played with.

Before I could begin on the next trunk, Ruth appeared at the bottom of the stairs with the much-needed water. I was already sweating like a polar bear in Hawaii.

"Find anything?" she asked.

I climbed halfway down to retrieve the glass. "Not yet." I gulped down half the water and turned to climb back up.

Ruth said, "I hear someone in the drive. Maybe a late caller coming to pay their respects. You be okay up there, Miss Abby?"

"I'll be fine. You go on."

I took the glass with me and had just dragged the second trunk over so I could look through the contents when I heard a voice I recognized. Sheriff Nemec.

I quickly opened the trunk, and this one proved far more interesting. I found several calendars, two photographs, and several sketchbooks. One photo showed a young woman standing by the gate to this house. The other picture was of Ben in an ill-fitting suit and the same woman in a simple white dress holding a bouquet of roses. I turned it over. *Ben and Cloris* had been penned on the back. I quickly switched my attention to the sketchbooks. Some of the colored-pencil drawings of birds and flowers were expertly detailed, stunningly realistic, but before I could examine these more closely, the sheriff interrupted me.

"You best come down from there, miss.

HPD might be interested in what you've found."

I turned and stared down at Nemec, who held his hat in his hand. "I believe Ruth would have given you the same chance at this stuff."

"Might have, Miss Abby," Ruth said. "But now I'm not so sure."

I pushed the trunk away from the attic opening and descended the stairs.

"Nothing but some old clothes and toys anyway," I said, brushing remnants of insulation off my linen skirt.

"Mind if I check myself?" He put a beefy hand on the stair railing and waved me aside.

Quickly I said, "Ruth, did he show you a warrant?"

"No, miss. Guess he needs one, huh?"

Nemec's jaw tightened. "Ruth, I never had no argument with you. I'm only doing my job, just like when I went after Ben."

"Then you do it proper and get that piece of paper," she said.

"I was hoping you'd let bygones be bygones now that Ben's dead and buried," he said. "Before you took a shine to him, you and I had a few things in common, as I recall."

"Are you thinking I forgot how you

hounded Ben year after year? And you didn't start with your tales of how he was going to hell until I turned your marriage proposal down. I take that kinda personal, Stanley."

The sheriff frowned and stared at the thin carpet that ran the length of the hall. "I couldn't believe you befriended a murderer. I kept telling you he done it. But I've been doing some thinking, and I may be willing to admit a mistake or two." He shook his head. "Never could pin Cloris's death on him. Been like trying to stack greased BBs all these years."

"Did you ever think maybe you couldn't pin the murder on him because he wasn't guilty?" I asked.

He stared at me. "If he didn't do it, then who the hell did?"

"Probably the same person who killed him," I said. "Have you pondered that since you heard about Ben's death, Stanley?"

He cocked his head and narrowed his eyes.

"Perhaps you were wrong about Ben?" I coaxed.

He didn't answer immediately, and the grandfather clock ticking in the front room seemed as loud as a skeet shoot.

Finally Nemec turned to Ruth and said,

"I'm sorry. I guess that's what I came over to say. When they laid Ben in the ground today — and this may sound strange — but I was mad! I wasted years blaming him when I should have given up. My chasing after him only made you cotton to him more." He paused and then said, "You heard me. And what in the hell good does that do anyone?"

I was beginning to think this confession could definitely do me some good. "You could make things up to Ruth, if you're truly sorry," I said.

"How's that?"

"Yes, Miss Abby," said Ruth. "How's that? I ain't sure I can forgive and forget, even though the Lord says I should."

"Finding out what really happened is what's important, right? I want to know who murdered Ben. But the Houston Police Department won't be cooperating with the likes of me. You know how they treated you on the phone, Ruth."

"I sure do, but what's this got to do with Stanley?" she said.

"The police *have* cooperated with you, Sheriff," I said. "I'll bet you know a lot about Ben's murder, don't you? You might even be privy to more information, if you asked."

"Wait a minute," he said. "I got a full plate here in Shade. I can't be traipsin' off to Houston huntin' up killers."

"You won't have to. I'll do the traipsing. All I need is a little more information about Ben's case, and a peek at the evidence from your investigation into Cloris's death."

The sheriff shook his head and stared at his boots. "I don't know if I'm supposed to do that."

"Stanley," Ruth piped in, "if you help Miss Abby — who's been very kind to me — I'd be inclined to serve you supper every now and then." She smiled slyly, even though I would have never thought she had a sly bone in her body.

"All right," he replied reluctantly. "For you, Ruth. Because I respect you, not because of some old pot roast." He pointed a stubby finger at me. "You follow me to my office, city girl."

He marched toward the front of the house, waving his hat this way and that, mumbling to himself.

And I climbed back up the ladder to gather anything belonging to Cloris I thought might help me before I met up with the sheriff.

9

The next morning, I was sitting at my kitchen table surrounded by my newly acquired sketches, a yellowed newspaper article, documents, police reports, and the photos. The color in the pictures had faded to variations of brown, but Cloris's dark eyes still grabbed me. So sad. So tired. The drawings in the sketchbook were signed simply with *C,* and I lingered over them. Ruth had told me before I left last night that according to Ben, Cloris had been happiest when she was drawing, and her art reflected a joy not evident in her face.

Just then the cat decided she was ready for her morning coffee — which she attempted to steal from the mug sitting next to me. The cream interested her, of course, not the coffee.

"Get out of here, Diva!" I shooed her away, knowing I'd pissed her off. But no one, not even her, messes with my Kona.

I heard Kate's footsteps on the back stairs, and she and Webster appeared seconds later. Stretching her arms over her head, she yawned, then said, "How was the funeral?"

"A lot less stressful than Daddy's. I think Willis did a great job with the arrangements."

"I'm glad Ben got a decent burial," she said.

She let Webster out into the backyard, and then microwaved water to brew her morning green tea.

Once she'd finished, she sat across from me with her cup. "I hope the funeral brought some closure to all this guilt you've taken on concerning Ben."

"Closure? I love it when you talk like a shrink."

"That's me. Shrinkish through and through."

"In a way I do feel better — though I still intend to find out why Ben was working here and how it connects to his wife's death. Last night I gathered a few clues."

I showed Kate what I'd brought home from Shade, and after she looked everything over, she reexamined the HPD report that had been faxed to Nemec, the one documenting how the murder had occurred. "I can't believe there was cyanide in those rose containers," she said.

"Very sneaky way to arrange a murder. Not only were there cyanide pellets in every pot, the watering can had been filled with the acid used to shock the pool. When Ben poured that acid on those plants . . . well, chemistry took over. The acid even burned Ben's arm when he collapsed from the fumes."

"Cyanide and acid," Kate said, shaking her head. "That's horrible and devious and . . . and . . . plain evil. Whoever killed him created a gas chamber right in our backyard."

"Makes me mad as a wet hornet," I said. "More reason to find out who did this and why."

"But how can Cloris's drawings — wonderful as they are — help you find anything?" Kate asked.

"I'm not sure, but artwork is almost like a fingerprint. And don't forget the calendars," I said. "She noted a few names. Appointments, I presume. And one name on the calendar — Samuel Feldman — is even scribbled over and over on the back page of the sketchbook."

Kate picked up the newspaper clipping that I'd found. "Why do you think she saved this?"

The article reported the disappearance of a teenager named Connie Kramer from a small town in East Texas. "I'm not sure, but I'm hoping to find out."

"But that happened more than thirty years ago, Abby."

"The Internet is a wonderful thing. Useful for much more than researching schizophrenia or obsessive-compulsive disorder, which is all you've ever done online."

"That's all I've had time to do on-line in the last three years. You really believe you can find answers on the Web?"

"I do," I said.

Kate sipped her tea. "I know your curiosity is piqued, but you'd better be careful. Both Ben and his wife died horrible deaths and, well . . . if anything happened to you . . ." She stared into her cup.

I reached over and laid my hand on hers. "Nothing will happen to me."

"Are you absolutely sure Ben didn't kill his wife? I mean, maybe something happened between them. Maybe he desperately needed the insurance money for, say, a sick mother or father, and —"

"He didn't kill her, Kate. I know he didn't."

"How can you be certain?"

"I trust Ruth. She knew him better than anyone, and if she says he's innocent, that's good enough for me."

Kate said, "Okay, then why not go to Sergeant Kline and tell him what you think?"

"You mean the man who was raised on pickle juice? Why should I willingly subject myself to him?"

Webster barked, wanting in, so Kate went to the back door.

Aunt Caroline had arrived and came in with the dog — early for her, I thought — and an overdose of Sunflowers perfume permeated the kitchen when she made her entrance. Dressed in a fuchsia-and-gold warm-up, she wore what looked to be new running shoes. She deposited her handbag on the baker's rack by the door and sat down.

Kate reclaimed her chair.

Staring at my bare thighs — I hadn't even dressed yet — Aunt Caroline said, "I have the best cosmetic surgeon. He does wonderful things with liposuction, Abby."

"And face-lifts, too, I'll bet. Course, when you get into double digits on those little operations, you —"

Kate kicked my shin. Hard. She said, "Can I get you coffee, Aunt Caroline?"

"I'm glad *someone* hasn't forgotten the manners I taught the two of you. Coffee would be wonderful." While Kate went for the coffee, Aunt Caroline addressed me. "So is that man buried yet?"

"You mean Ben?"

"Yes," she said.

"If he is buried, does that mean you can obliterate his memory?" I said coldly. "Deny he existed?" I tossed a crust of my leftover toast to Webster.

He held out for more, though Diva, obviously irritated at my favoring the dog, twitched her tail and left the room.

Kate placed a mug in front of Aunt Caroline and refilled my cup from the glass pot she carried in her other hand.

"What is all this?" Aunt Caroline waved at the papers on the table.

"Abby's found a new calling. Detective," said Kate. She set the pot on a trivet in the center of the table.

"What does she mean, Abigail?" Aunt Caroline added two packages of artificial sweetener to her coffee.

"I'm interested in the murder," I said. "Curious and concerned, you could say."

She sipped carefully, protecting her artistically made-up lips. "I'm not surprised you're getting involved. Even as a child you constantly overstepped. Got caught up in causes, brought minorities home, picketed and petitioned. I'm glad you've toned down, but a certain naïveté still clings to you, my dear. Professionals are being paid to deal with this crime, and you have neither the knowledge nor the experience —"

"I'll pass on the lecture. I don't think that's why you came over this morning." She wouldn't push my buttons today. Not if I could help it.

Aunt Caroline rose and retrieved her Gucci handbag, then produced two handwritten pages. "I have the list we discussed, a few sentimental items I'd like to have when you two move out."

I took the pages. She'd named almost every antique and piece of art Daddy owned. "A few items?"

I passed the list to Kate, who forced a smile. "Could Abby and I review this and get back to you?"

"Of course, dear." She took a gold compact from her purse and patted face powder on her nose. "Get back to me as soon as possible on the disbursement. I'll pay for a moving van to transport everything to my home."

I took a deep breath to ease the tightness in my gut. Why did our mother have to die and leave us at the mercy of a female role model as mean as a rattlesnake with a headache?

Aunt Caroline said, "Time for me to leave. I'm due at the health club for an appointment with Hans, my personal trainer. Quite a striking and knowledgeable young man." She brushed imaginary crumbs from the front of her warm-up, then bent and retied her running shoes.

"I need to shower," said Kate. "But please stop by again soon." She kissed Aunt Caroline's forehead; then she and the dog disappeared up the back stairs.

"Before you leave, Aunt Caroline," I said, "could I ask you about something I found?" I took the safe-deposit key from the antique sideboard, deciding that if anyone would recall anything to do with a bank, Aunt Caroline would.

"You'll make me late, Abigail," she said impatiently.

"Do you recognize this?" I held out the key.

Her eyes flickered with interest. "Where did this come from?" She plucked it from my hand.

"Daddy's house in Galveston."

"But I went through the files and boxes down there after he died. I never saw this."

"You went there?" I said, surprised.

"I wanted to make sure Charlie hadn't, well . . . that something important hadn't been overlooked for probate."

Hmmm. Could things have disappeared

from P Street that Kate and I knew nothing about? "So you had access to the Victorian?" I asked, thinking maybe Aunt Caroline broke the padlock and that was how the intruder got in.

"Your memory's failing you, Abby. I added the padlocks after Charlie's funeral. The old locks were flimsy, making that vacant house an easy target for a break-in. Don't you remember? I gave you the keys the day we met to go over Charlie's will."

"Forgive me for forgetting. I was distracted that day. I think it's called grief."

"That's why I put things in order down there. To spare you from having to confront the memories I knew you'd find."

"Right. And I've got some swampland in Antarctica I'd love to sell you. Did you take anything?"

She blinked. "Certainly not. Despite our differences, I do love you, Abby, and would never betray you in that fashion." She handed me the key. "But I expect you'll share the contents of that box when you open it, since I, too, am an heir. Now, I absolutely must be on my way."

She left, and I sat there wondering if she'd made more than one trip to Galveston — and more recently than right after Daddy died. I wouldn't put it past her to bash

126

Steven over the head if she thought she could benefit financially from assault and battery.

The phone rang and I picked it up. Willis was calling to say his secretary would be dropping him off so he could pick up his car. After I hung up, I showered and dressed. By the time he arrived, I'd even managed several calls to locksmiths in hopes of finding out who had made the key and what bank they worked for, but I'd had no luck.

"Have you forgiven me for making you ride in a hearse?" I said, after letting Willis in the back door.

"Yes, silly. I'm always willing to help you." He immediately noticed the police report on the table and went over and picked the paper up, his lawyer eyes sharp with interest. "What are you doing with this?"

"Research."

"Research?" he asked.

"On Ben's murder."

"And the police gave you one of their reports?" he said, surprised.

"Well, not the Houston police." I went on to explain what had happened since Willis left Shade in a hearse.

"As your lawyer, I have to advise you in your best interest. And what you are doing, or intend to do, is *not* in your best interest. No, not intelligent in the least."

"So you think I'm stupid to pursue the truth? You think I'm stupid to want to know who killed Ben? You think I'm stupid to —"

"Abby, I'm worried about you. Ben's killer hasn't been caught."

"And that's my point. So I don't care whether searching for the truth is in my 'best interest.' " I held up the safe-deposit key. "I found this at the Victorian. Look familiar?" I pushed the key across the table.

He picked it up and turned it over. "No. What bank is this from?"

"I have no idea. That's the problem." I noticed his tanned face was looking a little yellow, and a tiny line of sweat erupted above his upper lip. "Are you okay, Willis?"

He laughed, handing the key back. "I'm fine. Sorry I can't help." He stood, ready to leave.

"Thanks for the loan of your beautiful car. No hard feelings about your transportation back to Houston yesterday, right?" I walked around the table and put an arm around his shoulder.

"No problem," he said. "No problem at all."

10

Once Willis left, I headed to Galveston, now very late for my lunch appointment with Steven. We had planned to meet and talk about the renovation. When I turned onto P Street an hour later, I saw an exterminator's vehicle parked in the driveway. Steven was paying the uniformed man, and when the truck left, I pulled the Camry in.

After I slid from behind the wheel, Steven said, "You were supposed to be here at eleven-thirty." Without waiting for a reply, he turned on his heel, climbed the porch steps, and stomped into the house.

"Sheesh. Just what I want to do. Spend the afternoon with an alligator with chapped lips," I mumbled, following him.

Once inside, I saw he'd been hard at work. The scent of pine welcomed me when I entered, and the ceiling fan in the parlor was spinning furiously. The wooden shades were all open, revealing gleaming windows.

Steven was in the kitchen watching a few roaches squirm in the throes of chemical death on the tile floor.

"Looks like a different place. I'm impressed," I said, nodding in appreciation.

My reaction seemed to soften him up a little, because he almost smiled. "I paid the cleaning crew a hundred and the exterminator fifty. My treat. But where in hell have you been?"

"Sorry, but I had a few visitors this morning."

Steven pointed to a spray bottle on the counter. "While I remember, the bug man left extra juice in case a few critters need an extra push to roach heaven."

"There's always some who hang on. Have you eaten yet?" I asked.

"No, and I'm pretty darn hungry. Let's head for the beach and the shrimp. These chemicals may be odorless, but I don't like to hang around right after the exterminator has done his business. Stuff is pretty potent."

"How did you know I was craving seafood?" I said as we walked out through the back door.

Stan's Shrimp Shack, a tiny restaurant off Seawall Boulevard, had few customers, so we had our choice of tables. We sat in the corner farthest from the bar. Between mouthfuls of crab salad, I filled Steven in on what I had learned about Ben after the funeral yesterday and how I hoped to find answers.

"So you talked the county mountie out of his paperwork, huh?" He peeled a shrimp and dunked it in hot sauce. "I knew you couldn't keep your pretty nose out of this mystery."

"Hey, I can do what I want with my pretty nose."

"And how I love it when you remind me. Let's talk about the house. That's what I'm doing in Galveston, right?"

"I know the place is in bad shape," I said.

We spent the next thirty or forty minutes discussing the needed renovations, and by the time he finished, I wondered if we might be better off tearing the place down and starting over.

Steven, who could still read my mind as well as ever, said, "And don't even think about razing the Victorian. I contacted the city, and the house is more than a hundred years old. You don't tear down hundred-year-old houses in Galveston without dealing with reams of paperwork and getting multiple stamps of approval."

"Okay. But this sounds like a huge undertaking. Can you handle this project alone?" I asked.

"No way. But I will get the house in good

enough shape to last through hurricane season. Fix the roof, replace windows, that kind of stuff. Meanwhile, I've arranged to have a more experienced renovator come by and take a look."

I nodded. "You've impressed me twice in one day, Steven. Sounds like I hired the right man. But we haven't discussed your fee."

He stiffened. "I don't want your money. I got enough when we divorced."

"That's not what you told the judge."

"Hey, I was knee-walking, spit-slinging drunk the day we finalized. You can't hold me to anything I said back then."

"Okay. Maybe that's so. But I'm still paying you for your work. I want this to be a professional relationship."

"You don't want to owe me? Is that it?" He sat back, arms folded across his chest.

How did he always manage to turn things around? I took a deep breath. "If you want, I'll have Willis work with you about payment. That way you and I can stay clear of touchy issues like money."

He said nothing for several seconds; then his face relaxed in a smile. "Good idea."

I smiled back, relieved. If Steven stayed sober and if we both controlled our tempers, this renovation might actually be fun.

We went back to the Victorian after lunch, and he showed me where we needed the most urgent repairs, pointed out the phone he'd had installed, and then went upstairs to work on a leaky toilet. Meanwhile, I returned to the vandalized room. Maybe I could find bank records that would lead me to the mysterious safe-deposit box. But after an hour of searching, I settled for the next-best option — canceled checks. Since Daddy must have paid for the box's rental somehow, and since he used checks for everything, maybe I could find the name of the bank that way.

I was placing rubber-banded stacks of paper in a box when Steven appeared in the door, wrench in hand. "I need a few plumbing supplies. Can I get you anything while I'm out? A Coke or something?"

"No, I'm on my way home. You can carry this box to my car, though."

He set down his wrench, came over, and picked up the box. "What's in here? Bricks?"

"Three decades of canceled checks." I explained about the safe-deposit box and my plan to find out where the box was hiding.

"Good thing Charlie saved everything," Steven said snidely, heading for the stairs.

"He's providing for your entertainment even after he's gone."

I chose not to answer back, but all the way home I kept wondering why Steven had to ruin what had almost been a pleasant afternoon.

When I arrived back in Houston, Kate had left a note saying she was at Terry's place. Time for a chore I had been putting off. I told Ruth I would gather whatever belongings Ben had left in the garage apartment once the police removed the crime scene tape, which they had done while I was at the funeral. I went outside, found a cardboard box in the garage, then climbed the stairs.

The air-conditioning had been turned down to sixty degrees, probably by the cops, and they left the ceiling fan running, too. Goose bumps rose on my bare arms, and I immediately reset the thermostat.

The apartment we furnished consisted of only two rooms — a living area with a small kitchenette, and a bedroom. The chenille couch cushions lay on the floor, and the cabinets below the sink and microwave stood ajar. I found a crocheted afghan by the recliner that I didn't recognize and folded the blanket into the box. After a brief search of the room, which yielded only a coffee mug and several *Handyman* magazines, I went to the bedroom.

I stopped after stepping inside, a lump in my throat. A quilt similar to those Ruth had shown me up at her place, ones she made by hand, had been pulled off the bed, and a worn Bible rested on the end table. Pillowcases and sheets had been tossed in the corner, and the mattress was off center on the box springs. Every dresser drawer stood open, their contents removed. Ben's meager wardrobe — work clothes, Levi's, cotton shirts, and underwear — lay in a crumpled pile in the closet. All the pockets in his trousers were turned out.

I sat on the floor and packed up his clothes, feeling sad and also a little angry at how the police had discarded his belongings. I then folded the quilt and remade the bed before turning to the Bible. For some reason, I didn't want to even touch the book. Bibles seemed such private things.

Feeling like I was somehow betraying Ben, I opened to the first page. What I saw made me blink hard and swallow that tennis ball in my throat. The inscription read, *To Ben from Connie. All my love. July 24, 1971.*

Connie? Not his beloved Cloris? Was this the Connie mentioned in the newspaper article? The one who had disappeared? Seemed a logical conclusion. So what happened to Connie? And why would an article about her be packed away with Cloris's belongings?

I quickly boxed up Ben's things and hurried back to the house, anxious to research the newspaper article. I took the clipping into Daddy's study and booted up the computer. The byline in the Marysville *Sentinel* clipping belonged to a Larry Kryshevski. The small newspaper did have a Web site, but the archives went back only a year. I called the phone number provided on the site, but the young woman who answered had never heard of the author. Heck, the article was probably written before she was born.

With so much time having passed, the writer seemed like my best bet to learn more than what meager facts were provided in the article, so I plugged Larry K's name into a search engine. It seemed he was a syndicated freelancer, and I found pages and pages of Web articles from newspapers all over the country. And I also found his mother's obituary, which offered the name of his hometown. Finding his phone number was as easy as catching fish with dynamite.

After I dialed, he answered with, "Kryshevski here. I don't want any."

"I'm not a telemarketer," I said quickly. "I'm calling about a story you wrote years ago."

"Years ago I might remember; just don't ask me about anything I wrote yesterday." His raspy, gruff voice sounded like he was a smoker.

"My name is Abby Rose, and the article in question concerned a teenager's disappearance. Very brief story in the Marysville *Sentinel*. I'm hoping you know more than what appeared in the paper."

"Hold on a second." He didn't bother to cover the receiver when he started yelling at whoever was in the room with him. "Can you tell I'm on the phone? Or have you added deaf and blind to the hypochondria list?"

I heard a female respond, but couldn't make out what she said. Larry answered her with, "Now I understand why you sneeze all the time. To remove the dust from your brain." He cleared his throat. "Sorry, Ms. Rose. Continue."

"The teenager's name was Connie Kramer," I said, hoping to end this conversation quickly. Larry K wasn't exactly my kind of guy.

"Yeah. Connie. She disappeared."

"So you do recall the story?"

"The kid, more than the story. In places like Marysville you get to know people."

"And what do you remember about her?"

"Hold on again," he said, then barked, "Chicken again? Are you hoping to put enough salmonella in my system to kill me, Phyllis?"

Sounded like a decent plan to me, I thought.

This time the woman's response was audible. "Kryshevski, you're living proof there are more horse's butts than horses. Eat your dinner and shut up."

It seemed she didn't need anyone's help to handle this jerk.

Larry said, "I'm having a conversation with someone far more interesting than a fucking chicken. She wants to know about something I wrote, which of course would never interest *you*."

"Uh, maybe I should call you back later?" I said.

"No. Me and the chicken will go in the other room — if that's okay with *you*, Phyllis?"

Another muffled response that I was glad I couldn't understand.

"Women," said Larry K, and then I heard

a door squeal shut. "Okay. Blessed privacy. Now why are you asking about Connie Kramer?"

"I was cleaning out an attic after a friend died and found the article. Looks like it came from one of those 'police beat' sections," I said. "The last line is what caught my interest. You wrote, 'Foul play is not suspected.' "

"Ah, yes," said Larry K with a laugh. "Snuck that past the night editor and got in trouble with the big boss when he read the copy."

"Why would that get you in trouble?" I asked.

"Back then," he answered, sounding like he had a mouthful of food, "you weren't supposed to confuse gossip with the news. See, I was ahead of the times."

"And do you remember the gossip?"

"Depends on why you're asking. Dispensing information is my bread and butter, and it sounds like you want me to work for free."

"How much?" I said, stifling my irritation and hoping there really was salmonella in his chicken.

"You tell me why this is important to you and we can work something out. If it's a good enough story, it won't cost you a dime.

My newspapers will pay me."

No use shooting myself in the foot just because I didn't like the man. What harm could it do to tell him the truth? So I began with Ben's murder and ended with finding the inscription in the Bible.

"Hmm. Interesting," he said when I was finished. "Maybe we can work together on this. You say you found sketchbooks?"

"Yes, but I'm more interested in —"

"And you have a photograph of this woman, Cloris?"

"I do."

"Can you scan one of the drawings and the photo and send it to me, along with a signed commitment that I get first shot at doing a piece on this?"

"Okay, sure," I said. Obviously the guy knew something, and I wanted what he had. He gave me his fax number and I hung up.

Thirty minutes later I had him back on the line.

"Okay, here's the deal," Larry explained. "Kid ran off because someone knocked her up. And in Marysville, seventeen-year-old unwed mothers were about as welcome as piss in a punch bowl."

"And they never found her?"

"Not that I heard. Anyway, when you mentioned the sketchbooks, I remembered something else about Connie. She'd won this little art contest sponsored by our paper. I was one of the judges. She was good."

"Are you saying Connie and Cloris are the same person?"

"That's her in the picture you faxed. That's Connie. And that sure as hell is her artwork."

I didn't speak for a few seconds, wondering how this might connect to Cloris-a.k.a.-Connie's murder.

As if he'd read my mind, Larry K said, "When and if you find out what exactly happened to that girl, you remember we have an agreement, Ms. Rose." He was all business now. No attitude, no sarcasm. In fact, he sounded downright excited. And I was, too.

I hung up, thinking how everything I'd learned so far seemed to lead to a bigger mystery. Ruth had never mentioned any baby born to Cloris and Ben, in fact, I clearly remembered Sheriff Nemec saying there were no children, no other relatives period.

Okay. So maybe the man's name that Cloris had written in the sketchbook and on her calendar would shed some light on why she felt compelled to flee town and change her identity. I turned my attention to

Samuel Feldman and plugged him into the same search engine I'd used to find Larry K. Ten pages of hits popped up. Not bad. Could have been a thousand. And I soon discovered a number of these hits showed one particular Samuel Feldman lived in Galveston. After scrolling through all the pages, I could find no other Texas connection. So I visited the yellow pages on-line and typed in Feldman's name. When a number carrying a Galveston area code popped up, I dialed and was greeted by an answering machine.

"You have reached Parental Advocates," said a soft, professional-sounding female voice. "Our business hours are nine a.m. to five p.m. Tuesday through Saturday. If you would like to leave a message, please do so at the tone."

I hung up, wondering if I had the right number. But when I tried several other on-line phone books, the same number appeared. So was Parental Advocates Feldman's business?

The message said they were open tomorrow, and I decided I'd pay a visit. Who knows? Maybe I'd get lucky and come face-to-face with someone from Cloris's past.

11

I dragged myself from bed early the following morning and had little memory of the drive to Galveston, despite the double espresso I picked up at Starbucks. I found Parental Advocates without difficulty, located in a restored house in the doctor-lawyer-accountant section of town. I'd been considering what kind of business Parental Advocates might be. The most common options for unwed mothers back in the 1970s were adoption or abortion. Didn't sound like abortion, not with that *advocate* word, so I figured adoption was the most logical explanation.

The building was freshly painted, and gold-leaf lettering on a sign next to the leaded-glass front door confirmed I had the right place. The door chimed when I entered, and a woman was seated behind a sleek walnut desk across the large once-foyer-now-office. She looked to be around my age, close to thirty, with stylish straight hair and wearing an expensive-looking summer-weight pale green suit. I took in the burgundy velvet window seats, gleaming oak floors, and expensively draped bay window. No cheap storefront operation, that was for sure.

"May I help you?" she asked.

"I was looking for Mr. Feldman. Is he in?"

"Mr. Feldman?" Her eyes narrowed. "Did someone refer you to *him* for an adoption?"

Why did the woman sound so surprised? I didn't know, but she seemed so darned suspicious I found myself saying, "Uh . . . yeah. I was referred here."

"To Mr. Feldman? How odd. I'm Helen Hamilton, by the way." She gestured to a leather chair in front of her desk. "Please have a seat. I'm very curious to know who referred you, Ms. . . . ?"

"Deer. Jane Deer. Actually, the person asked me not to use their name."

"I see."

Whatever she "saw" wasn't sitting too well, so I decided to say nothing, hoping she'd offer more. Meanwhile, I scanned the walls for a framed state license confirming this was indeed an adoption agency, but there were only prints of sailing ships and the more famous Galveston mansions.

Finally she succumbed to the silence and said, "Mr. Feldman has . . . retired. I run

Parental Advocates now. How can I help you?"

Retired could mean the man was old enough to be Cloris's Feldman. "So has he moved to Florida or Arizona to play golf every day?" I said, trying to probe and sound lighthearted at the same time.

"I don't see how that information could possibly help you. I, on the other hand, arrange adoptions and would be happy to assist you. That is why you came here, correct?" she said.

"The fertility drugs just haven't worked," I answered. Never let the truth stand in the way of a good story, as Daddy used to say.

"Let me inform you first, Ms. Deer, that we're reluctant to place children with single parents. You're not single, are you?" She was staring at my left hand — my ringless left hand.

Couldn't manufacture a wedding band, so I just plowed on. "My husband couldn't come with me. He's out of town."

"If you want to proceed, then I'll meet with you both when your spouse returns. What's his profession?" She slid a stack of papers across the desk.

"Uh . . . computers. He owns a computer business." I glanced at the heading on the top sheet. It said, *Family History,* but nothing on the top page identified Parental Advocates as an adoption agency, either.

Hamilton rested her elbows on the chair's arms and smiled. "I hope you understand that finding the right child can be expensive."

"Money's not an issue." I leaned toward her, shaking my head sadly. "We've exhausted all other alternatives."

My response seemed to erase Hamilton's paranoia. Her body language — relaxed shoulders, welcoming smile — struck me as hugely sympathetic and accepting now.

She said, "I assure you, we'll do everything to find you the perfect child, but first we'll need your husband's input. If you'd like, I could arrange a meeting in a less formal setting. Dinner, perhaps? Say at the Galvez Hotel?"

So she wanted to meet me and my fake husband at an expensive restaurant, where no doubt she'd offer a smooth sales pitch. For a human life. I forced a smile and said, "I'll discuss this with my husband when he returns, but could you answer a few questions now?"

"If I can."

"How does Parental Advocates work? See, we've been through so many agencies and talked to so many —"

"We'll clarify everything after we receive the processing fee." She floated an elegant hand at the forms lying in front of me. "For purposes of confidentiality, all our transactions are in cash."

Cash? Definitely a fox in this chicken coop. I decided to mention Feldman again, since his name had provoked such a strong reaction earlier. "Are you sure Mr. Feldman is permanently retired? I really hoped to talk to him."

Did her cheeks lose a little color or was it my imagination? "Mr. Feldman no longer practices law," she said coldly. "We have several very good attorneys on board. Now if you'll excuse me, Ms. Deer, a client is due here any minute." She stood, extending her hand. "Call us in the future and we'll see if we can proceed with your application. A pleasure meeting you."

Her gray eyes were as icy as a pawnbroker's smile, and her "please let me take your money" attitude had transformed to "let me *think* about taking your money," all after my bringing up Feldman again.

She led me to the door and offered a frosty good-bye.

After I climbed into the Camry and turned the key in the ignition, I sat there wondering why the mere mention of a name had caused the ambient temperature in that room to drop twenty degrees. These thoughts were interrupted, however, when I spotted Hamilton in my rearview mirror. I pulled out and started down the street, still keeping an eye on her in the mirror. She took off in a silver BMW, heading in the opposite direction.

And I made a U-turn.

12

Helen Hamilton's hot little Beamer steamed through Galveston at an urgent clip. As I followed, I wondered if Daddy and Mom were forced to pay a "processing fee" when they adopted us. And worse, had they dealt with someone as mercenary as Hamilton seemed to be?

And why, if Hamilton had a client coming, as she claimed, did she leave her office? Had the mere mention of Feldman sent Hamilton speeding through town? Because she *was* speeding, weaving between cars on Broadway and passing on the right. I kept my distance, but the main street is long and wide, and I had no trouble keeping her in sight.

She made a right turn, and at first I thought she might be taking a shortcut to Seawall Boulevard. I made the same turn just before the light changed, knowing I had to be careful now. We were in a residential area with little traffic, and she might spot me. I let her have a two-block lead. We drove into a run-down neighborhood, and a minute later she made a left, lurching to a halt in front of a small yellow house.

I drove on past the intersection and parked by a sagging beige two-story on the corner. I adjusted my side mirror and saw Hamilton walking briskly up the walkway to the yellow house.

I waited, considering whether I should continue to follow her once she came out. I guess I thought she'd simply lead me to Feldman, but this was certainly no retirement community.

Then, five minutes into my self-appointed stakeout, I learned another little detecting lesson. I'd never make a good cop. I was stir-crazy. What was going on over there?

Knowing I shouldn't, knowing I'd be sorry, knowing I'm about as patient as a two-year-old in front of a birthday cake, I slid from behind the wheel into the humid morning air. Maybe the drapes were open and I could see what she was doing. Or maybe I could listen at an open window.

I started for the corner, noting that even the lawns looked defeated. Clumps of Saint Augustine grass choked the life out of the gentle Bermuda, where there was any Bermuda, and not merely blemishes of dusty ground.

"You selling something?" called a voice from behind me.

My heart skipped. Some surveillance expert I was. I hadn't noticed anyone within a block of here. I squinted back at the house I'd parked in front of, but through the screen door all I could see was a shadowy face and the whites of his eyes.

"Not selling," I said. "Hope you don't mind if I park here, but I want to surprise a friend, and if she recognizes my car, it would ruin everything."

He opened the door about six inches. He was a tall kid, maybe sixteen or seventeen. "If your car's gone when you get back," he said, "don't go telling the police I had anything to do with it."

A small child appeared at the teen's knees, peeking out at me with giant brown eyes. He couldn't have been more than five. "Yeah, white lady, don't go telling the police."

"Get back in the house, man," the teenager said. "Didn't Momma tell you about talking trash like that?"

The little boy answered this by running out onto the porch, skipping in circles, and chanting, "William can't get me. William can't get me."

William did get him, however, with a rapid swoop of one long, gangly arm. To the delight of the child, he was lifted to a horizontal position on William's hip, well above the slatted, uneven porch.

I smiled, then started off again, saying, "No one will have the time to steal my car. Besides, Camrys are hard to break into." I had no idea if this was true, but it sounded convincing. Their front door clattered shut as I walked away.

Sweat already soaked the back of my T-shirt and dampened the waist of my khaki shorts by the time I reached the yard surrounding the yellow house. It had to be a hundred degrees though not even ten a.m. yet.

That was when my impatience caught up with me. Helen Hamilton was coming out of the house she'd entered only a short while ago. I scurried to a nearby mimosa and stood behind the tree, but mimosas aren't exactly live oaks and I'm not exactly Kate Moss. I definitely had a camouflage-deficit problem.

When Hamilton descended the porch steps and I saw what she was carrying, my hand flew to my mouth. A baby. A baby in a car seat. Guess the "client" couldn't quite come to her. And then I wondered why she hadn't told the truth. Adoptions and babies go together, so —

"Hey! White lady!" said the little kid from

the beige house. His words seemed to echo through the waves of heat zigzagging off the blacktop.

Damn! Hamilton might hear him and spot me.

I grabbed the kid by his tiny shoulders and moved him in front of me, ducking so his chest was between me and her. I put my finger to my lips. "Shhh, I'm playing hide-and-seek."

His dark eyes grew wide with the pleasure of conspiracy.

I peeked over his shoulder. She was putting the baby in the car and did glance our way, but quickly refocused on the infant, whose tiny wail drifted across the lawn. Her high heels clicking on the pavement, Hamilton then walked around to the driver's side and opened the door.

The boy said, "Lady, you gotta listen!"

I covered his mouth with my hand and whispered, "Don't give me away. It's her turn to hide, and maybe I can see where she's going." I continued watching Hamilton, ready to head for my car and follow when I thought it was safe.

The boy twisted free, took my face in his small, square hands, and pulled my head so we were eye-to-eye. "But, lady," he said, those soft, wide eyes close to my nose,

"James Franklin is stealing your car."

A second passed before I grasped what he'd told me; then I started running like Satan's breath was on my neck.

I didn't know if Hamilton saw me bounding across the grass. I didn't know if she saw the kid right alongside me, taking three strides to my one. I wouldn't be finding out where she was taking that baby, and about then I didn't care.

I felt momentary relief when I saw that my car wasn't gone, and was about to deliver a lecture about lying little brats when I noticed the open driver's-side door.

A pair of what had to be size-fourteen athletic shoes rested on the curb. Shoes with feet in them. And legs attached. The remainder of this person's body was wedged under the dash of my car.

"Hey! You!" I shouted, hurrying toward the Camry.

Obviously James Franklin's give-a-damner was broken. He kept right on with his hot-wiring activities.

"Get the hell out of my car!" I shouted, giving the nearest size-fourteen a good kick.

"Yeah. Get the hell out of her car," came the small voice beside me. I noticed the kid had his hands on his hips just like me.

My kick got James Franklin's attention —

unless he was afraid of a five-year-old with an attitude. When his ugly mug appeared, his eyes bloodshot and looking in every direction at once, I should have known "Get the hell out of my car" would have about as much impact as a dart hitting an elephant.

Sure, he got out, but he was swinging my saddlebag of a purse, the one I'd left on the front seat.

I have reasonably sound reflexes. I ducked.

A mistake. My purse met the little guy on the downside, right on the head, sending him sprawling onto the sidewalk.

"Will-iam!" the kid screeched.

But apparently William had already heard the commotion, because while I knelt next to the screaming child, William tore after the retreating James Franklin, calling the thief a nasty name, which included references to a maternal parent. The car thief–turned–purse snatcher was running like a bullet with feet, my bag clutched to his chest.

I turned my attention to the whimpering boy, unsure how to handle him. "What's your name, kid?"

He didn't seem to be bleeding anywhere. But his nose was running, his face was streaked with tears, and his lower lip trembled.

"Sho . . . mar . . . i," he said, the syllables separated by sobs.

"I'm sorry, Shomari, I shouldn't have ducked." And then, since I didn't know what else to do, I hugged him.

His thin but strong arms came up and around my neck and I picked him up. Snot and tears joined the sweat on my shoulder as I carried him over to the much cooler porch and sat down.

A minute later William returned. Perspiration dotted his shaved head and ran in rivers down his neck, joining the widening stains on his T-shirt front.

"Why you come around here making trouble, lady?" he said, tossing my purse toward me.

Even though I was already flushed and sunburned, I felt my face grow even hotter. "I don't know how to thank you. I don't have much cash, but I could —"

"You think you can throw your money at us and make this okay? Shomari could have been hurt bad." He looked at the boy. "You all right, man?"

Shomari nodded, eyes down, fingers in his mouth.

Now I felt like *I* had taken the hit with the purse.

"So," William continued, "why don't you

take your purse and your money and your crazy red hair and —"

"Now, wait a minute. I may be a self-serving white bitch, but my hair is not red; it's auburn."

His eyes widened, and by gosh if this intense black giant didn't have a sense of humor. "Lady, you look like you combed that mess with my mama's skillet."

I laughed and so did William.

Then Shomari said, "Since you're not mad no more, William, can she give me some money now?"

I quickly said, "I have gum — will that do?"

Shomari nodded eagerly.

I found two sticks in my purse and gave them to him.

While Shomari unwrapped them, William said, "I need water. Looks like you could use some, too."

He went into the house and returned with two glasses. "It's not cold. Momma says you shouldn't have ice water when you're over-heated. Says it can shock you or something."

"Wet is all I care about. Thanks."

Shomari poked my arm and looked up at William. "She was playing hide-and-seek with the white lady who came and took Tannae's baby."

"So she gave the boy up." William shook his head, appearing disgusted.

"I followed the woman over here," I said. "The one who took the baby. I really parked here because I'm sort of investigating her."

"Tannae's brain could use some investigating, too," said William. "She sold that baby. That's not what she'll say, but she sold him, all the same. Got herself a color TV and a private doctor so's she wouldn't have to wait down at the women's clinic. Told everyone at school it was adoption, but everyone knows she sold him. Momma said she'd go straight to hell if she went through with it."

"This girl goes to your school?" I asked, then finished my water.

"Dropped out when she started to show."

"Ever hear her mention a man named Feldman?"

"I never heard her say nothing except Gerard Smith knocked her up and wouldn't give her no money, so she had to go for this adoption thing."

Shomari had the half-chewed gum in his hands and was trying to make a cat's cradle with it.

William grunted in irritation. He lifted Shomari by the elbow and stood him up. "Let's get that stuff off your fingers, man."

158

"Sorry again," I said. "And thanks for getting my purse back."

He paused by the screen door. "Wasn't me. Stupid James Franklin ran smack into some big black dude I never seen around here. Guy took back your bag and tossed it to me. Last I saw, he and James were, uh . . . talking."

"Still, thanks anyway." I left then, and as I went down the three rickety steps, I heard Shomari say, "Know something, William? She stinks as bad as you do."

On the way to the Camry I lifted an arm and risked a whiff. Geez. He was right.

13

On the drive back to Houston, I thought about all I had learned in the last two days, trying to fit these new pieces into the puzzle. One thing linked Ben with Kate and me — adoption. Was that why Ben showed up at our house? Was our adoption and Cloris's giving up her own baby somehow connected? And since these events happened around the same time, could Parental Advocates be that connection?

I always assumed Willis handled our case, but perhaps Ben sought out Daddy after learning they shared the same adoption broker. And maybe he was in Houston not to find his wife's killer, but to find a child given up years ago. I had to get with Willis on this. He hadn't reacted to the name Feldman when I told him all I had learned, but maybe Parental Advocates would ring a bell.

I turned on the radio, pleased with how far I had come with such few clues, just in time to hear the weather report. It seemed our summer drought could end soon. A tropical depression was forming in the gulf, though the disturbance was currently stationary. Since only fools made light of Texas weather, I would have to keep an ear tuned to the news.

When I turned onto my street in Houston forty-five minutes later, I realized I'd forgotten all about Aunt Caroline's planned visit today, but the U-Haul in the driveway reminded me. She and a muscular escort were just leaving, and I couldn't help but focus on my aunt's tiny white shorts and chartreuse halter top.

"Hello, Abby," she said when I greeted them on the walkway. "Have you met my trainer, Hans? He's been helping me load." She gazed up at him with her surgically correct smile.

"Nice to meet you, Hans." I looked at Aunt Caroline. "I forgot you were a woman on a mission today. Take everything on your list?" As if she'd miss a straight pin if it took her fancy.

Hans gazed down at me, or should I say at all my body parts, beginning at my feet and ending with my eyes.

"Caroline has told me so much about you," he said, his voice deep and accented.

Where did she find this one? At the Arnold Schwarzenegger look-alike contest at Cyclone Willy's Nightspot?

He massaged Aunt Caroline's naked shoulder, but never took his eyes off my chest.

"Where's Kate?" I stepped past them.

"She's in the study with Willis," said Aunt Caroline. "But where have you been, Abby? You smell like you've got goats under each arm."

I faced her. "Thanks so much for embarrassing me in front of someone I've just met. You can be sure I wasn't over plundering *your* house."

"I think we'll leave before this turns nasty." She started down the walkway toward the U-Haul.

Hans called over his shoulder, "I like a woman who doesn't mind getting dirty." He winked and then followed after Aunt Caroline.

I shook my head as I entered the house. I swear the inscription on Aunt Caroline's tombstone will read, *The only time she has ever slept alone.*

Willis and Kate were bent over Daddy's desk in the study, documents spread in front of them. Kate seemed harried, her hair a tangled mess, a fist on her hip. She was holding a paper in the other hand.

When our eyes met, I realized she might be more than a tad cranky.

"This is not my idea of fun, Abby. Not after a morning of trying to keep Aunt Caroline from calling Allied Van Lines and stealing everything in sight. What took you so long?"

"Glad to see you, too, Kate."

Her eyes flashed. She had to be the nicest, most flexible soon-to-be therapist this side of the Mississippi, but she was at her irritable worst right now.

"I'm not apologizing," she said. "Not this time. You deliberately avoided dealing with Aunt Caroline, didn't you?"

The last time Kate was this pissed off at me was when I went to the prom with the biggest flirt in the senior class just because the guy had a great ass. She believed I'd compromised my values. Actually, I had compromised *her* values. Great male asses rank right up there with chocolate and French-kissing, as far as I'm concerned.

The tension between us seemed to make Willis uncomfortable, probably because he'd never seen Kate have an almost-tantrum before. I had, of course, but not in a long time.

"Answer me, Abby. Did you purposely stay away?" she said.

"Well, Kate, you've spent a gazillion dollars at Rice University so you can call yourself an expert on unconscious motivation. You figure out why I didn't want to witness the pillage. And by the way, what's that?" I pointed at the paper in her hand.

"The stupid contract. We had an offer on the house." She threw the paper on the desk.

I looked at Willis. "Is this the real reason she seems ready to chomp a chunk out of my butt?"

Willis cleared his throat again, impatiently thumbing through other papers. "Bad offer. I'm guessing the prospective buyer wants to see how low you'll go. The small matter of the recent, uh . . . *death* in the greenhouse does affect marketability."

"With Kate's plans for a serious lifestyle adjustment, maybe we'll have to cut our losses," I said.

"Oh," she said sarcastically. "So if we make a mistake about selling, it's all my fault?" Her chin jutted a few inches, and her cheeks now raged scarlet.

What in the heck was wrong with her?

I kept my voice level. "You're entitled to a life of your own with Terry, so maybe we shouldn't be selling merely to spare me having to care for such a huge place alone. In fact, maybe Willis and Aunt Caroline are right on this one. Selling so soon after the murder could be a mistake."

Her shoulders relaxed and the tension around her mouth eased. "Good. Because I feel the same way."

Willis said, "I'm glad you've come to your senses about something." His hazel eyes narrowed behind his glasses. "Where have you been, by the way? You're sunburned."

"In Galveston, trying to find out about someone. Pretty frustrating day, though."

"Did this frustration concern Ben's death?" Willis asked.

"What if it did?"

"You're carrying this too far, Abby," he said. "What if you ended up face-to-face with Ben's killer?"

"Good question." One I was too tired to consider. I picked up the contract and looked at Kate. "Can we trash this?"

"Please do." She pushed aside the hair flopping on her forehead. "I'm sorry I overreacted. I've been worried about leaving you alone when I go live with Terry."

"I'll be alone, whether here or in a smaller place. About time I fended for myself," I said.

Willis cleared his throat. "If you ladies will excuse me, I'm meeting Simon Holloway for eighteen, though he probably

165

won't be able to finish nine holes in the afternoon heat. He eats porterhouse steaks and slurps Manhattans for lunch. No wonder he can't even walk back and forth to the golf cart."

"Thanks for coming over," said Kate.

Kate and I walked Willis to the front door and I said, "By the way, who handled our adoption, Willis?"

He stopped at the door, looking like he'd just put on barbed-wire Jockey shorts. "What? Where did you pull that question from?"

"Just wondering."

"I handled the legalities," he said, his tone curt.

"So you didn't go through an agency called Parental Advocates?"

"We dealt with your biological family's lawyer directly after the plane crash."

"And that lawyer's name wasn't Samuel Feldman?" I said.

He stared at me, eyes narrow. "Oh. I remember you mentioning Feldman and how he was somehow connected to Ben's past. Is that what you've been up to today? Digging up skeletons?"

"I was thinking Ben may have sought Daddy out because Cloris used the same adoption agency years ago."

"Cloris used an adoption agency?" Kate said. "When did you find that out?"

"I'm not sure she even did. And the adoption angle might have nothing to do with why Ben came here, but it's better than no explanation at all. I have another question, Willis."

He checked his watch. "I really should have left here by now."

"This won't take a minute. Do you need a license to run an adoption agency?"

"No license is required that I'm aware of. Texas has more liberal adoption laws than most states."

"What do you mean by liberal?" I asked.

"Can we leave this alone? I have to go." He turned the knob.

"Does liberal mean it's okay for someone to pay a birth mother?"

"Is this a roundabout way to ask about your own adoption? Because I assure you, Charlie and Elizabeth did everything in their power to provide you and Kate with a good home. If you start questioning their —"

"Who says I'm questioning anything they did?" But his defensiveness had me wondering. Now was not the time to press him, however. I'd already flustered him enough. So I said, "Actually, Willis, I'm asking all these questions because I'm thinking of adopting. I figure I've had plenty of experience raising Steven."

"I take it you're joking, but whatever you're up to, I advise you not to upset the wrong people. Adoption means money to some, and when you mess with their money, they often react unpleasantly. I'll see you Sunday for dinner."

He left and Kate closed the door. "What have you been up to, Abby? Because if I know you, you didn't get that sunburn on a Galveston beach."

"It's a long story, and I'm dying to share the details."

We went arm in arm back to the kitchen, fixed iced tea, and moved out by the pool so we could enjoy the tiny breeze that blessed us today. I recounted my interview with Hamilton and my first attempt at shadowing someone.

"That kid who tried to steal your car could have had a gun, Abby! What were you thinking?"

"Obviously I wasn't thinking."

"And I suppose you're not done with Helen Hamilton?"

"She's connected to Feldman, and Feldman is connected to Cloris and Ben."

"Sounds like you made her plenty suspicious with all your questions."

"I figure she'll get less suspicious when I return with a husband and some cash." I smiled.

Kate didn't.

"He won't go for this," said Kate as we pulled into Terry's driveway a few hours later. His small brick home was on a tree-lined street in one of my favorite sections of the city, near Rice University.

Kate hopped out of the SUV and went around to open the back gate on her 4Runner. She let Webster out and he bounded toward the front door, stopping briefly to lift his leg and spray the huge oak in the front yard. He likes Terry's house. Not as much square footage to wear him out.

"I know Terry will be reluctant to help me, and that's why you have to convince him," I said.

"I'm willing, but I'm not guaranteeing anything," she said.

We entered the house after a cursory knock, Webster leading the way through the narrow hall to the living room. Terry had been slowly modernizing the old house, but he had yet to work on the living room. Brocade drapes and floral wallpaper clashed with his black leather sofa, contemporary end tables, and sleek entertainment center.

Terry, dressed in his usual khakis and polo shirt, emerged from the kitchen, and Webster greeted him by barking and doing a few whirligigs.

"Hi, fella," he said, rubbing the dog's head. Terry grinned at me. "And hello, Abby. Didn't know you were coming for dinner, too."

"Never miss a chance to visit with my favorite soon-to-be brother-in-law," I said.

His eyes turned in amused inquiry to Kate. "What does she want, Kate? More police info, I suppose?"

"Me?" I said. "Ulterior motives? Never."

He laughed. "I'll set another plate for supper."

He had fixed fruit salad, grilled chicken, and poppyseed muffins, and we ate in the dining room, whose walls bore the scars of recently stripped wallpaper.

While we ate, I told him about Feldman, Hamilton, and the plan I'd devised to learn more about Parental Advocates. Once we'd finished the meal, Terry sat back in his chair, considering what I'd said.

I pushed pineapple tidbits around my plate, feeling his resistance, even though he hadn't come right out and said he wouldn't help me. Kate wasn't doing any generous lobbying in my favor, which bothered me. But she loved the guy and certainly knew how to handle this situation better than I did.

Indeed, the affection and respect between Kate and Terry was obvious. Love and respect. If I'd only weighed their importance before I married Steven. Passion and Bud Light weren't exactly the best foundation for a lasting relationship.

Kate picked up the pitcher and we passed the iced tea around, refilling our glasses.

"Why didn't you ask me for help before you went wandering around Galveston?" Terry finally said.

I added a lemon slice to my drink, saying, "Are you in the early stages of Alzheimer's, Terry? Remember that day in your office when you said you couldn't help me?"

He said, "I was a little ticked at you, remember?"

"I know. I'm sorry." I attended to the frayed edge of my napkin.

He went on, saying, "And you've gone a little overboard again. I mean, is it a good idea to follow a woman who may have been conducting an entirely legal business transaction?"

"She didn't know she'd been followed," I said.

"There's no give-up in you, is there?" He sighed. "I suppose I could check a couple of sources at HPD and see if they know anything about this Feldman guy."

"Maybe he's been dead for years," said Kate. "Or he moved away."

"Hamilton said he was retired. And if he's still in the area, maybe I can find him."

"Okay," Terry said. "So you find him. But if the man's guilty of anything, he certainly won't tell you." Terry's tone, edging closer to condescension, reminded me of an earlier conversation with Willis Hatch. Why did all the men in my life think they had to protect me?

Figuring I needed a time-out before I shot myself in the foot with Terry, I said, "Talk to him, would you, Kate? I'm going to the bathroom."

"Use the one in my bedroom," said Terry. "That hall bath is torn up."

And so was Terry's bedroom, though not from remodeling. He was plain messy, something Kate might have a problem adjusting to. The comforter was wadded at the end of the bed, and dirty clothes littered the floor.

I, however, considered this a point in the man's favor. I never trusted neat men. Neat men called their mothers on odd-numbered days and collected stamps. Dodging a trail of towels, I made my way to the bathroom. A minute later, when I moved a shirt strewn over the sink so I could wash my hands, three or four business cards fluttered from the pocket. I picked them up.

Police-issued business cards. An embossed gold shield was prominent in the upper center, and beneath this was printed, *Terry Armstrong, Ph.D., Houston Police Department, Consultant.*

Hmm. These could prove useful. I pocketed them and returned to the dining room.

"Guess what?" said Kate. "Terry's agreed to help with your plan to find Feldman."

"Really?" I said, genuinely surprised. "How'd she convince you?"

"By being Kate." He smiled and squeezed her hand. "I think she's right, though. There's nothing illegal about checking out Parental Advocates by pretending to seek their services. Investigative reporters do things like this all the time. A little play-acting, right? Besides, you are practically family. Tell me where and when, and I'll be there, Abby."

"Thanks . . . I'll call you when I'm ready to execute the plan." I ran my fingers over the edges of the small rectangles in my pocket. "But are you absolutely positive?"

"Sure," he said. "It's not like I'll be impersonating a police officer or anything. Now, that can get you in big trouble."

14

The following morning I was finishing a bagel in the kitchen and listening to the Weather Channel reporter banter about the possibility of the tropical storm becoming a hurricane. She bubbled with anticipation as pictures of those upper-level disturbances and low-pressure systems came in via satellite. She was orgasmic about potential ratings, rather than the storm, was my guess. Folks would be glued to their televisions up and down the coast. When she got to the important part, I jotted down the coordinates of the storm, making a mental note to check our supply of batteries and bottled water.

Kate had gone out for the Sunday paper, and when she returned, she noticed what station I was tuned to. "When should we expect the duck drencher's arrival?"

"Not sure. It's a slow mover. Meanwhile, I have more pressing concerns."

"Like what?" she said. "I was hoping we'd loaf by the pool today."

"Sergeant Kline called, and in his best evil-mannered delivery, he suggested I come and see him. Today."

"Doesn't sound like fun," Kate said. "Did he say why he wants to talk to you?"

I shook my head. "Maybe I'll be calling you from jail for bail money."

"Should you phone Willis? Have him meet you downtown?"

"I was kidding. I can handle a few questions without benefit of counsel."

"I could go with you for moral support," she said.

"I'm a big girl. By the way, have you seen Diva? She's pulled another disappearing act."

"She always comes back when she gets hungry," said Kate, gathering up the newspaper and her green tea before heading for the pool deck.

I hope she comes back before bedtime, I thought, heading for the stairs to dress for my trip to police headquarters. One night without her was enough.

With my visitor sticker plastered to my cotton camp shirt, I made my way down a narrow carpeted aisle bordered on both sides by partitioned cubicles in the Homicide division at HPD. Phones were ringing, computers whirring, and I heard more than one pager beeping as I made my way to where Sergeant Kline sat behind a desk piled with folders and papers. He indicated a plastic chair and I sat across from him, again confronting that unwavering stare.

After I refused the gum he offered, he folded a stick into his mouth, chewed a second, and said, "I have a few concerns. This shouldn't take long."

"Shoot," I said. "Or is that a bad word to use in a police station?"

He didn't smile. "First off, this case has few leads." He leaned back in his chair and rested one foot on the edge of the desk.

"So no one's confessed. That won't stop you, right?"

"No. But it takes an awful lot of legwork, paperwork, and brainwork to solve a who-dunit like this. From what Sheriff Nemec tells me, digging around in thirty-year-old dirt might not even lead us anywhere. Even if I'm not the one to dig that dirt up." He raised his eyebrows.

So the sheriff had gone and told him about my visit to Cloris's attic. "Why not be direct, Sergeant? Might save us both some time."

"Okay," he said, "I want whatever evidence you took from the Grayson house."

"Have you decided to investigate Cloris's death, then?"

"Maybe. Two people in the same family

dying from cyanide poisoning — even if the murders were years apart — is no coincidence," he said.

Ah. There was intelligent life in the police universe after all. "That's exactly what I thought, and I figure —"

"So," he interrupted, "either you cooperate and turn over what you found, or you could be investigating the inside of a Harris County jail cell."

I sat back, my enthusiasm melting like a chocolate bar left on the dashboard. "When have I not cooperated?"

"I don't call taking away evidence cooperation. But if you had a motive to kill Mr. Grayson, I haven't found one. Not even blackmail. And now, with the similarities between Ben's death and Cloris Grayson's, I —"

"Wait a minute. Blackmail? Why would Ben blackmail me?"

"I don't know. Yet."

"So you still think I might be hiding something?" This was ludicrous. Clearly Ben's death was related to a murder that occurred fifteen years ago, one I knew nothing about until last week.

He chewed languidly for a few seconds before speaking. "Ben Grayson was probably living on your property because he had a good reason to be there — which logically might involve the people who live in your house. Your father's dead, your sister spends every waking hour in the library when she's not with Terry Armstrong, and you . . . ? Well, I've learned you have a less restricted schedule."

My cheeks tingled. "And what, exactly, do you know about my so-called schedule?"

He said nothing.

"Oh. I get it. You've been watching me. Following me."

He shifted in his seat, looking uncomfortable for the first time since we'd met.

"Has this been going on since the day of the murder?" I knew I was glaring, but hell, this pissed me off.

He put both feet on the floor and squared his shoulders. "Routine stuff. Nothing personal."

"You haven't answered my question. How long?"

"After Nemec phoned and said he screwed up and let you take stuff from the Grayson house, we had to watch you more closely. And that's the reason I brought you down here. Following people can get you in lots of trouble. You nearly got more than you bargained for with that car thief in Galveston."

"So the big black dude who nailed James Franklin wasn't merely some good Samaritan, huh?"

"Not exactly."

Another tension-filled silence followed before I said, "You're wasting time and taxpayers' money pursuing me. You could have been up in Shade, where you might actually find answers — like I did."

His neck was blotched, the fire spreading up to his ears. "Carting off evidence before the police have a chance —"

"Nemec came to Ruth's house earlier and chose not to take anything, so I figure she could give me whatever she wanted."

"You figured wrong. I'm dropping the polite approach with you, Ms. Rose, so quit —"

"You actually believe you possess a polite approach?" I said with a laugh.

He leaned toward me, arms folded on his desk. "Okay. You think you're a detective? Why don't you just tell me what you know about the cold case?"

I took a deep breath and exhaled, realizing this was not about egos — his or mine. This was about murder. And if I could help, I wanted to. More than anything.

"Here's what I know." I told him what I had taken from the attic, then said, "I think

Cloris Grayson was actually a teenage run-away named Connie Kramer. She may have had a child out of wedlock that she gave up for adoption thirty-odd years ago. I believe she was looking for the adoption agency when she was murdered."

"She waited fifteen years to look for her kid?" said Kline.

"No Internet back then. And from what I can tell, the lady was poor. It might have taken her that long to get a lead."

"So maybe Ben killed her because of this baby rather than for the insurance money?" he said. "That doesn't work for me."

I wanted to shake the man by his ears, but I stayed calm. "Read my lips. Ben did not kill Cloris."

"If I accept that as fact, tell me how this ancient history relates to his murder. You think he started looking for his dead wife's child after all these years?"

"Yes. He had money after the insurance paid out."

He nodded, seeming to consider this. "And someone didn't want him snooping around in old business. Not out of the realm of possibility. Still doesn't explain why he showed up at your place using a fake name."

"I'm working on that," I said.

"See, that's a huge problem," he said.

"You have no business working on this. I can't afford to keep a man on you."

"You didn't need one 'on me' to begin with."

"You just don't get it. I can foresee arriving at a crime scene to find you've become the victim of an ingenious new method of killing with cyanide. And I wouldn't like that, okay?"

I crossed my arms. "So now I've gone from suspect to potential victim?"

He closed his eyes, looking frustrated and tired. "There's a whole lot about this case neither of us knows. But let me explain something. I've got six fresh homicides right here." He slapped a stack of folders. "That means I can't spend all my time on one case. Especially one with ancient connections."

"Oh. So you'll slide this case over to the 'too tough to solve' column and move on to another murder?"

As soon as the words left my lips, I knew I'd gone too far.

He stared at me for a full ten seconds, chewing the life out of that gum. "You know," he finally said, "you've got way too much time on your hands. I have priorities, Ms. Rose, and I'm sure you do, too. Difference is, no one's judging yours."

Sometimes I can accept the truth, even

when I'm upset. This happened to be one of those moments, but I wasn't willing to give Kline the satisfaction of knowing that. Instead, I stood and turned to leave.

"I like that," he called after me.

I stopped, still facing the other direction. "You like what?"

"A woman who knows when she's wrong."

I whirled. "I never said I was wrong."

"Bet you never do, either. I can't spend any more time and manpower watching you, even if you might need protection."

"Protection?" I craned my neck toward him. "Why should I believe you care one ounce about my safety, Sergeant Kline?"

"Because I called you here to warn you. Not to arrest you for interfering in an official investigation, like I could have. Do me a favor and stick to computers. Something you know about." He removed two more sticks of gum, unwrapped them, and aimed the wadded-up papers at the neighboring trash can. He missed.

"You hate it, don't you?" I said.

He smiled. "On the contrary. This sparring match is the best time I've had in a while."

And that was when I really noticed him for the first time — through this, his first real smile. Those tiny creases surrounding his eyes probably signaled too many sleepless nights and his having been the bearer of bad news day after day. But right now his smile was young and his stare had softened to one more simple and honest.

In a quiet voice I said, "No . . . I mean you really hate giving up on something, even though you may have to close this case."

The smile faded. He averted his eyes and grabbed a handful of papers, shoving them angrily into a manila folder. "This case will not be closed. And what the hell, do you know about it, anyway?"

"More than you could hope to comprehend. I had to give up on my marriage, a decision that still keeps me awake nights. I appreciate your concern for my safety, Sergeant, but I have priorities, too."

Later that evening, when the doorbell rang, I was actually looking forward to Aunt Caroline's and Willis's arrival. I usually went along reluctantly with these Sunday dinners Kate planned, but I'd been examining canceled checks for hours, hoping to unearth a clue to the mysterious safe-deposit box, a task that had progressed from downright humdrum to seriously tedious. Visiting with Willis and Aunt

Caroline seemed a stimulating alternative in contrast.

"Abby, leave this stuff and join us for a drink," Kate said when she entered the study with Willis on her heels.

"You won't have to twist my arm." I rose from the desk chair.

"Whatever are you doing?" Willis took in my pile of checks.

"I figured I could locate the bank where Daddy rented that safe-deposit box by hunting through these. He had to pay for the lease, right? Unfortunately, Kate and I didn't put the checks back in chronological order after the break-in on P Street, so those from 1960 to the present are all mixed together. A rabbit in a frying pan could have more fun."

"What will you glean from all this sleuthing, Abby?" said Willis.

" 'Gleaning' and 'sleuthing'? Is that what I'm doing? Gosh, that sheds a much more interesting light on this thankless task. They never taught you about gleaning and sleuthing in East Texas, did they, Willis?"

He flushed and took a gulp of his club soda.

The doorbell rang again, and Kate left to let Aunt Caroline in. From his expression, Willis didn't appreciate my jab at his humble beginnings — beginnings he had spent a lifetime disguising with fancy cars and expensive suits.

"Let me be straightforward, Abby," he said. "What do you hope to find inside this safe-deposit box?"

"Something linking Daddy with Ben's murder."

"Do I need to remind you that your father died three months before Ben's murder?"

"Daddy may have known more about Ben's past than he let on," I said.

"Like what?"

"Ben's using an alias, for one thing. Maybe Ben told him why, and Daddy hid away anything concerning Ben in that box — maybe for Ben's protection." I wouldn't bring up my theory on the adoption connection again — not until I had hard facts rather than guesses.

Willis smirked. "Abby, you're cooking up stuff to entertain yourself now."

I stacked the checks I'd just gone through back in the box. "Okay. Sure. Whatever you say."

"I didn't mean to discount your very creative ideas," he said. "But have you considered the much simpler possibility that Ben owed someone some money and was murdered when he didn't pay that person back?

I'd say that's much more plausible than your speculation about Charlie and Ben's relationship."

"Are you implying Ben was a mob hit? Aren't they more into assault weapons and concrete? I can't remember the last victim they rubbed out with poisoned spaghetti, can you?"

He raised both hands. "Obviously you've abandoned common sense completely." Willis turned his attention to the lime sliver floating in his drink.

"Common sense was never her strong suit," said Aunt Caroline from the arched doorway. She'd gone from underdressed the other day to looking as if she were ready for dinner at La Reserve in her black crepe pantsuit.

"What's this? Gang-up-on-Abby night?" I could tolerate Willis chastising me. He meant well. But Aunt Caroline had as much right to talk about common sense as about the benefits of monogamy.

"Let's have a drink before dinner and forget this for now," said Kate.

"Sounds great to me," I said, anxious to get away from the check search for today.

We retreated to the family room, where Aunt Caroline sipped white wine and prattled on about how well she would protect the paintings and sculptures we'd entrusted to her. Then she pumped Willis for information on the insured value of every piece of art she'd confiscated, making sure to point out that she planned to will everything back to us. That was when I had a chance to extract a small measure of revenge.

"Good. We wouldn't want anyone else to get his 'Hans' on our things when you die, Aunt Caroline," I said.

Her eyes sparked with anger, and I had to turn away to hide my grin.

Whenever Diva disappeared, which wasn't all that often, I usually had trouble sleeping. By one a.m. I was still awake, my eyes focused on the interlocking circles in the plaster ceiling of my bedroom.

Where did cats go when that urge to wander hit them? Did they have prearranged meetings with each other in the night? Hold little cat conventions to reaffirm their independent spirits? I closed my eyes with a renewed effort to find sleep, and that was when I heard her faint but distinctive meow. I sat up and strained to hear more, then realized where the sound was coming from.

How in the world did she get into the

attic? It was only accessible through the back of a closet.

I left my bed and crept down the hall, not wanting to wake up Kate. She had to be at school early tomorrow.

When we were kids, she and I had plotted our escape from the world into our "secret room" in the very attic Diva now inhabited. But once we'd dragged a few prized possessions up there, prepared to disappear from the face of the earth, we immediately realized that anyone who spent more than a few minutes in those stifling confines would shrivel up and die from the heat. Poor Diva was probably melting.

I went into the guest bedroom, pushed aside the clothes in the closet, and opened the door. A rush of hot, humid air threatened to suck me in.

"Diva!" I whispered into the darkness. I reached over my head, trying to locate the ceramic pull for the light. "Here, kitty-kitty." I found the chain, but after several tugs I realized the attic bulb was burned out. Meanwhile, I could hear plaintive cries in the blackness beyond.

The bedroom light would have to suffice, but though I waited awhile for my eyes to adjust, I still couldn't see her. I needed a flashlight, and on my way down the hall to find one, I asked myself why all important cat business had to be conducted in the dead of night.

Wiping my sweaty hands on my boxers, I tiptoed toward the stairs, certain I'd seen a flashlight in the kitchen drawer not too long ago. But about halfway down the front stairway, I stopped abruptly.

I'd heard something. A squeaking sound. Did it come from outside? I couldn't tell, so I called out Kate's name, thinking maybe I'd woken her. No response. And no more noises.

I grasped the banister, slowly followed the railing down to the foyer, and flipped on the lights. I walked down the hall to the kitchen and started clawing through the catchall drawer. No flashlight there, so I stooped and looked in the cabinet beneath the drawer, mumbling, "If and when I move, half this stuff is getting thrown in —"

I heard another noise. Behind me.

I spun in time to see the back doorknob slowly turning.

15

My heart thudded against my chest, and I was about to grab the phone or scream for Kate when Steven opened the door. My whole body went limp with relief. "Steven Bradley! You gave me a mouthful of my own heart!"

"Sorry," he said. "Thought I could sneak in and out without waking you."

"I know I locked that door. And the alarm was on."

"No alarm, babe. You musta forgot, as usual." He then held a key with a sheepish grin. "Found this a month or two after the divorce. Couldn't sleep, thanks to all the Dr Pepper I drank, so I thought I could sneak in and pick up the blueprints for the Victorian. I saw them in Charlie's study one time."

"Give me that key. Seems it's slipped your mind that you don't live here anymore."

He walked over and placed it in my outstretched palm.

"You smell like a wet hog, by the way." I waved my hand in front of my face.

"Huh?" He was focused on my T-shirt, which read, *Let's put the fun back in dysfunctional* — a phrase that I realized might well have been Steven's motto.

"You stink, Steven. Have you taken to living in a ditch these days?"

"Sorry, the truck needs Freon and it's about ninety degrees outside."

"Do you happen to have a flashlight, by the way? Diva is stuck in the attic."

"How'd she get in there?"

"How would I know? Have you got one?" I said impatiently.

"Got what?" He had renewed his interest in my chest, and not because he was a slow reader.

I crossed my arms and whispered hoarsely, "A flashlight!"

"Sorry. Yeah. In the truck."

He left.

I grabbed a quick drink of water and was just about to get those blueprints when I heard voices outside. Now what?

I walked to the door, the sound of raised male voices carrying from the back driveway. Though not exactly dressed to meet the neighbors, I went outside, and the night immediately enveloped me in its sticky August embrace.

I jogged in the direction of what was now

a considerable commotion, considering the possibility that all the residents in this particular zip code might be congregated in my yard. But I stopped dead when the glow from the small lights that marked the drive revealed only two men — Steven and someone else — locked in a struggle.

The assailant's back was to me, and, figuring I had the advantage, I ran up behind him. Maybe I could stick my fingers in his eyes or pull his hair, but instead my hands slid down his sweaty cheeks. The guy's elbows flew out, and one strong arm tossed me off his back like popcorn.

I landed hard on my tailbone, legs flailing. Steven, meanwhile, had freed himself, and his fist was drawn back.

"Don't hit him!" I hollered, realizing who the assailant was. "He's a cop."

For once Steven listened.

"You know this bozo?" said Kline between gasps, brushing his clothes, then dabbing the cut near his eye. Blood wound in a thin trail down his cheek.

"Yes, I know him." I stood. "Sorry for scratching you, but I *am* immunized against most diseases."

As usual, Sergeant Kline was in no mood for jokes.

Nor was Steven, who took a menacing

step forward. "I'm no bozo."

Even in the dim light, I could tell the tips of Steven's ears were scarlet, and that meant trouble. Several guys at the Frontier Club, where we used to party before I became acquainted with the term *codependent,* knew what sort of trouble.

"Why don't we go inside before we wake the neighborhood?" I said. "Besides, I'm half-naked."

Those words got their attention. Despite preoccupation with fistfights or territorial disputes, most men remain on full alert for a less-than-adequately-clothed female.

As I started walking toward the house, I said, "I don't recall inviting either of you for this two-man square dance."

Neither of them responded. They followed in silence up the walkway and into the kitchen. I hated to leave the two of them alone, but I couldn't comfortably converse in my underwear, so I said, "Make coffee, Steven," hoping that would keep him occupied.

I took the back stairs two at a time, and Webster raced past me in the opposite direction, barking frantically, tail wagging.

"Better late than never, Wonder Dog." I glanced back as he trotted down to greet the guests. "Better go see if you can lick those intruders to death."

Sleepy-eyed Kate was coming out of her room when I entered the upstairs hallway. "Did I hear people yelling?"

"We had a little Pecos promenade on the lawn. One of the yellers — Steven — is making coffee, so join us, if you're so inclined. And by the way, do *you* have a flashlight?"

"In my nightstand. But who else is downstairs?"

I explained about Steven and Kline as we walked to her room. Kate did have a flashlight — exactly where she knew it would be.

"Would you mind rescuing Diva from the attic while I get dressed?" I asked. "Then I need to play referee downstairs. Those two might not be able to stay in the same room together without doing severe damage to each other's faces."

Kate agreed to find the cat, and I went to my bedroom and quickly pulled on shorts and put a bra on under my T-shirt. When I arrived back downstairs, well armed with questions for my policeman friend, I realized I might need a meat cleaver to cut the tension.

I smiled. "So maybe we can have introductions now. Or have you two already done that?" I glanced back and forth between them and was rewarded with a surly grunt from Steven and an "are you nuts?" look from Kline.

I took a deep breath. "Okay, then. Guess you've already exchanged names."

"Not exactly," said Kline. "He's not talking. Since you obviously know him, why don't you enlighten me as to who he is and what he's doing here?"

"Uh, sure. Sergeant Kline, this is Steven Bradley, my ex-husband."

"Oh," said Kline, his tone frosted with sarcasm. "Did I stumble in on one of those kinky 'ex-spouse' things?"

Steven was on his feet faster than a prairie fire with a tailwind. He grabbed Kline by the lapels of his sports jacket.

This set Webster to barking and racing around the table.

"Who the hell do you think you are, asshole?" Steven said. He was spraying bits of spit into the cop's face, but Kline had no trouble turning the tables. Within a millisecond, he had Steven restrained.

I jumped up. "Stop acting as if this is recess at elementary school. He could arrest you, Steven." I focused on Kline, trying to contain my anger. "What Steven and I do in private is none of your damn business, so I suggest you let him go."

Kline pushed Steven away and straightened his jacket. Both of them sat back down.

I reclaimed my seat as well, my hands shaking as I raised the coffee mug Steven had set on the table for me.

To his credit, Kline said, "Sorry. I was way out of line." He pulled out a handkerchief and dabbed the bright slash on his cheek produced earlier by my fingernail.

"Why were you in my driveway in the middle of the night, Sergeant Kline?" I asked. "I thought you said you were finished with the surveillance."

"Thought I was." Kline offered his pack of Big Red to Steven and me. It was definitely the worse for wear.

I declined, and Steven ignored the olive branch.

Kline put two sticks in his mouth and chewed for a second before continuing. "As I waded through the paperwork on my desk after you left the station this morning, I came across a fax from Galveston Police Department. Why didn't you tell me about the break-in on P Street, Ms. Rose?"

"You didn't ask. You had other priorities, remember?"

Kline flushed.

My turn to gloat. "But I like a man who

can admit when he's wrong."

Steven perked up at this exchange. "Maybe I ought to leave the two of you alone so you can like each other in private." But he didn't budge from his chair.

That figured. He wasn't about to leave me alone with Kline. I said, "You didn't exactly call at a reasonable hour, Steven, so don't pull that 'poor me' stuff." I turned back to Kline. "Tell me, Sergeant. How does a break-in on P Street lead to this fight with Steven?"

"I was working late on a case tonight, another surveillance, and after my partner took over I decided it wouldn't hurt to swing by and make sure everything was okay over here. What went down in Galveston concerned me. The report said someone dinged your ex-husband and — Wait a minute. I guess that was you, huh, hero?" Kline smiled.

Gosh. He could actually do more with his mouth than chew gum tonight.

"It was only a scratch," said Steven, staring intently into his coffee.

"Anyway," continued Kline, "seemed like a good idea to keep an eye out here until I figure out if that break-in is connected to the murder. But what do I see when I get here? This jerk — excuse me — him" — he thumbed at Steven — "creeping away from the house. How would you expect a cop to react?"

"I wasn't creeping," said Steven with undisguised contempt. "I was doing Abby a favor."

"And I was watching out for the lady, okay, Bradley?"

The knuckles on Steven's clenched fists grew white. "The lady already has someone to —"

"Hey! Abby!" Kate called from the back stairs. She appeared seconds later and stopped in the doorway, pulling her robe around her. "I didn't realize you still had company."

"You remember Sergeant Kline, Kate?"

"Yes." She nodded at both of them. "Listen, I need help. I can hear Diva, but I need more than a flashlight before I step inside that attic. I think a lightbulb and some reinforcements are in order. I remember the last time she pulled a stunt like this, she nearly shredded my arm during the rescue attempt."

And that was how we all ended upstairs five minutes later — and discovered that rescuing Diva from the box where she was trapped was the least of our problems.

Someone had done the P Street number

all over again. The small attic was a ran-sacked wreck.

I slept late the next day, with Diva har-bored once more in her usual place, purring contentedly each time I reached out to stroke her. She wouldn't be visiting the attic again in the near future, judging from the amount of food and water she'd consumed after rediscovering the kitchen.

Last night, Sergeant Kline — his first name was Jeff, I'd learned — had called for reinforcements to dust the attic for finger-prints and to determine if we'd been a victim of vandalism or theft. They couldn't decide, and neither could we. I hadn't ex-actly done an inventory prior to the ran-sacking. The police left around four-thirty in the morning, and then Kate and I had dragged the contents of the attic into the guest room so we wouldn't have to pull things out tomorrow in the daytime heat to reorganize the mess. We had a huge pile of old clothes, picture albums, and household rejects, as well as more proof that Daddy's need to save things had bordered on psy-chotic.

Last night, and now again this morning, I wondered whether this assault on the attic was somehow connected to Ben's murder.

Or could it be related to that safe-deposit box key? After all, I had found the hidden key right after a similar incident at the Victorian. Of course, I had no proof the key was even what the P Street vandal had been looking for.

Before I could think of any other possible reason for people tearing into our old belongings, the phone rang. I turned on my side and picked up the phone.

"Ms. Rose? Jeff Kline."

"Oh, hi." I sat up.

"I'm sorry, did I wake you?"

"No," I said.

"We found no identifiable prints last night. Lots of smudges on those dusty boxes, but my fingerprint expert thinks the perp wore gloves."

Diva crawled into my lap and climbed halfway up my chest, rubbing her head on the hand holding the receiver. "Why would anyone be interested in a bunch of old family mementos?"

"Maybe they were looking for something else. Did you give any thought to the question I posed last night about how this person found the attic?"

"As far as I know, that attic could have been messed up for months. I haven't been up there since right after Daddy died."

"I checked the reports, thinking maybe my crew made that mess after Ben's murder, but the person assigned to search upstairs said everything was in order that day."

"So," I said. "This must have happened in the last week."

"Right. As for what's-his-name, the ex," Kline said. "He says he came for those blueprints you handed over to him last night, but I've learned about his DUIs and drunk-and-disorderlies. Not exactly your model citizen. Are you sure that's all he came for?"

"I happened to be in the kitchen when he arrived, so he had no chance to go upstairs without me seeing him. As you saw first-hand, he's still protective, despite the divorce, so don't judge him too harshly."

"I leave judging to the judges. Just filling you in on the work we've done since I left this morning."

"Did you get any sleep at all?" I asked. That morning after Ben was killed, this guy could have hired on as an extra in *Night of the Living Dead*. But after what couldn't have been more than an hour or two of sleep, he sounded downright energetic.

"*Nada,*" he answered.

"You sound awfully alert, while I'm feeling like I've been run over by a mobile home pulling a horse trailer."

He laughed. "I've consumed more bad coffee than one human can safely tolerate, but other than that, I'm revived. I'll let you know if any leads turn up."

I hung up, liking the idea that he intended to stay in touch. Liking it plenty. I mean, the guy was a hunk, and he was even laughing at my jokes now.

Terry arrived for a late dinner that evening, and we ate our grilled tuna out on the patio by the pool. The amber antimosquito torches surrounded us, flickering against a starry sky. Kate had already called and told him about last night, making him once again hesitant to help me with my plan to investigate Parental Advocates. But I was certain that finding Feldman might lead us not only to Ben's killer but maybe Cloris's, too, and after a little pleading on my part, he finally succumbed. His renewed cooperation then resurrected the guilt I felt over the business cards now in my purse. But they were still staying in my purse.

"Hon, you look exhausted," said Terry, reaching over and resting a hand on Kate's cheek. He brought her to him and kissed her briefly.

"Abby needs to tell her gentlemen friends

to call at more reasonable times," said Kate. "I missed school, thanks to everything they stirred up."

"Steven and Kline? Gentlemen friends?" he said.

"I didn't invite them," I said. "And I hope you're using the adjective 'gentlemen' loosely. Did you know Kline put a tail on me, Terry?"

"Nope. Those Homicide dicks tell no secrets. Besides, they know Kate and I are a couple, so they wouldn't say anything. By the way, what was your cat doing in the attic in the first place?"

"Someone must have left open the attic door," I said. If I could remember the last time I saw Diva, maybe I could pinpoint when the room was trashed.

"I can narrow the field," said Kate. "Aunt Caroline was all over the house Saturday — she and her strongman, Hans."

"You mean the guy she found in the yellow pages — listed under 'recreational facilities'?" I said.

Kate smiled. "That's the one."

"So you think Aunt Caroline's our culprit?" I said.

"Don't tell her I was the one who fingered her," Kate said. "She still likes me."

I smirked. "Maybe I can change that. I

think you should share the joy of genuine animosity."

Kate and Terry laughed and then we cleared the table. After we finished the dishes, they went to catch a movie and I tackled the chaos in the guest room. I carried packing crates upstairs and Diva soon joined me, the lure of a box too enticing to refuse.

But instead of finishing up quickly, I found that the task stirred memories, and the work took much longer than I expected.

I hadn't seen many of the photographs in years. I quickly set aside the ones of my mother in her wheelchair. I didn't want to think of her like that. I only wanted to know her as I had for the last thirty years, as the woman Daddy spoke of so often and had loved so much.

Instead, I confronted my father's smiling face in the albums, his healthy grip enclosing the small hands of Kate and I as we stared adoringly up at him in front of the Alamo or Disneyland. Those photos brought a fullness to my chest I hadn't felt since that day he collapsed in front of me.

I turned more pages and witnessed the progression of men through Aunt Caroline's life, each a blur in my memory. None of them ever stayed around long.

Willis made his regular appearances in the pictures as well — at Christmases or birthdays, usually alone, but occasionally with some strange female. The nannies were familiar, some Kate's favorites and some mine. But one thing stood out, page after page — Daddy's enduring grin. His light-hearted smiles diminished as the strain of my collapsing marriage appeared in all our eyes in the newer photographs.

The camera truly doesn't lie.

Christmas . . . right before the divorce. We stood side by side, mouths forced into bleak crescents, my gaze not toward the lens but focused on the longneck in Steven's hand. I skipped past those pages, eager to forget, then piled the albums in boxes, wishing I could pack the sadness away as well.

I missed Daddy . . . missed him terribly. He always insisted he was the small end of nothing, whittled down to a point, said we were specks of dust in the big picture. But if that were so, why did he occupy such a huge part of my heart?

A tear escaped, and I wiped it away with the back of my hand, shifting my attention to bags and boxes of clothes.

16

Terry had agreed to be my husband on the visit to Parental Advocates, and we held hands when we walked into the foyer-office for our appointment the next day. Kate, who would wait for us at the Victorian, assured us when we dropped her off that we indeed looked like we could be a married couple. This time I was in full costume, my old wedding band burning on my finger. I hated the thing.

We decided I would play the "I'll do anything for a baby" role, and Terry would act like the skeptical consumer. I had done a little acting in college, but I felt none of the exhilarating tension I had experienced before a stage performance. With my palms sweating and my mouth feeling wiped dry inside, I was plain scared.

Hamilton wore an emerald-green tailored shirt, and her newly cut hair was feathered around her face, a style that softened her angular features. Thin wasn't always flattering, but she'd made a successful adjustment.

She reached across her desk and offered

her hand to Terry. "Nice to meet you, Mr. Deer." She nodded at me. "Good to see you again, too."

She folded her hands in front of her and smiled expectantly. "You've had a chance to fill out the paperwork, I assume?" she asked.

Terry said, "We'll get to that, but I'm sure you won't mind a few questions, Ms. Hamilton. See, I'm not ready to commit to anything in writing."

"As I explained to your wife, putting things in writing in this business *can* cause problems, and that's why we only ask for the family history, which is promptly shredded after we put the information into our computer. We do this for your protection, so you won't be tracked down years later by the birth mother."

"Is this how all adoption agencies work?" asked Terry.

Her eyes shifted for an instant. "Basically, yes. But don't let me alarm you. We protect your investment and do ten times the business a charitable operation might in a given year."

"Ten times?" I said, not bothering to hide my surprise.

She nodded. "You're fortunate to live in Texas. The baby market is booming here."

I kept my eager smile in place, even though I didn't feel the least like smiling. If I truly did want to adopt, her words might be music. But markets for babies didn't excite me. It sounded as if we were talking about racehorses, not children.

I said, "So our chances are good?"

"Like anything worth having, it depends on what you're willing to spend, both monetarily and time-wise. This agency specializes in privacy, and we will serve you well, but surely you understand I'm unwilling to discuss details until I have a cash commitment."

"How much cash?" asked Terry.

"The processing fee is ten thousand."

"What do I get for my processing fee?" he asked, sounding wary.

"Part will pay for adoption insurance. Then we meet with you for several hours and assess exactly what you're looking for in an infant. I assume you want a white child, or you wouldn't have come to us."

"You only deal in Caucasian infants?" I asked. I knew for a fact she didn't, after what I'd seen the day I followed her, but I was curious to see if she would tell the truth.

"We have a few black couples, but we're talking supply and demand, aren't we?"

I could read her demeanor, and she didn't

need to add, "Black babies aren't profitable." It was getting harder to keep my fake smile in place.

"Are you ready to work with us, then?" she asked, focusing on Terry and ignoring me.

"You mentioned adoption insurance," Terry said, skipping over her veiled reference to the processing fee she was itching to get her hands on. "I've never heard of such a thing."

"We connect you with an independent insurance broker. If you lose out on the first birth mother we match you with, you are insured for the ten thousand. So you see, the processing fee is actually covered if there's a disaster. We can start all over." She smiled as if she'd just invented water.

"And what's the actual cost of the insurance?" he asked.

Her smile shrank to a tight pucker. "Twelve hundred."

"And the rest of the ten grand is just to meet with you people? That doesn't even include the actual cost of the adoption?" he said.

I didn't think he was acting anymore. He sounded too astounded.

"That's correct," she said. "Each adoption is unique, sometimes quite complicated."

"Darling," I said quickly, "it's worth it. They'll find us the perfect baby and make sure we don't lose her." I smiled at Hamilton. "We want a girl."

"Can I set up a meeting?" she said, switching her pitch to me.

"Yes. We're ready," I replied.

Terry put a hand on my shoulder. "I'm not forking over ten thousand dollars until I know more about this company. Do you have lawyers? Doctors? Where do these mothers come from? How do we know we won't get some poor child with AIDS or —"

"I'm sorry," said Hamilton. She still sounded pleasant, but her steel-gray eyes hardened. "What is it you do for a living, Mr. Deer?"

My throat tightened. I'd forgotten to fill Terry in on his background. *Please say "computers,"* I begged silently. *The whole frigging world does something with computers.*

Thank goodness Terry slithered away from a direct answer. "I'll save my answers for the expensive processing meeting, if we decide to go ahead. After all, you people have ten thousand dollars to earn."

"Touché," said Hamilton. "I only wanted to point out that you wouldn't give away computers, would you? So you can't expect us to provide valuable counseling services free of charge."

So she did remember what I had told her the other day. She was slick, all right.

I said, "Did you notice Ms. Hamilton's computer, darling? It's one of the brands you sell. And she has a point, because I'm sure she paid good money for it." Though I was cueing Terry, the computer itself interested me: a CompuCan model, with the ribbonlike cable I recognized — very expensive. Wired for special electronics.

Hamilton said, "I think Mrs. Deer and I are on the same page. But perhaps you need more time to mull things over, which is understandable. I might add, we currently have an excellent supply of babies on the way, and the chances are good you'd find a match. We can't always offer such variety."

So the crop was exceptional this year? This was making me sick.

When Terry didn't even nibble on the bait, she stood. "I do have another appointment, but please call on me when you're ready."

We were being dismissed. No money, no more information.

Terry and I rose.

She walked around the desk and accompanied us to the door, saying, "Mrs. Deer, since we work on a referral basis, I wanted to ask you again where you heard about Mr. Feldman."

That threw me, her bringing up Feldman. "I have confidentiality issues myself, Ms. Hamilton. Especially when my friends have told me not to mention their names."

"I understand," she answered, her face as blank as stone.

But her eyes held even more suspicion than the last time I'd been here.

Steven's truck was parked in front of the house on P Street when Terry and I arrived back there to meet with Kate.

"He's probably working on the roof and windows before the storm hits," I said as Terry and I climbed the porch steps.

When we got inside, I saw that Steven had brought over the blueprints and they were spread on the parlor floor. He looked up when we came in.

"So how was your adventure?" he asked. Obviously Steven knew where we'd been.

"I guess Kate explained. But don't take it personally, Steven. I divorced Terry, too — in the car on the way back here. He doesn't want to adopt and I do."

"You think this is one big joke, don't you?" said Steven. "But messing with

213

murder and pretending to be someone you're not is like bucking in the rodeo without a pickup man."

"Since when did my life become a province and you took over as dictator?" I said.

Terry cleared his throat. "I'll find Kate while you two finish slinging arrows."

Steven turned his flushed face toward Terry. "You're as bad as she is, Terry. You work for the police, don't you? Isn't what you two did today on the hot side of the law?"

"It's not illegal. And the visit proved enlightening. In fact, I may call up the Galveston County district attorney and ask her to take a serious look at this Parental Advocates agency."

"Not yet," I said quickly. "Let me find out about Feldman before you send Hamilton into a panic."

"Maybe you should listen to Steven," said Kate. She'd come in through the dining room. "Sergeant Kline might not be working as fast as you like, but —"

"I'm not giving up, Kate," I said. "In fact, I may take ten thousand dollars over to Parental Advocates tomorrow and see if a few greenbacks will persuade Hamilton to discuss Mr. Feldman."

"What?" came the simultaneous cry from Kate and Steven.

"You always were a few bricks shy of a load," said Steven.

I said, "What makes you think —"

"Hold on, Abby." Terry put a hand on my arm. "I already told you I've put out feelers at the precinct and courthouse. I may hear something any day about Feldman."

Steven said, "Let her throw her money away, Terry. Interfering with Abby when she wants something is like standing in front of a runaway locomotive."

Breaking the uncomfortable silence that followed, Terry said, "Sounds as if you guys need to clear up some issues if you expect to work effectively on this house project together. I can help. I know several good marriage and family counselors who could —"

"Our marriage is over," I snapped, sticking my ring hand in my skirt pocket. "There's nothing left to counsel." I thought I'd gotten past the bitterness, but apparently not.

Steven closed his eyes, took a deep breath, and then looked at me. The green sea was calm. "I apologize. I promised I'd help fix this place up, and I'm following through on my commitment. I've got things to prove, to you and to myself. Are you okay with that, Abby?"

I felt my shoulders relax. "Yes. Sorry if I went off on you."

Steven smiled. "Good. Now, there's a problem with the house we need to discuss."

By gosh, wasn't he improving on his apologies?

Kate's mouth had the white-ringed traces of her reaction to witnessing what she thought she wouldn't have to listen to again. "Is it safe to leave you two together?" she asked.

"I agree not to call Steven things like sawdust-head. He, in turn, must not tell me I have the mentality of a screwdriver or that if I had twice as much sense I'd still be a half-wit. He actually told me that once, by the way."

Steven smiled. We all smiled. Storm over.

After Kate and Terry left, I said, "What's this problem?"

"Come over here and I'll show you."

I walked across the room and we both knelt to better view the blueprints.

He tapped a spot on the paper. "This upstairs bathroom was added on above the mudroom, which was also an addition."

"You mean that little laundry room leading from the back door into the kitchen?"

"Right. Don't know what fool approved

216

those plans, but old houses rarely had extra bathrooms way back when, thus the need for the addition. Never would have put one there myself, though. Too many heavy fixtures and not enough support. We should tear out the tub and commode and start over."

"Put in a shower, maybe?"

"That's an option, but I'd prefer to make this a closet and relocate the bathroom here." He fingered another spot on the plans.

"Sounds like a good idea." I could feel the warmth of his body where our shoulders touched and remembered how we used to make love after we'd fought and made up. I was feeling like one of Pavlov's dogs, my body conditioned for pleasure after pain. When would I stop wanting him?

I stood, knowing I had to put space between us before I did something stupid.

But before I could move, he grabbed my hand. "I meant what I said. I am sorry."

"I'm sorry, too." I gently withdrew and stepped back. "I have to go. I promised I'd pick up contracts from CompuCan."

"Ah, yes. Keep the Rose money machine cranking out bucks. Who knows when you might want to blow off ten thousand dollars."

★ ★ ★

CompuCan basically runs itself, but since Kate and I had inherited the business, I visited the corporate offices in downtown Houston on a regular basis. After I returned from Galveston, I drove there and spent an hour chatting and meeting new faces, then picked up the documents that I'd come for.

While waiting for the elevator, I decided I shouldn't leave the building without sticking my head in at Willis's office two floors down.

Several minutes later, his secretary waved me through the reception area. As usual, my stomach lurched at the breathtaking view of sleek corporate castles displayed through the wall of windows behind Willis's desk. He'd spared no expense decorating the place. A wet bar gleamed with Waterford crystal decanters and glasses to my right. Barrister bookshelves lined the wall to my left. Three leather wing chairs surrounded a rectangular coffee table near the window, and a humidor was open and ready to serve clients. Willis would never think of smoking. He worried too much about his health, but clients were a different story.

"This is a surprise," he said, rising. "What brings you up here?"

"I couldn't ignore CompuCan any

longer, although the staff's doing great without my help."

"What have you been up to, little lady?" He came around and sat on the desk's corner.

I chose a tapestry-covered client chair facing him and set my paperwork and purse on the floor. "Still trying to find out about Ben and the adoption angle."

"You have enough to handle without adding in detective work, don't you think?"

"You mean, besides which best-seller I'll read this week?"

"That restoration, for one thing. It's a major project."

I nodded. "True. Steven tells me the bathroom is ready to fall into the first floor."

"See? You need to focus on the house, on making the place into something you'll be proud of, even make a profit on. Real estate is a very sound investment."

"I'm not giving up on finding Feldman. I want to keep my promise to Ruth to help hunt down this killer."

Willis shook his head. "When you start something, you clamp onto it like a pit bull, don't you?"

"Do you know how down and dirty the adoption business can get, Willis? I never realized we deal in human beings in this country. You deal cards . . . or stocks and bonds. You don't deal babies."

"Money can buy almost anything," he said.

"I refuse to believe that. And you know what else? I don't think I'd even shed a tear if every penny I inherited disappeared to-morrow."

"That's because those billions of pennies won't disappear. Playing what-if is not like being without. Your father and I knew about being without. We were so poor, the hogs wouldn't eat our slop. Being poor means being powerless, and groveling for what you need leaves a nasty taste in your mouth — one that never goes away." Willis's eyes glistened. "Until you die, of course. Like poor Charlie."

Seems he was still struggling with grief as much as I was. "I know you loved Daddy," I said.

"Charlie was my first client," he said. "And God, I was so green. We both were. Lost our shirts more than once trying to make deals, thanks to either my stupidity or his impulsiveness. But we hung in there. Back to Feldman, though. How do you expect to find him after all these years?"

"I was thinking of talking to one of the more traditional adoption agencies. See if anyone there has ever heard of Feldman. Maybe Catholic Charities or —"

"Since when have you acquired an interest in religion, Abigail?" said Aunt Caroline from the open office door.

"Come in, Caroline," said Willis. "Abby was in the building, so she dropped by."

She wore a peach suit today, and her white hair held a blue hue. New dye job.

"You mentioned Catholic Charities?" she said. "Getting philanthropic as you age, dear?" She took the seat next to me.

"I'm still less than half as old as you," I said sweetly.

She chose to ignore my remark — this time. "If not philanthropy, does this mention of a charity have something to do with your insistence on pursuing criminals?" She leaned forward and placed her handbag on Willis's desk.

"I'm pursuing the truth, and I have a few questions for you. Remember when you and Hans came over the other day?"

"I remember."

"Did you go into the attic?"

"The attic?" she said, with overplayed innocence.

"Yes. The one you go through the closet to get to."

"What could she possibly want in the

attic, Abby?" said Willis.

"I'll do the asking," I said sharply. "What were you looking for, Aunt Caroline?"

She fussed with the lace peeking out high on her thigh, the tight, translucent skin on her face burning with color. "When I was young, I made a mistake and wrote things to a man. Private things. Take it from me, Abigail, if you have something to say to a lover — if you ever have another — don't be foolish enough to declare it in writing. You see, I happened to be married to my second husband at the time, and this other man I fancied, the one I'd written to, decided my letters might be worth something to my husband."

I couldn't keep from smiling. She was more than capable of penning some real scorchers. "Go on. I'm waiting to hear about the attic."

She glanced at Willis, who encouraged her with a nod. "Your father bailed me out. Paid the blackmailing scum. But Charlie kept those letters, kept them because . . . well, let's say he had his reasons."

"What reasons?" I pressed.

"To keep me in line. He said I'd cost him too much money over the years." She folded her arms and her mouth drew tight. "But I never forgot about them, and when I had an opportunity Saturday, I found them. Who knows what hands they could fall into with the two of you moving out and stirring up a mound of dust better left swept under the rug?"

I wondered who she thought gave a flip about her ancient history. "And what did you do with them?"

"I destroyed them." She raised her chin.

"Good move — but do me a favor, Aunt Caroline? The next time you go snooping around, clean up your mess. We ended up calling the police because we thought we'd had a break-in. You and your boyfriend left that attic a wreck, and what's more, you forgot to close the door. Diva got stuck in there and —"

"Wait a minute," Aunt Caroline said, shaking her head. "I didn't disturb anything. I found the letters almost immediately, second box I looked in. Granted, I may have left the door ajar, but it wasn't intentional."

"Sure. If you say so," I said. If she was telling the truth, that meant someone had come in after she left and torn the place up. I didn't believe it for a minute. Either she was lying or good old Hans went back up there when she wasn't looking, hoping to find something of value for himself.

"You have my admission, Abigail. Now

could we please change the subject? Or would you prefer to humiliate me further in front of Willis?"

I glanced at him. He shook his head as if to tell me to leave well enough alone. "Okay, we can drop this. For now," I said.

"Good," said Aunt Caroline. "I'm hosting a dinner for the CompuCan board of directors tomorrow. Could you please show up this time? I will be entertaining the executives, as I have done in the past, but you and Kate should make an appearance. The country club, eight o'clock. Perhaps you could accompany Willis?"

"I'd be delighted to escort Abby," said Willis.

"I . . . I sort of have a date," I lied.

"A date? Not that do-nothing ex-husband, I hope?" said Aunt Caroline.

"Steven is not a do-nothing. He happens to be a very successful contractor." *Successful* might be stretching the truth a hair, but I felt the need to defend him.

"Oh, I understand your attraction to him. Always have. There's something sexy about those redneck types. Feel free to bring your gentleman friend, whoever he is."

"Okay," I said, and sighed. Now I'd have to make up another lie when I showed up without a man.

17

After returning home from CompuCan and my enlightening visit with Aunt Caroline, I decided to try on-line resources before contacting Catholic Charities. I logged on to the Texas Central Adoption Registry, and learned that only adoptees born in Texas, their siblings, and birth parents could even request information. And I discovered two other interesting facts. A list of thirty-three "voluntary child-placing agencies" on the site did not include Parental Advocates, but there were eighty-six such agencies in Texas. Why were those other fifty-three not included? Even more interesting, any out-of-business agency was required by law to forward their adoption records to the registry. This told me that even if Feldman had retired, perhaps in some file, somewhere, lay evidence of Cloris Grayson's child. But who could access that information now that both Cloris and Ben were dead? No one. And maybe someone wanted it that way.

Chewing on the pencil I'd been using to jot notes, I considered hacking into the system to find Cloris's records, if they existed. After all, any system was vulnerable.

Then I rose abruptly.

Not a good idea. The last thing I needed was to be arrested for a cybercrime involving a government agency.

I had to get out of this room, away from the computer, and think this through.

I hurried down the hall to the kitchen to sneak a diet Coke before Kate came home — she knew nothing about my stash of diet Cokes. I walked circles around the kitchen island, sipping aspartame and caffeine, hoping to find clarity. When had curiosity turned into an obsession to find answers?

And then it dawned on me that there would be nothing illegal about learning how the adoption system in Texas worked first-hand. Nothing illegal about me, an adoptee, searching for my own records. The state of Texas told me I had the right to do so on their very own Web site. Even provided an application form on-line. This would be a perfectly legal way to see what information was kept in the registry database. Then maybe Jeff Kline could take over from there.

I went to Daddy's study and printed out the brief two-page document. Thirty minutes later I drove to Mail Boxes Etc and FedExed my application, surprised at how my hand trembled when I handed the envelope over to the clerk. This seemed all too personal now. And sending off the application reminded me that, though Daddy had shown us our court papers many years ago, I hadn't seen them during all my searching for the mysterious safe-deposit box. Willis probably had them, I decided on the way back home.

In Daddy's study once again, I renewed my search through the remaining canceled checks for any clue to the safe-deposit box. I'd never realized how many pieces of paper a human being could accumulate in a lifetime. Daddy could have saved a hundred trees, maybe even a thousand, if he had used cash even occasionally. But he'd told me once checks always came back as proof you took care of your business, and I guess that made sense.

By the time Kate arrived home from her evening therapy session, I had one last stack to go through.

"Any luck?" she asked, carrying two glasses into the study. She placed one in front of me and sat down in the red leather wing chair.

"Not yet," I answered, removing the mint sprig and silently praying this concoction wasn't herbal. But alas, it tasted suspiciously like grass. "Mmm, yummy," I lied.

"I have to say this check hunt has produced some interesting moments."

"Interesting? How?"

"Aunt Caroline profited from Daddy's generosity more than I ever knew. Every other check seems to have her name on it. No matter which one of her husbands she was married to at the time, Charlie Rose kept her outfitted in green."

"I didn't think she needed Daddy's money. I thought she only married rich men." Kate took a hefty swig of her drink and I half expected her to bleat like a goat.

"I think the husbands ended up rich by marrying her," I said. "By the way, I ran into her this morning. She told me a boyfriend blackmailed her over letters she wrote to him while she was still married to Number Two. The one with the odd first name. Remember him?" I pretended to sip my drink.

"Marion something. Hand me a bunch of those checks and I'll help you."

"Be my guest." I handed her a stack.

"She told you about these letters willingly?" asked Kate, removing the rubber band. "Had she been sipping brandy at Willis's office?"

"I confronted her about searching the attic and she confessed."

"She actually admitted she made that mess?"

"She says she went up there, but emphatically denies disturbing anything, which has to be a lie, of course." I continued scanning checks, pulling a few current ones that didn't help with the safe-deposit box situation, but matched the two already in my shorts pocket.

"What about this one?" Kate said. "Community Savings and Loan. Thirty dollars. Dated last fall." She passed me the check with a satisfied grin.

"I've spent endless hours searching; then you bop in and bingo! Does that tell you who inherited the strand of DNA with the luck genes? You should go out and buy a lottery ticket."

I picked up the glass of herbal whatever, making her think I might be interested in actually consuming this iced horror. "We can visit the bank tomorrow, but now that you've released me from this thankless task, I can run an errand."

"Pretty late for errands," she said.

"I need to pay someone a visit." I headed for the hallway, carrying the glass with me.

Kate called after me, "You don't have to drink it, Abby. It won't hurt my feelings."

I smiled and poured the contents in the sink before leaving.

Nights on Houston's freeways bear great resemblance to the days. Nothing keeps people out of their cars in this city. I joined the stream of traffic on the Southwest Freeway and followed a thousand taillights past the glossy office buildings populating this side of town. It could take as much as an hour to navigate the sprawl of Houston, depending on where you came from and where you were going, but I arrived at the Greenleaf Apartments in thirty minutes.

"This is a surprise," said Steven when he opened his door.

"I had a surprise myself this afternoon." I dropped my purse on the table by the door and walked past him into the living area.

"How's that?"

He'd redecorated since the last time I'd visited — or someone had redecorated for him. Steven never had much sense of color. The expected grays and tans had been transformed into a salute to the Southwest, with pale green, blue, and mauve fabrics on the couch and love seat, and various desert scenes hanging on the walls.

"This is sure different," I commented.

"A friend told me a change of everyday

scenery might help me readjust to being single."

"Did your friend help you with this or did you hire someone?" I asked, sitting on the sofa.

"She helped. Can I get you a drink?"

"If you swear on the Bible no herbs are involved."

"Another reason you should take me back, if only to serve as a buffer between you and Kate the holistic. How about a Dr Pepper?"

"On second thought, I'll pass. This won't take long." I took the canceled checks from my pocket and held them out. "Can you explain these?"

He looked at them briefly, then shoved them back. "Yeah. But I'm not sure I will."

"I thought we were friends," I said softly. "You borrowed money from Daddy behind my back, didn't you?"

"I needed help, okay? And Charlie offered." Steven's face tightened with tension, and his green eyes darkened.

I was sorry then, sorry I'd come here without thinking through how to confront him more tactfully.

"Must have been hard asking him for money," I said.

"I had debts after my rehab, and I didn't

think you'd help me out. Charlie agreed to tide me over."

Oddly enough, I felt a certain relief at hearing this information. "Daddy *would* help you with something like that. He really tried to like you. Still, I'm surprised you didn't do a wide dance past him and ask me for the money."

"You stopped hanging your wash on my line the day that paper made us officially divorced. I wasn't about to ask you for anything."

"No, especially since you left right after I stopped financing your self-destruction," I said.

Though Steven's expression indicated he didn't like what I had to say, he didn't shoot back with something sarcastic. Instead an uncomfortable silence followed, and when he finally spoke, his voice was calm. "That's the fairy story you like to tell yourself about why I left. In truth, I had to get my head together. And yeah, it took me longer than I thought. And yeah, I've regretted losing you every day since I got sober."

This was a new wrinkle in an old shirt. Might even pass for insight. "I'm sorry, Steven. I made a mistake. This is really none of my business." I rose and circled around him to retrieve my purse.

But he reached out and grabbed my arm.

"Hold on." He pulled me to him, his lean body fitting into mine the perfect way it always had. Though my brain screamed for me to break away, I couldn't pile rejection onto distrust. His sobriety might be too tenuous.

He lifted my chin. "I think that's a first. You said four words I never thought I'd hear from you."

"Four words?"

" 'I made a mistake.' "

He kissed me then, with all the passion I remembered, and it was the best thing that could have happened.

There were no lights, no sirens, no stomach flip-flops. None of the things I had dreaded for months happened. Could this be the beginning of the real end to my wanting him? I drew back and rubbed my knuckles against the stubble on his cheek. "We can be friends, Steven. I know we can. That's all I can handle."

He released his grip on my arms and stepped back. "Whatever you say, Abby. But I've changed. Changed because . . . Never mind."

I turned to leave.

But as I walked to the door, I noticed a pair of shoes tucked under the coffee table, a name brand I recognized, Pappagallo. I could never wear a pair of those shoes in a million years. They were designed for tall, skinny women with matching long, thin feet. One shoe had a pair of black panty hose stuffed in the toe.

I didn't say anything. If a woman had left her entire wardrobe at his apartment, it meant nothing to me, because I no longer felt the presence of that maddeningly ambivalent voice saying, *I want you, Steven; I hate you, Steven.*

Tonight I neither wanted him nor hated him. And maybe, just maybe, I could simply accept him for the flawed, overgrown boy I had lusted for but never truly loved.

Back home half an hour later, I found Diva sitting on the counter awaiting my arrival, her amber eyes matching the light on the answering machine as it flashed eerily in the darkness of the kitchen.

Kate had left me a message on the two-way memo telling me Terry had called with information about Feldman.

My hand hovered over the phone; then I glanced at my watch. Past midnight. "Come on, Diva; let's go to bed. It's too late for phone calls."

18

The next day, Terry wouldn't reveal what he'd learned over the phone, but rather asked me to meet him at his office. As I sat by his desk around nine a.m., I recalled how I had keyed on his computer right after Ben's death, determined to discover the truth — something that had proved far easier said than done. But Daddy always said that lick by lick, any old cow can polish off a grindstone.

Terry, wearing a soft green shirt and lightweight sports jacket, had a gleam in his eye. A good sign. After our meeting with Hamilton, he had seemed almost as interested in this case as I was, so maybe he'd caught the detecting bug, too.

He opened a manila folder and said, "I haven't located Feldman, so no address. But an old desk sergeant named Grant, who started out as a bailiff at the Galveston County Courthouse years ago, remembers a lawyer named Feldman who made regular appearances in family court for his adoption business."

"You're kidding. This is fantastic, Terry."

"Grant says Feldman was a shady baby broker linked to hints of a judicial scandal. A judge named Hayes left the bench after being tied to Feldman and some questionable adoptions." Terry leaned back and smiled.

The rush of pleasure I felt at finally getting a solid lead surprised me with its intensity. "We could search back," I said, "and if Feldman has a record, maybe Jeff Kline will help me locate him."

"Hold on. I said there were *hints* of a scandal. When Hayes left the bench, the investigation ended. Apparently lots of wheeling and dealing went on behind closed doors. She resigned and everything quieted down. Feldman wasn't seen around the courthouse much after she left."

"Did Grant tell you anything else?"

"He remembers the judge better than he remembers Feldman. Quite a few of the 'good ol' boys,' Grant included, said they knew she played dirty. Their take was that if she wanted to make it in a man's world, she had to cheat."

"How typically Texan of the boys. Is Judge Hayes still around?"

"I don't know, but her son is a big-time real estate salesman in Galveston. Here's his number." He handed me a piece of paper. "If Mr. Hayes isn't happy that you're resurrecting unpleasant rumors about his mother, do me a favor and don't tell him who sent you."

Several hours later I was cruising toward Galveston for the umpteenth time in a week, excited at the prospect of following this lead. David Hayes, the judge's son, had been more than cooperative. He gave me Eugenia Hayes's address with his blessing, as well as directions so I could visit her. I didn't mention her past indiscretions and he didn't either. I simply told him I was a reporter writing a story about pioneering women in the judicial field. If he knew anything questionable about her past, he made no mention. But then, she probably didn't share the bedtime story of how she nearly got kicked off the bench. David Hayes might not have a clue about her questionable past.

The fact she now resided in a nursing home might present a few problems. Not to mention her Alzheimer's disease. But I wasn't discouraged. In fact, I hummed the Beatles' "Here Comes the Sun" as I followed the brick-lined path leading to the front door of Faircrest Haven.

A kind-looking woman, with tight salt-

and-pepper curls and wearing a name tag with *Lorna* printed in giant letters, greeted me from behind a U-shaped desk several feet beyond the entrance of the two-story building. She abandoned her *People* magazine to offer a friendly smile.

"I'm here to visit Judge Hayes," I said.

Her face clouded as she flipped through a Rolodex of laminated plastic cards.

"Judge Hayes?" questioned the woman. "Is he inpatient care or a day resident?"

"I think *he* is a *she*, if that helps any," I said, peering over the desk and wondering if they'd ever considered indexing the patients on a computer.

"Oh, my goodness." Her eyes widened and she shook her head. "You must have the wrong facility. They do *those* surgeries down at the University Hospital. We only have old people here, not any of those sex-change folks." She pointed back out the front door over my shoulder. "To get over there, you go back to Seawall Boulevard and turn —"

"No, you misunderstood," I said with a laugh. "Judge Eugenia Hayes," I clarified. Or so I thought.

"You're telling me our Eugenia used to be a man? Doesn't that pop the wax out of your ears? You know, she doesn't make sense half the time, so that explains her problems. It's hard enough making it in this world, and then you go switching your body parts and —"

"I'm really in a rush," I interrupted. "Could you tell me her room number?" I realized I wouldn't straighten this out in Lorna's mind, now or in the future.

"She's in two-thirty-one. Take the elevator to the second floor and turn left. You know, I always thought Eugenia was a weird name, but now I understand. She used to be Eugene, didn't she?" She smiled and gave me a conspiratorial wink.

There was a good reason for Lorna to use laminated cards. Trusting her with technology would have been far too risky.

When I exited the elevator on the second floor, an overpowering blend of disinfectant and room deodorizer greeted me. I followed the signs and was soon tapping tentatively on the door of two-thirty-one, not sure what I'd find. I'd never visited a nursing home before.

"Come in," commanded a woman from within.

I opened the door and paused, surprised at the size of the voice coming from the tiny person propped up in bed.

"Shut the door!" boomed the gray-headed lady, her frame nearly lost in the swath of white sheets and pillows surrounding her. "It smells like a goddamn nursing home in that hallway!"

I quickly complied and moved into the spacious room. I'd expected IVs and oxygen tanks at the very least, but instead, the place resembled a jungle. A huge corn plant stood in one corner, leaning toward the light of the picture window. Potted plants, bursting with blossoms of violet and pink, spread out to line the wall with bright green foliage. Framed by the window, the seething Gulf of Mexico angrily foreshadowed the approaching storm.

"What do you want?" she demanded. "Because if you're selling insurance, you can turn around and march right out. Odds are I'll be dead soon, and no living soul will profit from that event. Not if I can help it." She opened her arms wide. "Besides, this glorified tomb has taken every penny." She turned and started fumbling around for something on the bedside table.

"Can I help you?" I asked, hurrying over to her.

But she located her glasses before I could reach her side, stretching the wires behind her ears, then scrutinizing me from head to toe. "No. You're no salesperson. You don't have their sneaky eyes. God knows I can pick out those idiots at a hundred yards."

"Your son told me you lived here," I said, sliding a dieffenbachia away and pulling a chair up alongside the bed.

"My son?" Confusion muddied her already hazy brown eyes.

"He told me you have a problem remembering things sometimes." Actually, he told me she had trouble most of the time, but did better with the distant past than with recent events. My hope lay there. "Could I ask you a few questions?"

"I run a tight courtroom, young lady, so don't think because you're fresh out of law school you can get one past me. I've seen every trick in the book." She folded her arms across her chest and stared at me expectantly. "Go ahead. Ask away."

"I-I'm not a lawyer, but —"

"I told you not to argue with me," she snapped.

"Yes, ma'am," I said. Even through her disorientation, she exuded an authority not unlike that of the second-grade teacher who had sent me to the principal for chewing gum. "I wanted to ask you about another lawyer, Judge."

"You came to the right place, because I've known a bunch of them. Professional liars, for the most part." She laughed, turning her face to the ceiling and guffawing loudly before the outburst mutated into a fit of coughing.

I helped her sit up straighter, concerned about the faint blueness around her lips and alarmed by the parchment quality of her skin. I feared her bony shoulder might crumble beneath my touch. "Are you all right?"

"Of course not. Who is? Ask your questions, counselor." She leaned back into the pillows and closed her eyes.

"Do you remember a man named Feldman? Samuel Feldman?"

She bolted upright and hatred raced across her heavily wrinkled cheeks to settle in the tight line of her mouth. "Did that snake send you here? Because if that's the case, get out!" She started to lift the blanket off her legs.

I took her hands in mine. "I swear I don't even know him," I said quickly. "He hurt someone and I want to see him punished."

I'd come up with the right response through pure dumb luck, because she calmed immediately. "You don't want to find him, nurse." She squeezed my hands and shook her head emphatically.

Within the span of a few moments I had

gone from lawyer to nurse. Getting information out of her might be more difficult than I thought.

"Do the world a favor and skip the CPR on Samuel Feldman," she said. "Nothing wrong with him that reincarnation wouldn't cure." She grinned, and I saw teeth too large for her shrunken gums.

"I have to find him first," I said. "And unfortunately I've misplaced his address."

"Check hell. I think he's stringing barbed wire down there."

She seemed quite sure how much she hated Feldman, but maybe if I mentioned the adoptions, she'd focus more on facts than emotion. "I heard you placed many babies with families over the years. Could you tell me about that, Judge Hayes?"

"Ah, the babies. Sent hundreds to fine homes. Sad part was, the birth mothers were babies, too. Children having children. Tragic. Absolutely tragic. I had to make some hard decisions, but that's why they elected me."

She squared her thin shoulders and I could picture her, robed and dignified, running a courtroom.

"Um . . . I also need information on a woman named Cloris Grayson. She —"

"No!" Her face went gray and she

clutched both my wrists. "You promised me. You said I wouldn't lose my good name. You claimed you were a fair man." She stared off past my right shoulder, obviously focused on the past. And what I saw in her eyes seemed like pure terror.

I decided to play along, to pretend I was this man she'd spoken of. "I am a fair man, but I need to know about the baby."

She cocked her head and appeared lost by my remark. "If you don't know, who does?"

"Oh, I know, all right, but I still need help locating Feldman. Finding him will solve my problems."

"He went to see Cloris. That's what he said, anyway. He promised he'd convince her to quit. But don't trust him. Don't *ever* trust him. Look where it got me." A tear slipped from the corner of one eye. "My career is ruined."

She started crying, the room echoing with her long, whimpering sobs while I rubbed the tissue-paper skin on her hand. I'd never intended to upset her this much.

When she finally regained control, she said, "Tell them the truth, nurse. Tell them I'm not a bad person."

"Of course you're not a bad person," I said quietly. "Even good people do bad things sometimes."

"And child?" she said, slowly closing her eyes. "Water the plants before you leave, would you? We breathe for each other, you know."

I stopped at the house on P Street after leaving the nursing home, and, as expected, Steven's truck was sitting in the driveway, as well as an expensive foreign car.

I burst in through the back door, anxious to tell him about my conversation with the judge, and found him and another man poring over books and blueprints laid out on the kitchen counter.

"Hi," I said, addressing the stranger and extending my hand. "Abby Rose. I take it you're the renovation expert here to help Steven with my house."

We shook, with the man casting a puzzled glance toward Steven.

"Guess I forgot to mention the owner is my ex-wife here," said Steven. "Mr. Gibson is the man we hope to contract, Abby. He knows his stuff."

"Nice to meet you, Mr. Gibson. The house really belongs to Steven at this point in the renovation. I've put this project in his very capable hands." Maybe that would salve Steven's ego a little, as I could see he was embarrassed by my blundering in here unannounced.

Gibson said, "You've given me what I need, Mr. Bradley. We'll have a more thorough consultation in a few weeks." He gathered one set of blueprints and said, "Nice to meet you, too." He bowed stiffly in my direction, then hurried out through the back door.

"I didn't mean to interrupt," I said. "But I've had a breakthrough on Ben's case, Steven."

"Wonderful. Maybe you should think about applying to the police academy."

I ignored the sarcasm and told him about my visit with Hayes and what I considered to be a confirmed connection between Feldman and Cloris. He listened with half an ear, obviously anxious to return to his blueprints and books.

"How much weight can you put on the ramblings of an old woman with a brain disease?" he asked when I'd finished.

"I'm certain what she told me was founded in reality. I mean, the name Cloris is so unusual. The next step is to convince Jeff to help me find Feldman."

"Jeff, is it? How cozy." Steven slammed one book shut.

"He's a friend, like you are," I said.

Steven abruptly gripped my shoulders. "I

246

love you, Abby, and not like a friend. And one day you'll be back with me, where you belong."

I stepped back, away from his grasp. "This is too intense, okay? Can we drop it?"

"Sure. Sorry." But that small fire of desire in his eyes remained.

As for me, I felt nothing but regret.

19

The next afternoon Kate was free, so she and I turned our attention to the safe-deposit box. We'd driven in Kate's 4Runner to Willis's office first, picked up the needed paperwork to gain access, and were now on our way to the small bank located south of the city near the Space Center. A thick layer of rolling gray clouds covered the sky as the slow-moving storm marched ever closer.

"Refresh my memory on what those happy weather people are saying," I said. "Will this become a hurricane?"

"Probably won't get that strong before the thing slams into us," said Kate. "Which exit do we take again?"

"NASA Road One. About two more miles down the freeway," I said. "The summer's been so dry, when the skies do open up, it will be like a cow peeing on a flat rock."

"Let's hope the rain waits until tomorrow," Kate said. "We have that country-club thing Aunt Caroline arranged, remember?"

"I remember," I said.

"Terry's coming over about six and we'll

leave from our house."

"With all the construction on the interstate, we should plan on forty-five minutes' travel time," I said.

"You bringing Steven?" Kate asked.

"No way. Slow down, Kate. Here's the exit coming up."

"Right or left once we get off?"

"Right, then over the freeway."

We found the bank without problems, and after wading through yards of red tape — paperwork no doubt designed to discourage any but the most tenacious person from removing anything of value from inside the four walls of Community Savings — we carried the safe-deposit box to a cubicle.

But if I thought a miraculous revelation, complete with videotaped documentation, would rise from the depths of that small metal receptacle, I was mistaken. We found an unlabeled computer CD. Nothing else. Still, I held out hope that my theory about Daddy was correct and this CD would reveal something about Ben's presence at our house.

When we arrived home, I hurriedly stuck the CD in the computer while Kate ran upstairs to shower. But did I find any evidence connecting Ben and Daddy? Not a chance.

The CD contained a spreadsheet and word processing program, and an ancient one, at that. All my slaving over mounds of canceled checks for this!

I rushed through the program once more, noting that the word processor seemed to lack all the features of the one he'd eventually marketed. Maybe he'd copied the original onto this CD as some sort of keepsake. But why? He'd never seemed the least sentimental about the software he created. Maybe this was a rough draft of sorts, or maybe he'd removed aspects of the program for updating. As far as I knew, he could have been planning to get back into software after all these years.

One thing balanced my discouragement, though: Aunt Caroline would be more disappointed than I was. We had found no money in that box. Not one penny.

The Pines Country Club, hidden in the lush forests north of Houston, was perched on a manicured rise near a man-made lake. For business purposes, Daddy considered membership a necessity, so we'd appeared regularly, dressed up like poodles in a dog show. Tonight I made sure not to wear the "plump" dress, opting instead for a one-shoulder forest-green number. I even dug out the panty hose, but passed on the high heels. Nothing would make me submit to that self-punishing throwback to foot binding.

Walking up the path to the club with Terry and Kate leading the way, I smiled, breathing in the smog-free air. The night was almost cool. I glanced up at the tall trees and first few stars, thinking maybe I'd move up this way once I was ready to sell the house in River Oaks. But before I could consider this possibility further, a chance look to my right had me doing a double take.

I saw the silhouette of a man I recognized, leaning against a tree on a small rise.

"Uh, Kate?" I said.

She and Terry stopped and turned.

"Tell Aunt Caroline I'll be in shortly. I'd like to enjoy this glorious night for a few moments by myself."

Kate looked at me skeptically. "Everything okay?"

"Sure. Be right in. Promise."

They went on, and I strode over to confront the man.

As I got closer, I saw his mouth working the ever-present gum. "Hi," he said.

"Hi? Is that all you have to say?" I stopped in front of Sergeant Kline, arms folded across my chest.

"What did you expect?"

"I want you to tell me why you're still following me."

"I have a job to do. Let's leave it at that. But since you spotted me, answer me one question. Why are you here?"

"I do have a life," I said.

He raised his eyebrows, waiting for the real answer.

"Okay," I said. "If you must know, this is a business dinner."

"Ah. For CompuCan. I get it."

Smarting from the knowledge that he obviously still suspected me of something, I said, "Is there anything about my life you don't know?"

"I don't know how you like your coffee."

"What does that have to do with anything?" I said, exasperated.

"I thought maybe you and I could get coffee. The expensive kind, for the rich kid."

"That's a pretty condescending way of asking me out. You are asking me out, right?"

"You game?" he said.

I didn't reply, weighing his possible intentions. Did he think I had withheld something about Ben? Or could he possibly want to share my company?

He grinned. "Please?"

I had to smile, too. "Okay, but I have to make this dinner. I'm obligated."

"No problem. I can meet you right here in, say . . . two hours?" he said.

I agreed and left, feeling his gaze on my back all the way to the front door — an uncomfortable, but at the same time interesting, feeling.

When I entered the club, the maître d' led me to Aunt Caroline's table, the scent of designer perfume overwhelming whatever pleasant aromas might have wafted from the kitchen. Most of the time the food served here was excellent, but since most guests remained preoccupied with who was eating with whom, the cuisine went mostly unappreciated. The dimly lit dining room, its tables dressed in starched white cloths and crystal, hummed with quiet conversations.

Aunt Caroline was holding court at the best spot in the room. Willis, the board of directors of CompuCan, and their spouses, along with Kate and Terry sat near the picture windows overlooking the lake. Aunt Caroline's peek-a-bosom dress of black crepe — probably purchased at Nieman Marcus, or Needless Markups, as I preferred to call that particular store — seemed wildly inappropriate for a woman on the shady side of sixty.

My late arrival didn't win any points, and she made sure I knew it. Terry bailed me out with a story about how the SWAT team had recruited him this afternoon to help with a paranoid woman threatening to drop her child — a boy supposedly possessed by the devil — off the walkway spanning the freeway between the amusement park and the parking lot. Luckily, he'd talked her out of hurting the poor kid.

Meanwhile, his heroic tale seemed to activate Aunt Caroline. Always willing to drop her line and troll for whatever she could hook, she now took what I considered a disturbing interest in Terry. Kate noticed, too. This flirtation continued on through appetizers and salad, and then finally managed to ruin my stuffed flounder. I even refused dessert.

Once the last of the board people departed, I'd had about all I could stand. Aunt Caroline needed to be distracted, so I said, "You'll be interested to know I tracked down the safe-deposit box."

Predictably, her gaze strayed from Terry to me. "And what did you find?"

"A software program Daddy created back when such pursuits interested him." I nodded as the waiter offered more coffee.

"That's all?" said Willis. Unlike Aunt Caroline, he didn't seem the least bit disappointed.

"Yes," I answered. "A copyrighted program, Willis. We're not looking at stolen software or any other cryptic explanation for his hiding this CD, are we? I mean, I'm certain we even have a duplicate of that on disk at the house."

"I have no clue why he would do such a thing," said Willis.

"Did this particular program generate exceptional revenues?" asked Aunt Caroline, leaning forward and revealing even more cleavage.

"All Daddy's software made a profit," I said. "And you already got your slice of that pie." I wondered then if she'd had help from her plastic surgeon with those extremely perky breasts.

But before I could ask, Kate must have picked up on the edge in my voice, because she tried her own brand of distraction. "Abby was telling us in the car about the progress she's made on Ben's murder. Tell them about the judge you met today."

"Uh, Kate. Why would they care?" I said.

"I'd love to hear, Abby," said Aunt Caroline. "Is this someone I might know? Because several of my friends have husbands who are judges, and —"

"I don't think this is the time or place to discuss the murder case," I said sharply. "Mainly because some of you" — I raised my eyebrows at Willis — "think I'm crazy to pursue Ben's killer."

"I have never, for one minute, considered you crazy," said Willis. "I may have cautioned you, but that doesn't mean I'm not interested. Please tell us what you've found out."

He did seem genuinely interested, so I said, "The judge's name is Eugenia Hayes, and she was elected to family court in Galveston several decades ago. Poor thing is living on borrowed time, with a couple late payments added on. Her son says she has Alzheimer's and her story *was* fragmented, but she knew Feldman and didn't much care for him."

"Feldman?" questioned Aunt Caroline. "You've lost me, Abby."

If only that were true, I thought. "Feldman may have arranged an adoption for Cloris Grayson — her real name was Connie Kramer — about thirty years ago. I think I told you about her."

"Oh, right. The day you showed me the key," Aunt Caroline said.

For some reason her demeanor had

changed. Suddenly she seemed . . . almost subdued. Tired of holding her shoulders back all night so the entire dining room could appreciate her boobs, maybe?

"Anyway," I went on, "I met Judge Hayes and learned that the rumors Terry heard from some old bailiff might be true. Hayes could have been taking money from Feldman, and was perhaps involved in illegal adoptions. I'm wondering if both Cloris and Ben died because they tracked Feldman down and threatened to expose him as a baby stealer."

"But you said this woman has Alzheimer's, right?" said Terry.

I nodded.

"How reliable can she be, then?" he said.

"I only know I believe her," I replied.

Willis piped up with, "She's basically senile?"

"Well, yes, but —"

"I have a question," Aunt Caroline said. "Why did this woman change her name?"

"You mean Cloris? I've thought about that myself, and I'm not sure," I said. "But I filled out an application to acquire my own adoption records, and one question on the form asks if the birth mother used an alias. I'm guessing it's not an uncommon practice. She did run away from her family, after all."

You could have heard an ant sneeze; that was how quiet it got.

Willis finally found his voice. "W-why did you request your adoption records, for heaven's sake? I have everything you need in my office. All you had to do was ask."

"Just testing the system," I said. "Wondering how the adoption registry worked and what you got back for your twenty bucks."

"Twenty dollars?" said Aunt Caroline, who looked like she'd been zapped by a stun gun. "Quite a bargain. You know I'm awfully tired. Willis, could you please take me home?"

"Certainly," he said, popping out of his chair like a jack-in-the-box.

They were out the door faster than wind can snuff a match.

Kate's mouth hadn't closed. She still looked shocked. "Why didn't you tell me you'd requested those records?"

I leaned back in my chair, surprised by everyone's reaction. "I didn't think it was all that important."

"You know how sensitive Daddy was about the adoption," Kate said. "I remember once asking him about our biological parents, if he thought they died instantly in that crash, and even though he answered me, his next question was whether I thought he was a good enough father. He seemed so . . . hurt that I even asked about them."

"He's past being hurt, don't you think?" I snapped back.

"Don't you see that Aunt Caroline and Willis were reacting to what they consider yet another betrayal of Daddy?" she said.

I stood, angry now. Maybe irrationally angry, yes. But Kate seemed to have jumped the imaginary fence to their side, and I was feeling betrayed myself. I said, "Daddy's dead, and I refuse to feel guilty about wanting control of my life."

I marched away, Kate hot on my heels.

"Wait," she cried.

I stopped, fingering my beaded bag and not making eye contact.

"You're right," she said. "I'm sorry. Now let's go home."

"I have a ride. Don't wait up for me," I answered. I whirled and left her standing there, knowing I'd feel guilty later, but for now, not caring.

I had time for a few deep breaths before meeting up with Jeff Kline in the parking lot. We stopped for cappuccino at a tiny coffee bar on Montrose Boulevard. His beeper sounded as soon as we sat down with our cups, so he excused himself to make the call in a more private corner.

I swirled a stick covered with rock candy into the foam, breathing in the wonderful aroma, watching the cinnamon blend into the coffee. I needed this reprieve from family interference.

"Do you need to leave?" I asked when he returned.

"No. My partner had a few questions about a case we're working. I'm supposed to be off tonight, not even on call, but for Homicide cops, real days off exist only in theory. No one's figured out how to actually make them happen." He held the rock candy up for examination and instead added three bags of sugar to his cup.

"You're off duty? You aren't officially assigned to follow me tonight?"

"Did I say I was following you?"

"Well, no, but —"

"Let's drop it," he said. "I can't discuss the case." He took several swallows of coffee and then produced a new pack of gum from his jacket pocket and offered me a stick.

I refused by shaking my head. "You know, I've learned a few things since we last spoke."

"And what have you learned?" he asked, smirking.

I explained about the adoption angle, Feldman, and Judge Hayes, and finished by saying, "I really thought we could help each other out, especially since you no longer consider me a suspect, but I'm wondering now if you haven't changed your mind."

"You're not a suspect. You're also not my partner. End of discussion." He said this in a far friendlier tone than he would have on the first day we met, but I must have pouted anyway, because he leaned toward me and said, "I asked you out on an impulse, and I hate making mistakes probably as much as you do. Don't turn this into one, okay?"

"You keep saying you can't tell me anything, but do you have any idea how frustrated I am?" Okay, I was whining, and thus had moved a rung below pouting. "Ben didn't deserve to die, and he wasn't a murderer, either. I'm not sure I can explain this, but for the first time in years, I'm certain of something . . . and if I let go of this investigation, it's like . . . like I'm giving up on Ben."

"Very noble, but I'll let you in on something. If a murder's not solved in the first eight hours, twenty-four hours max, you'd have better luck faxing it to *America's Most*

Wanted and letting the media have at it. I can think of a few exceptions, but that's the unpleasant truth."

"So this is already a cold case?"

"No. Cloris's murder is a cold case." A tense silence followed; then Jeff said, "You know, I really do appreciate your concern. In fact, I'm amazed a privileged little heiress like yourself cares enough about a middle-class guy like Ben Grayson to go hunting up people from the past and pursuing the clues. Pretty impressive."

"Privileged little heiress? Is that how you think of me?"

"Aren't you?"

"Well . . . I don't think of myself like that. Sounds more like a description of Aunt Caroline."

"Yeah. Maybe you're right."

"You know Aunt Caroline?"

He smiled. "I know your whole life story. Parents died. Adopted with your twin by Charlie and Elizabeth Rose at the age of six weeks. Mom died when you were three. Auntie helped Daddy raise you. Graduated from the University of Houston. Married Bradley four years ago. Divorced last year."

I sat back. Hearing him recite these things made me feel so . . . strange. More surprised than angry, really. "What else do you know about me?"

"That would take us into forbidden territory. So let me return to my lesson on murder in the big city. As I've told you already, I have to be selective about where I concentrate my energy. Usually you find relatives and neighbors out there destroying each other, and most of them leave plenty of evidence. But the Grayson murders? Hell, I spent a whole day finding out his real name. I can't waste twenty-four hours on every murder. I'd never solve anything. We bank on percentages and statistics in Homicide . . . and the probability a perp will screw up or brag to half the city about the crime."

"Those priorities rear their ugly heads again." I took my napkin and dabbed the cappuccino foam clinging to his upper lip.

He took my hand when I finished and held on, his once-icy stare having warmed considerably since our first meeting. I was liking this little date. A lot. I mean, Jeff Kline was brainy and broad-shouldered, and I had the feeling I could learn a lot from him — about things not involving police work.

About then the lone worker made enough sweeping and cleaning noises in the background for us to take the hint, so we left. After Jeff dropped me at home, I locked the front door, regretting the conspicuous lack of a good-night kiss.

"Not even a measly peck on the cheek," I lamented, climbing the stairs with Diva in my arms.

I worried about my breath for a second, but knew he had to keep his distance while on the case. I also understood an important difference between Jeff and me. He had all the patience I lacked and then some. He took things slowly. But Sergeant Jeff Kline still appealed to my senses. Every single, tingling one of them.

Fueled with the gallon of coffee I had consumed during the evening, my brain wasn't ready to quit. As I brushed my teeth, I decided that just because Jeff could squeeze my toothpaste anywhere he wanted didn't mean I'd leave the investigating to him. I had an idea of how to locate Feldman, but the plan needed refining. Like Daddy used to say, it would take a lot of river water to float this boat.

20

The next day, Kate's guilt over our little spat at the club came pouring out over breakfast, but though I had planned to ask for her help finding out if a connection still existed between Feldman and Parental Advocates, Kate was too vulnerable right now. She felt so guilty she would have agreed to wear pajamas to the university, had I asked. Besides, I needed a little more time to think through my plan. Although Hamilton knew Feldman, I wasn't sure exactly what their relationship was. And there could be plenty of information lying behind Parental Advocates' leaded-glass door, information about Cloris Grayson's baby. So maybe my sister, whose face was unfamiliar to Helen Hamilton, could help me find out what I wanted to know.

Kate had only a morning session, and I heard her heading for her little office off the living room when she got home around noon. I followed her, and she smiled when I held my arms out and we hugged. "My turn to say I'm sorry for stomping out on you last night."

"We were both a little tense after that

dinner. Did you see the way Aunt Caroline hung on Terry's every word?"

"Hard not to notice," I said.

She plopped down into her favorite over-stuffed chenille chair and I sat behind her desk.

"I could use your help," I said, picking up a pen and doodling on her blotter. "I'm not giving up on the investigation. And the two of us might actually have a little fun with this."

"Like the fun we had when we were in first grade and you tied Buster the dog to the wagon and convinced me we could ride to school with him as our horse and you as the driver?"

"That *was* fun," I said, smiling.

"Until Buster saw the cat."

"Well, I didn't foresee cats."

"Four stitches." She pointed to her eyebrow. "Do you know how traumatic four stitches are when you're six years old?"

"I told you I was sorry."

"Yes, you were sorry then and sorry now. My question is, are you tying dogs to wagons again?"

"I want to say no. But —"

"But you can't."

"Please, Kate. Just listen?"

"I'm listening."

"I need to get into Hamilton's office. I'm sure I could find Feldman if I had a peek inside her desk. You get me in, and I'll do everything else."

"How do *I* get you in?"

"You bring Hamilton something that will grab her attention, making her think you're ready to cut a deal for a baby; then you'll have to get creative . . . I'm thinking a fake illness might work. Yeah, that's it. You ask for water or aspirin. She'd have to leave the front office to get it, and that's when I sneak in and hide in the closet. You depart, she goes home, and I'm free to explore."

"Are you crazy? At the very least, that's trespassing."

"I wouldn't be jimmying any locks, or climbing into windows. And no one will know but you and me."

"I — I want to help you, but this?"

"Terry told you how he felt after we left her office, didn't he? How disgusted he was with Hamilton's so-called business?"

She nodded. "He said he doesn't think you have to run an adoption agency as if you're working the commodities exchange."

"She's only in this for the money. Feldman probably operated the same way. She could be his daughter, for all we know, carrying on the family business for another generation. Help me? Please?"

"We could get in serious trouble."

"And if we do nothing, another woman like Cloris might have her children stolen from her."

"Okay, so what's this something you mentioned that's guaranteed to grab her attention?"

I smiled. "Money, of course."

"I don't know how you talked me into this," Kate said. It was late afternoon and we were on the way to Galveston.

"You agreed because you're my loyal, loving sister, not to mention my best friend," I answered, maneuvering through rush hour traffic. "Besides, behind your placid facade lies a spirit yearning for adventure."

"You really think this will work? Hamilton sounds like a fairly clever woman. I don't know how convincing I can be."

A light rain forced me to turn on the windshield wipers. "You can match wits with Hamilton any day, Kate. Once she sees you're willing to write a check, you'll have her right where you want her."

"But you said she insisted on cash."

"You'll say someone told you the price

was ten thousand, but never mentioned the cash-only stipulation. She probably won't even accept your check, but your eagerness to whip out a checkbook will add authenticity to your visit."

"And what if she's not there?"

"We try again on your next day off."

"And what if Hamilton comes back before you're in the closet? Or what if that door you remembered seeing isn't a closet?"

"Kate, don't get yourself worked up. That office was once a foyer, so that door has to be the front closet. And if she does catch me, I'll confess that my other visits and the one today were lies. I'll say I'm a reporter doing an adoption series."

"I see. I'm Jimmy Olsen and you're Lois Lane. Well, let's hope we don't need Superman."

Though the streets were damp in Galveston, the rain had stopped by the time we reached Parental Advocates. I watched Kate climb the steps to Hamilton's office, feeling like a mother sending her kid off on the first day of school. As much as Kate trusted my version of how this would go down, Hamilton could do something unforeseen. But still, the bottom line at Parental Advocates was greed, and I was certain Hamilton would be licking her chops after Kate got out her checkbook. Then, if the woman stayed true to form, Kate wouldn't have a chance to sign her name before the cash-only speech ensued.

A minute after Kate entered the office, I tiptoed up the porch steps, crouched under the railing, and waited there. Ten minutes later, Kate appeared in the window and gave the signal that Hamilton had left the room, probably to fetch the glass of water Hamilton's very "upset" visitor had requested. The plan was working perfectly so far.

I carefully opened the front door.

And realized I had missed something important.

The door chimed.

I quickly opened the closet and sneaked in, reading panic in Kate's eyes as I eased the door shut. Enveloped in blackness, I prayed Kate would think of an explanation.

When Hamilton returned to the office, I pressed my ear against the door to listen.

"Did someone come in?" Hamilton asked.

"I'm sorry. I felt so faint, I thought fresh air might help. But the humidity made me feel worse than ever."

Good girl. That ought to fly. I slowly released my breath.

"You did want ice water, Mrs. Rose?" Hamilton said.

"Yes," Kate replied. "Thanks so much."

"Please let me apologize again for upsetting you," Hamilton said, "but I must refuse your check. We only take cash. Believe me, you don't want to leave a paper trail."

Yes! The same song and dance she'd offered Terry and me.

"If all the contracts are legal, why should it matter?" said Kate. "I mean, do the birth mothers really come back that often to claim their babies?"

"Sadly, yes. That's why we've been so successful at Parental Advocates. We prevent problems like that from happening beforehand. Please bring your husband and we'll discuss the details."

"Thanks for seeing me without an appointment. I know you must want to go home," said Kate. Her chair scraped the floor.

Another chair moved, and Hamilton's heels clicked a few times on the hardwood. "Are you sure you're all right?"

"I guess I'm still woozy. I'll just take this cup of water with me," said Kate.

"Would you like a refill before you go?" asked Hamilton.

"No, thanks. I appreciate your time."

I relaxed at the sound of them walking away. I couldn't tell if Kate said anything else, but I heard the now-familiar chime as the door opened and closed, then the renewed *rat-a-tatting* of Hamilton's feet.

Coming toward the closet.

Then her feet obliterated portions of light shining under the door.

Damn! I was trapped like a lizard under a cat's paw!

I covered my mouth with my hand, as if that would somehow make me invisible. Then I heard the blessed bleat of the phone and her feet *clackety-clacked* away. I frantically felt around in the darkness, my heart thumping. I touched a large cardboard box . . . hanging clothes . . . stacks of folders . . . several umbrellas leaning in the narrow space between the door and the wall. I climbed on the box, moving what felt like a wool coat in front of me.

Insulated by the fabric, I couldn't hear her telephone conversation or even if she was headed back my way.

But sure enough, within seconds the door opened.

I held my breath again. Peeking through the coat's folds, I captured her lower body with my left eye. The crimson enamel on her nails flashed as she picked up an umbrella. The storm. Of course. Then she closed the door and darkness enfolded me again.

Lucky for me, all I'd lost was a little confidence.

I moved the coat aside in time to hear the metallic turn of — oh, no! That sounded an awful lot like a dead bolt. *Dead bolt, Abby. As in, How the heck will you escape once you're finished searching?*

I'd have to deal with that problem later.

I cracked the door and peered out. Storm clouds completely filled the Gulf of Mexico, and with the front drapes pulled, light barely eked into the office through the leaded-glass window. I had already spotted the motion sensor on my first or second time here and knew I could reach the computer by staying close to the wall. I sidled over, feeling simultaneously silly and scared. Creeping around someone's office uninvited wasn't something I had ever imagined myself doing.

The telephone intrigued me, but shutting down the security system was the first order of business. I might not have detectivelike observational skills, but the distinctive ribbon cord leading from the computer to the wall told me Hamilton's system was hooked up to an extra power supply for several modules behind the computer. This special cord handled electric current along with communication and control signals. Computer-controlled security like this avoided the very expensive rewiring usually required in these older houses for computerized security. I knew all this because CompuCan had an agreement with Intelli-Home, the company that sold this system, and my familiarity with the program would help me turn off the alarms.

I typed a few commands already prepared with an override for the Intelli-Home password, since I'd looked it up ahead of time. I walked through the necessary steps without a glitch, and a message soon flashed, informing me the security system was disengaged. I then started hunting through the files stored on the computer, but found only contract templates, word-processing files, and lists of adoption agencies in every state of the union. No information about clients appeared to be stored here, or they were well hidden.

I found plenty of disks and CDs in a box next to the computer, labeled only with dates, none older than a few months ago. I had no time to load and search all of them, and besides, what I really wanted was information from years back, or anything connecting Feldman to Parental Advocates. I turned my attention to the telephone, a state-of-the-art piece of equipment. Maybe I could find out about Hamilton and Feldman through whatever numbers were stored in the telephone.

I hunted in the desk for the instruction manual and found it within seconds. I perused the index for a last-number-redial feature, then read the directions. The phone displayed the date and time above the number buttons, and next to that, an orange tab labeled FEATURE protruded. To the right and above the numbers were more buttons. To autoredial, I pushed feature three. Not only did the phone dial the number, it displayed the digits where the date and time previously appeared. I quickly wrote the number down and hung up. So what else could Magic Phone do? Back to the manual.

I learned the phone could be programmed to speed-dial up to twelve numbers by using those unlabeled buttons. I pushed each one and jotted down five additional phone numbers on a Post-it note when they appeared in the display window. I stuck the paper in the pocket of my shorts and opened each desk drawer but didn't find an address book with Feldman's name agreeably printed under the Fs, nor an appointment schedule conveniently lying around.

I switched my focus to the hall door leading to the rest of the house. What went on back there? Were there filing cabinets chock-full of records?

Time to find out. I opened the door and discovered several lights glowing in the short corridor. But did I stop and consider why these lights were on? Of course not. I charged right in.

Another light, this one tiny and red, flashed up high near the end of the hallway. Miss Smarty-pants Rose had missed something else in her perfect plan.

Smile, Abby. You're on Candid Camera.

This video equipment, obviously not hooked up to the computer, needed the hall's brightness to adequately film unwanted visitors. Unfortunately I hadn't foreseen this possibility.

Now what? I went down the hall, stood underneath the camera, and squinted up. Could I turn the thing off? And where would the tape be? How could I get it out? The camera was too high for me to reach, so I decided to leave that little problem for now.

I retraced my steps and entered the first room off the corridor. A copier stood against one wall, with a fax machine and document shredder alongside. The filing cabinets tempted me, but they were all locked, with no key to be found.

I reentered the hall and took several steps toward the kitchen end of the house, once again facing the blinking camera.

Then I heard the muffled sound of the chime, the one that had nearly been my downfall earlier.

I stopped dead, my stomach tight with fear, then soundlessly took a giant step to the opposite wall and flattened against the wall. I edged toward the office, positioning myself behind by the door so that if someone came through, I'd be hidden — or so I hoped.

A female voice spoke. Definitely Hamilton.

Then a man responded — he was not as close as she seemed to be — but I couldn't understand either one of them. Could she have brought Feldman with her? Was the man I'd been hunting for in the next room?

Quick steps echoed beyond the door. Then I heard a familiar computer-generated ding. One of them was at the desk on the other side of this door.

And my right shoulder was no more than a foot from the hinges. I could feel my pulse hammering at my neck.

And then I heard her clearly. Sounding exasperated, Hamilton said, "The stupid security system is off. Second time that's happened. I'll switch to manual on the way out."

Her companion said something indecipherable. He must have been standing way on the other side of the room, close to the front door.

Hamilton then said, "I left the copy of the check in the machine. Wait here while I get it."

A copy of the check? Kate's check? God, I hoped not.

I made myself as pancakelike as possible, anticipating Hamilton coming on through.

And she did, the open door stopping within an inch of my cheek. Sweat dribbled down the hollow of my back, and I pressed against the wall, holding my breath.

She clacked into the room across from me, came back out quickly, and exited, shutting the hall door.

I slowly exhaled.

"Let's go," she said. "I've got to find out about this Katherine Rose. She was no more sick than I am."

Damn. Kate did write a check, and Hamilton had copied it.

Once again I heard a barely audible reply. After the lock turned, I counted to sixty before stepping out, wanting to be sure they were gone. I cracked the door to the foyer.

Without thinking again.

Hamilton had clearly said she'd activated the security system manually, and as soon as that door opened, an almost imperceptible whine started up. A not-quite-silent alarm.

I was knee-deep in manure now. I needed that videotape and then I needed out of here. The police or the hired security people would be arriving any minute.

I sprinted back down the hall and dragged a chair from the nearby kitchen, climbed up, and ran my hands along the outside of the camera.

Come on, come on! Where's the tape?

I paused, hands trembling, telling myself to calm down.

After taking a few seconds to slow my shallow, rapid breaths, I was able to locate and remove the palm-size tape.

I hurried into the kitchen and confronted a locked dead bolt. No surprise. But the alarm was already activated, so a broken window wouldn't matter now. In fact, a broken window would be expected.

I smashed through the nearest pane with a broom, but cut my trailing leg when I climbed out. I felt a sting, then a warm stickiness on my shin.

Dark clouds rumbled angrily above me, but thank goodness the rain hadn't resumed. I glanced around the small fenced yard, seeking the best escape route. Poor Kate was parked on the next block over, probably close to having a heart attack about now. And maybe I'd just join her.

I pocketed the tape and raced across to the hurricane fence. I gripped the top and I hoisted myself up. But one side of my shorts caught on a protrusion when I came over to the other side.

I was stuck. Hung like wash on the line.

21

Dangling there on that fence, I told myself to forget about the eight ball. I was behind the whole rack.

I glanced toward the house, expecting someone to rush out that back door. Galveston Island is only twelve miles long, so someone should have already arrived in response to the alarm.

I clung to the fence with one hand, and, craning around, I saw that one prong had twisted the fabric of my shorts into a knot when I swung my legs over.

All I could do was let go, hoping the cotton would give. And so I did, and immediately heard the wonderful sound of ripping fabric. I landed on my rear with a thud.

Jeez, that hurt!

I stood, realizing my shorts had split down one side, all the way up to my waist. *Great.* I could run around the neighborhood, clothes torn, leg bleeding, gasping for breath, then maintain my innocence if stopped for questioning.

I crouched behind a large ligustrum alongside the fence, trying to figure out how to deal with this new dilemma. Looking around, I saw a reclining lawn chair ten feet away. A magazine, a pair of sunglasses, and a glass of tea, the ice melted long ago, sat on the ground next to it. The chair and drink had probably been abandoned when the first rain fell earlier.

Hmm . . . Could I pull this off?

I looked down at my tattered shorts. They would be impossible to ignore if I were spotted leaving here. I might as well have *fugitive* printed across my forehead in lipstick. So I did the only thing I could do: I took my clothes off, tossing them under the chair, along with my sandals.

But my underwear would never pass for a bathing suit. Too much lace. So off they came as well. Self-preservation takes priority over modesty any day.

I donned the sunglasses, laid my shirt over the cut on my leg, and assumed the lounge position — something I'd definitely practiced before. I slowed my breathing so the frantic heaving of my chest wouldn't give me away, then opened the magazine strategically across my torso. Unlike Steven, who was good-looking enough to have a legitimate shot at showing off his body in glossy splendor, this might be my only chance at a staple in *my* navel.

I closed my eyes, and a second later, as expected, a voice hailed me from the other side of the fence.

"Ma'am? Pardon me for disturbing you, but —"

I opened my eyes, let my mouth fall open in appropriate shock, and allowed the magazine to slip an inch. "Where did you come from?" I said, feigning surprise. "And my goodness, what time is it?" I peered at my watch.

"Uh, I'm really sorry," he said. He came up to the fence and then, realizing I was naked, focused on the ground. "You didn't happen to notice anyone running out of your neighbor's yard within the last ten minutes?"

"No. I must have fallen asleep. Is there a problem?"

"Could be." He had a five-o'clock shadow and a potbelly, and he was peeking at me — one eye open, one squeezed shut. "Pretty cloudy for sunbathing. Uh, why don't I turn around while you put your clothes on?"

I sighed. "If it will make you more comfortable." After he turned away, I watched him rock nervously back and forth from his toes to his heels, hat held behind his back.

I put on my underwear, then said, "I've

read you get a much better tan if you lie out when it's overcast. Have you heard that, Officer?"

"Seems I did once," he answered, rubbing his bald head with the hand holding the hat.

Before I lay back down, I spied a smear of blood on my shin, so I placed the magazine over my legs this time. "Okay," I said. "All clear."

He turned and, seeing I was still not fully clothed, pivoted back. "Not exactly all clear," he mumbled, his earlobes coloring.

"Come on, Officer. Don't make me put those sweaty clothes back on. Galveston's a beach town. People walk around undressed all day."

He slowly faced me, obviously pleased with this rationalization. I noticed that his badge said, *Guardian Angel Security*.

"Guess you're right," he said. "I didn't think of it like that."

He ogled me shamelessly now, but I figured it was a small price to pay for sneaking into closets uninvited.

"You planning to call the police?" I asked.

"The Feldmans wouldn't like that. No cops for them." He relaxed, leaning against the fence and fanning himself with his hat. "Say, you busy tonight?"

"Married." I smiled apologetically. "You say the Feldmans didn't want you to call the police?"

"I answered an alarm over at their other house, the one down near the beach, a few months back, and —"

"They have a beach house, too?" I said, hoping he'd help me out some more. "Funny they never mentioned it."

"Yeah, on the west side. Anyway, I answered a call from them about a break-in. 'No cops,' Mr. Feldman said. 'Just get here sooner if there's a next time and catch whoever is causing trouble.'"

"Hank? What are you doing?" yelled another man from the back door.

Hank rolled his eyes and sighed with disgust. "Questioning a witness," he hollered back. "Listen, I better go."

I certainly won't detain you, I thought.

"If you ever have any security needs, I'm Hank." He pointed proudly to his badge. "Guardian Angel Security. Give me a call."

I waited a good ten minutes before I risked leaving, then sneaked between houses to the next block, where Kate picked me up and told me at least twelve times how she never should have agreed to this caper. We drove to the Victorian so I could clean up, and I exchanged my shorts and shirt for a skirt and blouse from the pile in my trunk. Both Kate and I seemed to always have half our wardrobes in the car, en route either to or from the laundry. We then sat on the floor in the parlor, Kate sipping on the jumbo iced tea we'd picked up on the way over.

"Despite my bungled detecting job, to-day's adventure wasn't a total loss," I said, unwrapping a Snickers. "The security guard confirmed the Feldman connection to Parental Advocates. And since I learned the general vicinity of Feldman's home, per-haps one of the phone exchanges from Hamilton's office belongs in the West Beach area."

"I don't know how you convinced the se-curity guard you were a neighbor, Abby. I would have blubbered and bawled like an idiot, then raised my hands and said, 'Take me to jail. I'm guilty.' "

"By the way, Hamilton made a copy of your check. You did give her a check, right?"

"I had to," Kate said. "That ice princess just sat there with her hand out after I wrote the thing, so I passed it over. She took it with her when she went for the water, then gave the check back and gave me the 'cash-only' spiel."

"Hey, I would have passed it to her, too. But I'm afraid that despite my getting away with the tape, she now knows where we live, and who knows what else."

Kate closed her eyes and shook her head. "Why did I ever let you talk me into this?"

"Because we're doing the right thing." I picked up the phone book lying next to me and started flipping through the pages.

"What are you doing?" Kate said. "We're sixty miles from home, and my nerves are frazzled. We need to leave."

"Be patient a little longer, okay?"

She stood and started pacing. "Okay. Sure. This is what I get for teaming up with you."

I soon discovered two of the numbers on my Post-it note were located in the West Beach area. I picked up the phone, dialed, and heard a man's voice on an answering machine. Feldman, maybe? I hung up and dialed the other number.

"Ellen Fulshear Home for Young Women," said the female voice.

"Could I have your address?" I asked.

"Nineteen forty-five Bay Street. But no visitors after seven," she said.

"I have a delivery. When's a good time?"

"We're used to deliveries here," she said, then laughed. "Of course, ours take nine months. You can come after eight in the morning. Let me guess. Flowers for Susan?"

"Why, yes, but how did you know?"

"That young man of hers won't leave her alone."

I said good-bye and hung up, smiling. Maybe my luck had changed.

Kate shook her head. "Abby, you've got to quit pretending you're someone else. With my name, address, and phone number in Hamilton's hands, we probably haven't heard the end of her, and —"

"I merely told the lady I had a delivery."

"Yes, but —"

"It's not my fault if people jump to conclusions. I didn't tell the security guard I was sitting in *my* lawn chair at *my* house, either. But don't mention what happened today, especially to Terry. I did steal a videotape and break a window. That's probably a misdemeanor, but —"

"Who do you think helped you with your misdemeanor? And who do you think could never justify that misdemeanor to Terry in a million years? Oh, no. I won't be confessing this to anyone."

"Ah, fodder for blackmail. I'll remember that," I said with a grin.

"Remember, that goes both ways."

Hard to believe my sister, who'd never let a lie past her lips, was worried Terry would find out. I liked it, though. A bonding experience, I decided.

Five minutes later we hurried out to the car, the rain little more than a mist now, but before we were even in the Camry, Steven arrived.

"Got that bathroom torn up for me, Abby?" he called, climbing out of his truck.

"That's a laugh. You want to see a disaster, hand me a few tools. Didn't you already put a day's work in over here?" I said.

He came over, nodded at Kate in greeting, then said, "I need to check a few dimensions before the crew pulls those fixtures next week. You ladies had dinner yet?"

"Is that an invitation?" The Snickers bar hadn't put a dent in my hunger pangs.

Kate said, "We'll have to pass, Steven. I promised Terry I'd meet him in town, and I'll be late if we don't leave soon." She cast an anxious glance at her watch as she climbed into my car.

"Maybe next time, Steven." I opened the door and slipped behind the wheel.

"I don't want to eat alone, Abby. I'll bring you home," he pleaded.

I was hungry, and still feeling the excitement of the afternoon's adventure. Why not?

Then a voice deep inside whispered, *Because it's not a smart move.*

But I chose to listen to my grumbling stomach instead. So Kate drove on home alone and I went with Steven.

Not until we reached the restaurant did that inner voice start sounding more ominous. Steven had chosen a place complete with candlelight and panoramic ocean view. I was afraid before long he'd be humming "When I Fall in Love" and pressing his knee against mine under the table.

The hostess seated us by the window, and I saw the gulf roiling and frothing in response to the huge, swirling mass of clouds churning overhead.

"That's an angry sea," I said.

"I'd love to be out there while everything's all stirred up," said Steven.

"You've lived half your life in a storm. Doesn't it feel good to be stable, regularly employed, and sober?" I regretted the words before they were barely out of my mouth. Why couldn't I keep these brilliant insights to myself?

"I guess so," came his halfhearted reply.

The waiter approached and I spoke

quickly, thankful for the interruption. "We're ready to order. I'll have the red snapper, house dressing, and iced tea."

"Scampi for me, the rest the same," said Steven.

The waiter returned momentarily with our drinks and a basket of bread sticks. I squeezed lemon into my tea with one hand and nabbed a bread stick with the other.

"Been a while since you saw a meal?" said Steven, watching me with amusement.

"Sorry, but hungry is not something you get better at with practice. Besides, I had a busy day. Made progress, even. After the disappointment of finding a useless CD in the safe-deposit box, I —"

"Wait a minute, back up. CD? Safe-deposit box? Did I miss something?"

"That key. Remember?"

He nodded. "Oh, yeah. So you didn't find any exciting secrets?"

"No. Only a spreadsheet and word-processing program Daddy wrote."

"The one I used when I got myself so messed up with the IRS?"

"That's the one. Maybe someday I'll figure out why that CD deserved royal treatment. But forget about that. I have proof Hamilton is connected to Feldman, and might even have his phone number."

"What do you mean, you might have his phone number? Either you have a phone number or you don't."

"I got the numbers off Hamilton's speed dial. Trouble is, I don't know who they belong to, and I still don't know where Feldman lives. But I'm close." I stuffed a bread stick into my mouth.

"Slow down before you choke yourself. So how did you manage all this in one day?"

"Kate helped me. She visited Hamilton's office and jotted down the numbers when Hamilton left for a moment." Okay, so it was variation on the truth.

I washed the last crust away with a gulp of tea as the salads arrived. I started in, avoiding his eyes. He could usually tell when I was lying. But if Kate was sworn to secrecy, so was I. Besides, I couldn't tell him about the security guard and leave out the naked part. The last thing Steven wanted to hear after that wingding on the lawn with Jeff was about me prancing around in my underwear again. If I wanted him to accept that a romantic relationship between us was no longer possible, I'd better not agitate him.

An hour later we were on our way back to Houston, rain sprinkling intermittently. I yawned as the rhythm of the windshield wipers threatened to put me to sleep. Exhaustion had been lurking beneath my hunger, and now that I'd eaten, I could hardly keep my eyes open.

Steven said, "If this storm turns out as bad as they're predicting, we'll be wading through the halls of that Victorian like ducks. I'll come back tomorrow and secure those windows, but it may not help much."

"I'm coming back, too. Should I meet you?" I said.

"I've got another job, but I could catch you over there, say, late afternoon. What's going on? You still hunting Feldman?"

"Maybe."

"You're convinced you can crack the case, huh? You always were the most stubborn human I ever laid eyes on. And the best-looking, too." He reached over and placed his hand over mine.

"I agree about the good-looking part, but stubborn belongs to you, hands down."

He laughed. "I won't argue. Don't pass out from surprise, but if it'll win you back, I'll agree to anything."

I gently pulled my hand from under his. "Steven, listen . . . I don't love you anymore. At least not like that."

"You told me I owned stubborn, right? You'll see I've changed and you'll find that love again. It's only turned up missing for a while." He stared at the misty road ahead, and the rest of the drive was very quiet.

22

The next day a steady, slow rain fell, foreshadowing tropical storm Carl's assault on the Gulf Coast. I delivered to CompuCan the contracts I'd signed, this time passing on a visit to Willis's office. But I ran into him on the elevator. He said he was meeting Aunt Caroline for lunch and asked me to join them.

Why would I want to willingly subject myself to double torture? But the words *no, thanks* hadn't made it past my tonsils before the doors slid open and there stood Aunt Caroline.

"Abby! Just the person I wanted to see." Her smile was as wide as that of a small dog with a large bone.

"How scary," I said. "You hardly ever want to see me. Kate maybe. But not me."

"I need to speak with you about the business, so let's talk over lunch."

Business. Couldn't very well wiggle out of that one, so I agreed. We ate at Carrabba's Italian Grill, and between bites of linguini I soon found out what this "business" involved. Monkey business. She wanted me to hire that muscle-brained Hans person.

We haggled through the meal, and Willis kept silent for the most part, concentrating on his *pollo Marsala*. I couldn't help wondering what would have happened had I not shown up at CompuCan today. Would the manager have found some job for Hans?

When reasoning with Aunt Caroline didn't work, I suggested Hans could work for Willis as a courier, but this idea didn't pass muster with either of them. So finally I played my trump card: I mentioned all the valuable items Aunt Caroline had taken from our house.

"I've put off selling for now, Aunt Caroline, so if you persist in your demand that I hire Hans, I insist you return everything. Sort of a trade, you see, because I'm certain I'd lose money trying to create a job for him. About the only thing he'd be good at is squeezing naphtha out of mothballs."

This got her wheels spinning. Hans might not be around forever, but the art and antiques would only escalate in value. She knew the fishing expedition was over. Time to cut bait.

Then Willis said, "How's my little detective doing? Have you moved on to more sensible endeavors?"

"Little detective? Could you be more condescending, Willis? But I've made progress, thank you very much. In fact, after I leave here, I'm following up on a lead. I've finally confirmed that Feldman and Helen Hamilton are linked. She happens to work in a house he owns."

"So what does that prove?" asked Aunt Caroline, now staring at her pouting lips in the compact she'd removed from her purse.

"That proves the man is still doing what he did thirty years ago — making money off human tragedies."

Willis said, "Aren't you being overly dramatic? Things aren't as one-sided as you may think. These days pregnant women can shop around for agencies that provide the best financial support if they want to give up their baby. This Parental Advocates operation sounds perfectly legal to me."

"I don't care if they have an endorsement from Dr. Spock's ghost. Something's not right there."

"So what is this lead, Abigail?" Aunt Caroline asked.

"Feldman or Hamilton or both of them are connected to some sort of home for expectant mothers, and I'm betting the place isn't exactly the Westin Galleria Hotel. I'm going to pay them a visit. And by the way, Willis, this Hamilton woman may start

297

asking questions about Kate or me. If by chance she reaches you, tell her nothing."

"Why would she be calling me?" he asked.

This perked Aunt Caroline up. "Yes, why, Abby? What have you done?"

"She managed to get Kate's real name, and I'm afraid she may be resourceful enough to find out everything about us, including our lawyer's name," I said.

"And you think this woman might be a criminal? How did you let this happen?" said Aunt Caroline.

I should have never agreed to do lunch with them. Having Hans take laptop orders for CompuCan would have been a less painful alternative. I took a deep breath and managed to say in a fairly controlled voice, "It's been pleasant. And now I have to go."

The gray-haired woman who answered the door at the Ellen Fulshear Home for Young Women smiled back at me and nodded at the bouquet of flowers in my hand.

"For Susan, right?" she asked. She was large, with soft, fleshy arms folded on a wide stomach.

"Yes," I answered, then squeezed my eyes shut and rubbed the space between them, leaning on the door frame for support.

"Are you all right?" She opened the screen door, concern replacing her laugh lines.

"It's this weather. When the barometer dips, I suffer with horrible sinus head-aches."

"I have some aspirin. Would that help?" She stepped back so I could enter.

Like Daddy would have said, easy as stepping in East Texas mud. Can't slam the door in someone's face if they're already inside.

She led me down a hallway, and I managed to catch a peek in the living room, where three very pregnant young women sat on a worn-looking velour sofa watching television.

We entered a country kitchen, and the smell of something wonderful cooking in a giant pot on the stove enveloped me. Chicken and dumplings maybe? The woman unburdened me of the flowers I had picked up at the local grocery store, and I sat at a gigantic table covered with a red-checked cloth. The woman placed a tall glass of lemonade in front of me. She then started struggling with the childproof cap on the aspirin bottle she'd pulled from a cupboard near the sink.

"My five-year-old grandnephew opens

these things in a flash," she mumbled. "The only ones they keep from the medicine are the arthritics like me."

"Please don't bother with the aspirin," I said. "See, I have a confession. I don't really have a headache, and I'm not delivering flowers."

She stopped fiddling with the cap, her face wary, her smile gone. "How's that, young woman?" she said sternly. "Are you selling something or fixing to rob me? Because if that's the case, I don't have much to take."

"Nothing like that. If you can spare a few minutes, I'd like to explain."

She poured herself a glass of lemonade and sat opposite me. "Are you in trouble? Is that it?" Despite her irritation, she seemed genuinely concerned.

"I'm troubled, yes, but it's not what you think. And so complicated, I'm not even sure where to start."

"The beginning usually works." Her smile returned.

"I've made up so many stories lately, the idea of simply telling the truth seems . . . strange," I said.

"If I can, I'll help you. There's still a few people in this world you can trust, and I'd like to think I've lived long enough to understand most of what human nature is capable of. Tell Sally Jean about this trouble."

"It's odd. I've never lied this easily before the murder."

"The murder?" Her eyes widened. "You didn't murder someone, did you?"

"Of course not. It has to do with Samuel Feldman. I got your number off the Parental Advocates office phone, and I want to ask him a few hard questions, but the only phone number and address I could come up with were connected to the office."

"I can tell you where he is, but first you need to tell me why I should."

"You know where he is?" I sat straighter in my chair.

"You must want to see him real bad to sneak in here with your daisies and your fake headache."

"I think he murdered my yardman. And maybe someone else . . . a long, long time ago."

She closed her eyes and made the sign of the cross. "It wouldn't surprise me one bit. It's a sad thing to believe that about another person. He's a cold one, he is. But start at the beginning, Miss . . . What's your name, honey?"

"Abby. Abby Rose. And yours?"

"Sally Jean Daniels. All the girls call me

Sally Jean, and you will, too. Explain about this murder you say Sam did, may God have mercy on him."

"I don't have hard proof, but the story began in a little town north of Houston called Shade. . . ."

By the time I finished my narration, I could tell nothing I'd said surprised her.

"I've lived here ages and ages caring for pregnant girls," she said. "Making sure they eat right and get enough exercise and all that. But not until Melvyn — he was my husband — not until he died did I begin to suspect the only light at the end of my tunnel was an oncoming train."

"What do you mean?" I said.

"I'm not good with math . . . figures . . . you know. I never saw the bills. Melvyn worked with Feldman on the business end of running this place. The Doc — that's what the girls called my husband — treated the girls; then Sam Feldman paid him for services rendered. But after Melvyn's funeral, I discovered that even though I'm bad with arithmetic, Melvyn missed more of the basics in addition and subtraction than I ever did." She shook her head. "A financial nightmare, let me tell you."

"Wait a minute. Young women giving up their babies for adoption stay here, right?"

"Going on thirty-five years now," she said.

"And you work for Parental Advocates?"

"That's what I was trying to explain. If you had said 'Parental Advocates' to me six months ago I would have looked at you like you were as nutty as a Corsicana fruitcake. But as I waded through those legal papers after the Doc's death, I learned how the whole thing works." She crossed her arms, barely spanning her broad bosom.

"You don't seem thrilled," I said.

"This business has changed, nothing like it used to be when Melvyn was alive, that's for sure. But he left me nothing but a bunch of worthless stock, so I gotta keep working, and this is all I know how to do."

"I take it Mr. Feldman hasn't been the best employer."

"He's just in it for the money, of course. But he stopped coming here a while back. Grew to be a hermit. We talk on the phone, but I don't see him anymore, which was working fine for me. But he married that skinny, fast-talking woman right before he took to his house. She's young enough to be his daughter, mind you. Anyway, she started bringing the girls over here and handling the business. She expects me to run this place like a prison, and I hate her ways.

These youngsters have made mistakes, but it doesn't mean they've lost their rights as human beings."

"Are you talking about Helen Hamilton?" I asked.

She nodded. "The two of them live in the fancy section of town. Do you realize what people pay to adopt a baby these days? Thousands and thousands of dollars, that's what. Yet my salary's not much more than when we first started here. Of course, Melvyn and I never did this only for money — not like those two."

"You've been doing this for thirty-five years?" I asked, wondering if Cloris had come here to have her baby.

"That's right. I'm not a registered nurse, just vocational, and Melvyn was only a GP, but I think we did okay. Only lost two babies in all those years."

"You and your husband delivered them?"

"Sure did. Not in the last ten years, though. Times have changed. Not that I don't know how to deliver, but I'd need a midwife certification from the state. We gave the girls the best, most inexpensive care for a good many years, though. After the Doc died, I discovered most of them could have had the finest room in any hospital for what those adopting families paid

Feldman, but he cut costs and pocketed most of the cash."

"Ben's wife, the one I told you about from Shade? Her name was Cloris. Do you remember her?"

"Cloris? Let me think." Her lips moved in and out as she concentrated; then she said, "Yes! Yes! I do remember her! Unusual name. Right after she gave birth she changed her mind about the adoption. Took one look at those beautiful twin girls and said she couldn't give them up."

"Twins?" My heart hopped. "But I never realized —"

"Wait a minute," said Sally Jean, holding up a restraining hand and shaking her head vigorously. "It's all coming back. Cloris got real bent out of shape once she realized she'd never see them again. Not that some girls hadn't balked before. But if they wouldn't sign the adoption papers, Sam Feldman would hire a family to keep the baby for a few days. That way the girl could reconsider without an infant snuggled up to her. Oh, Mr. Sam was slick, all right. He'd come and talk to those girls about how there'd be no more dancing or movie shows and how they wouldn't be having fun anymore; they'd be changing diapers. And I'll admit, I didn't argue with that approach.

Those infants deserved a decent life, one that probably wouldn't happen with mothers who were little more than children themselves. After a few days, sure enough, they'd forget and sign whatever Sam wanted them to sign."

"But Cloris was different?" I asked, a strange tightness constricting my chest. Twins. Cloris gave birth to twin girls.

"Way different. She came here with only the clothes on her back. A sad young woman, and bearing some trouble she wouldn't talk about. Had worried eyes, same color as yours."

"But she signed the papers?" I asked, my voice sounding small and faraway. Twins. This couldn't be real. There had to be an explanation other than the one I couldn't push from conscious thought.

"Well, see, I don't know. I assumed she did. But after the birth she took sick. Got to coughing so, and I couldn't get her fever down. She nearly gave up when she came 'round and found out Feldman had taken the babies already. But I wouldn't let her die. Uh-uh. No, ma'am. But though her body finally healed, her heart wasn't mended. She left the money behind, the five hundred Sam gave her to start over."

"She tried to get those children back," I

said quietly. "Tried for a long time. And was murdered for her trouble."

"And you think Sam killed her because she came too close?"

"Yes," I said, then lapsed into silence.

I heard Sally Jean saying, "I could kick myself from here to Lufkin for trusting the Doc and Sam so completely. As far as my husband's concerned, he probably didn't think he'd done anything wrong. And me? I cooked and cleaned and cared for the girls, thinking I was doing good works all those years."

I blinked, forcing myself back into the present moment. "You won't tell Feldman I came here, will you?"

"Do I look like I fell off the stupid truck?"

"Good." I stood. "If you'll give me his address, I'll be on my way. I can't thank you enough for the information."

"If he's killed two people, seems to me getting rid of you would be easy, girl. Best to call the police, don't you think?"

"Maybe," I said. But I would not be calling the police. Not yet.

"You be careful then, little lady." She took a piece of paper and wrote the address, handing it to me just as a voice echoed down the hallway.

"Sally Jean! It's me," a woman called

through the latched screen at the front of the house.

The door rattled. Thank goodness Sally Jean had fastened the hook, because I recognized that voice. Helen Hamilton.

"Is there another way out?" I whispered.

She nodded and gestured for me to follow her.

I hurried out the back door, then drove two blocks before calling Sally Jean on my cell. She picked up on the second ring.

"It's me, Abby. Is she still there?"

"Yes, ma'am," said Sally Jean.

"Standing near you?"

"Yes, ma'am," she replied cheerfully.

"Can you delay her so I can visit Feldman?"

"I'll try. Friday sounds fine," she said, covering for me.

"Thanks." I disconnected and sped west. I had to make a move while Sally Jean was delaying Hamilton or miss my chance at Feldman — even though I was no longer sure I wanted to know the truth.

No, I wanted to believe in coincidences. And the kindness of the only father I had ever known and the invalid mother I had not.

But I'd been fishing in troubled waters for more than a week, and it was time to reel in that shark Feldman.

An older man answered the door after I knocked, then backed up six feet inside. He looked seventy or close to it, with thinning silver hair and piercing blue eyes. Though I'd realized Feldman would be old, a geriatric murderer didn't quite jell with my image of a criminal.

"Terry Armstrong, Houston police," I said, extending one of the business cards I'd been hanging on to for a moment like this. "Are you Samuel Feldman?"

I'd told the *big* lie this time. The illegal kind. But with the word *twins* battering my brain unmercifully, I really didn't care.

"Yes, I'm Samuel Feldman," he said, stepping forward and snatching the card before retreating again into the shadowy foyer.

I was now face-to-face with this slimeball, and though he looked frail, his voice sounded strong and self-assured. I would have preferred weak and wavering.

"I'm a consultant in the Unsolved Crimes division, and I have a few questions," I said. "Can I come in or should we go down to the precinct?"

He hesitated a second, then replied, "What's this about?"

"It's about murder, sir. Would you like to

discuss this here or go downtown?" I didn't stop to consider what I'd do if he actually told me to take him "downtown."

"I can give you a minute, but I know nothing about any murder." He turned abruptly and I followed him inside, wondering if he'd noticed my trembling hands or an expression that surely must have relayed how sick I felt inside.

A winding staircase rose to my right, and the foyer ceiling opened up to the second floor. A gleaming chandelier hung above our heads, and this hallway alone could have housed a family of four. I couldn't help thinking that all this wealth had been achieved thanks to exorbitant fees paid by hundreds of desperate people over the past thirty years. Had I known one of those desperate souls? Lived with him all my life?

Feldman walked briskly to the left, into a formal living area furnished with an expensive-looking modular sofa and heavy white drapes on the picture window with a bay view. A palatial room, one that reminded me of winter.

"What's this about?" he said curtly.

He sat on the sofa near the fireplace, and I sat opposite him, seemingly a football field away. A heavily varnished coffee table fashioned from the trunk of a redwood filled the

U space between us.

"I'm investigating the deaths of a couple named Grayson," I said. "You may remember the wife. Her name was Cloris, and her children were placed in an adoptive home through your agency many years ago."

He crossed his legs and leaned back against the white cushions. "Thousands of children came through my agency, and by the way, I don't own or operate that business any longer."

Maybe not on paper, I thought. He'd no doubt covered himself there. "Let me refresh your memory. Cloris Grayson caused a bit of trouble in your life . . . before someone murdered her."

"I don't know what you're talking about."

"I think you do. We know you placed her twins, and we know she tried to find them. If she succeeded, then you would have lost. Big-time. I'd call that motive, sir."

He shifted his thin frame, paying considerable attention to his fingernails. "I think you're mistaken. I don't remember this woman."

I guess I had expected him to fall on his knees and confess. I should have planned this confrontation better, but I was too distracted by what Sally Jean had told me to even make much sense right now. Still, I couldn't leave without getting something out of this asshole. Maybe if I threw out a line about the judge, he'd squirm.

"You cooperated with a judge named Eugenia Hayes. We believe you made some shady deals with her, threw a few bribes her way. Is that not a fact, sir?"

"I told you I don't know anything about your murder, nor about bribery. Frankly, I'd categorize your information as flimsy innuendos. I haven't been in a courtroom in a long time, and I don't recall anyone named Hayes."

"Suffering from selective amnesia, sir?"

He got up. "I won't be insulted in my own home. Obviously you're grasping at straws."

I had forgotten he was a lawyer, a "professional liar," like Judge Hayes said.

"This isn't the end, Feldman," I said, knowing this was true, even if everything else I'd said was a lie.

"If you show up again," Feldman said, "you'd better have more than speculation."

He marched ahead of me, and I heard the phone ringing beyond a door across the foyer.

"I'll find my way out," I said.

He waited until I was out the front door,

but didn't come too close . . . almost as if he were afraid of what was out there. He certainly wasn't afraid of me.

It was raining like God opened the drain, and I hesitated before closing the front door behind me. Just then a gust of wind blew me backward and the door opened, horizontal rain spraying into the foyer. I stepped back inside, deciding to wait a minute or two for the weather to let up.

That was when I realized I could hear Feldman talking in the other room. He said, "When do you think you'll be here?"

Silence followed. I moved closer to the half-open door.

Feldman said, "I've had a visitor. Houston Police."

His voice drifted closer, as if he might be walking toward me.

Damn.

I hurried across the foyer and crouched behind a large statue of some naked Greek god. I sneaked a peek and saw Feldman step out, his attention on the open front door. He maneuvered around the puddle on the floor, shut the door, and practically jumped away after doing so. As he went back into the other room, I heard him say, "Stupid woman left the door open."

Taking a path close to the wall, I tiptoed

back, stopping outside the room just in time to hear him say, "I understand. But they're putting things together."

Another pause before he said, "I *know* they don't have any evidence, but she mentioned Eugenia Hayes, and she was one of the judges. If they dig deep enough, they'll find out Rose made her step down and — Hold on; I've got another call."

My knees almost gave way, and I steadied myself against the wall. Then, not caring whether Feldman knew I'd been listening in, I opened the door and ran out into the stinging rain. I didn't remember starting the car or navigating through the downpour, but soon I found myself on P Street.

I parked in the driveway and sat there in the Camry, not bothering to even turn off the air-conditioning, my soaked clothing molded to my cold, shivering body. Rain still poured in unrelenting intensity from the swirling slate sky.

I clutched the steering wheel, my knuckles protruding white and sharp through the stretched skin of my hands. The truth, the thing that was supposed to set you free and all that crap, ricocheted between the confines of my skull, cruel and punishing.

Then tears began sliding down my cheeks and under my chin.

23

The rain let up minutes later, but rivulets continued to trail down the windshield. I watched one and then another and another meander and disappear. I could have easily run to the Victorian during this temporary reprieve, but I remained paralyzed in my car.

Those words, *Rose made her step down,* kept replaying in my head like a broken car alarm, over and over and over.

I don't know how much time passed, but my tears had dried. I was left feeling numb and more alone than I could remember. That was when another man's words came back. Jeff Kline's words. *Ben Grayson was living on your property because he wanted to be there.* Yes, indeed. Ben had come to find Daddy, to find Kate and me.

"How very clever of you, Daddy," I whispered. Was anything he'd told us true? Had there even been a fatal plane crash right before Kate and I were born? I doubted it.

And did he have any idea how much this truth would hurt when it came pouncing out from the past? How did I reevaluate a lifetime founded on deception? Where did I begin?

I felt overwhelmed and unequipped to deal with any of this. I wanted none of such a messy past. But having made the first vital connection, my synapses continued to fire. My father made Hayes step down because someone threatened to expose the judge as corrupt, had threatened to reclaim her children.

Cloris. Also known as Connie. Also known as *my mother.*

I shook my head, sprinkling the windshield with water from my drenched hair. *Don't think about that part, Abby. Not now.*

Rain pummeled my car anew, and for some silly reason — maybe denial was kicking in — I entertained the notion that Daddy could have been honoring a friend's request when he forced Hayes to resign — simply been helping some friend protect their adopted children, not his own. After all, he had powerful business connections and measurable influence in political circles.

But I knew the truth, and the more I tried to push it away with implausible explanations, the more its presence grew. But that voice in my head came back with, *You don't have solid proof. All you have is an overheard sentence spoken by a cruel old man.*

And I had to be one hundred percent sure.

Eugenia Hayes knew everything. At least, she used to know. Could I drag the truth from the cloud of confusion fogging her mind? Maybe if I could hear the words from her, from the woman who sealed the deal, I could accept that I was raised by a man who then spent a generation lying to my sister and me.

The same curly-haired woman sat filing her nails at the information desk at the nursing home. When I marched past her, she spotted me and called out, "You can't go up there!"

Over my shoulder I said, "I'll only be a few minutes. I need to talk to Eugenia Hayes."

I continued toward the elevator.

"Don't make me call security. No visitors for her."

I turned and went back to the desk. "Has something happened? Is she sick?"

"You upset her last time, and her son had a fit. Seems she called him and rambled on about bribes and crooked lawyers. She got so worked up she had to have three breathing treatments. After that, Mr. Hayes told the doctor not to let in anyone else." She lifted her eyes, her withering gaze intended to shame me. "The son doesn't come here much, you know. Of course, after you explained to me about Eugenia's operation, I could understand his shame, but —"

"Wait a minute. I never said anything about any *operation*."

She kept on talking, ignoring me. "Then I knew what had upset her son so much. Mr. Hayes was worried that little tidbit about his mother's operation would get around town, don't you know." She paused, glanced around the deserted lobby, then whispered, "About her sex change."

She resumed her normal tone. "I told him I wouldn't tell — but he kept denying Eugenia started out as his father, *Eugene*. But we know better, don't we?" She winked. "So you're the one who got him so mad." She smiled, pleased with this logic, and started buffing her index finger.

I had to talk to the judge. Now. So I did what lately seemed to come so naturally to Charlie Rose's daughter: I lied.

Leaning on the desk, I said, "Eugenia told me about her son, how he keeps visitors away. How he's embarrassed by her. She's lonely up there. Craves company. Do you

318

want to contribute to making her last days on earth totally miserable? I don't think that's why you work with the elderly, is it?"

She set her nail buffer down. "Well . . . no."

"Please let me talk to her. I'm begging for a few short minutes."

"Maybe I could call the nurses' station . . . say you're an out-of-town relative and have the son's okay to visit." She pointed a finger at me. "But you have to give me your word you won't upset her."

"I promise." And that was probably another lie. But I didn't care.

Judge Hayes sat with the head of the bed propped up, her eyes clear and alert. "It's about time you showed up," she said. "I told that man who keeps insisting he's my son to find you, get you back here," she said. "Did you locate him?"

"Your son?" I asked, dragging a chair to the bedside.

"No, that snake Feldman. Don't tell me you forgot already?"

Judge Hayes was chastising *me* about forgetting? "Yes, I found him. But something he said troubles me. Do you remember the man who pressured you to resign?"

"Resign? I'll never resign. I've done

things I shouldn't, but always in the best interests of the children. So many children . . . beaten, forgotten, neglected . . ."

I sighed. Reality lasted for only the tiniest interludes with her. I had another trick I'd thought of on the way up in the elevator, though, and took my address book from my purse.

"What's that, counselor?" she said, obviously curious.

"This is evidence," I said.

"Evidence? You'd better mark it as an exhibit, then."

"I submit this as exhibit A. Proof Charles Rose illegally adopted the twin children of Cloris Grayson and forced you to resign when she came looking for them."

"That's inadmissible. Inadmissible!" Her face flushed to an unhealthy shade of purple, and she grasped the siderails of her bed.

I placed a hand on her bony knee. "It's all right," I said. "I'll keep your secret."

She collapsed against the pillows, closed her eyes, and inhaled feebly. "If I didn't resign, Rose told me the truth would come out about the forgeries."

"Were all the adoption papers Feldman presented in your courtroom forged?"

"No. But Rose would make sure every

placement I'd made would be investigated."

"And children might be returned to their mothers?" I said.

"To mothers who didn't want them. Or they'd be forced back into orphanages." Her cloudy eyes were filled with sadness.

"So if you resigned, he'd make sure that didn't happen?" I said.

Her features hardened again. "He promised that snake Feldman would be out of business, too."

"And the twins' documents were forged?"

"Yes, yes." She tossed her head and kinky gray wisps of hair fanned out on the pillow. "He said if his girls had to go back to their mother, their hearts would break."

I closed my eyes, tears burning against my lids.

Judge Hayes touched my arm. "Bobbie? I'm tired. This has been hard on an old woman."

I blinked hard, pushing down the emotion. So I was Bobbie now. "Can I get you anything before I leave?" I said.

She nodded at the water pitcher and I filled her glass. She took a sip, then handed the glass back.

"I don't blame the man for wanting to protect those children, do you?" she said.

I shook my head no, not wanting to upset

her any more than I already had. But I was lying again. I did blame him. God, how I blamed him.

I returned to P Street and waited for Steven, no longer doubting that my father had deceived my sister and me all our lives. I paced in front of the window, trying not to think, wondering how I would tell Kate, and realizing that working through the emotions that had flooded me in the last few hours might take me a lifetime. First I had to come to terms with the knowledge that Daddy could have had a hand in murdering my mother. Yes. He might have murdered her to keep her from staking her claim on her own children. Or had he helped Feldman do the job? They certainly both would have benefited from her death.

My head throbbed and I still couldn't seem to arrange the facts in logical order. Did I know for certain Daddy had had anything to do with killing Cloris? Or did I merely fear he might have been involved?

I wasn't sure. I only knew I would stick to this investigation until I had enough hard proof to bring Feldman and the ghost of Charlie Rose to justice. Nailing Samuel Feldman was now the most important thing in my life.

I stopped pacing and took a deep breath, aware of the stuffy room, my clenched fists, and the awful headache. Darkness had descended early, the smoky-black clouds transforming the late afternoon into night.

And that noise? What was that noise coming from above me?

I had been so distracted, I had no clue whether the sound had just begun or had been going on since I arrived. The way the wind was blowing, and with all Steven's construction work, something could be very wrong upstairs. The repetitive banging persisted, so I climbed to the second floor to investigate. I smelled rain. A window must be open.

But when I reached the landing, the mystery was solved. The door to the bathroom was swaying back and forth, and every few seconds it swung hard enough to hit the wall.

So where was all the wind coming from? The tiny window in there couldn't possibly be allowing these huge gusts. I walked over, grabbed the door as it swung toward me, and peered into the bathroom.

A gaping hole replaced what had once housed a commode, sink, and tub. All those fixtures were below me now, a pile of rubble resting on the mudroom ceiling. As Steven had predicted, the bathroom had collapsed and the far wall had crumbled into the yard.

Just then a violent cracking and crunching started beneath my feet. I had no time to grab for the door frame as the damaged entrance gave way.

Down I plummeted, into the saturated mound of broken wood and insulation, the journey a horrible aberration of a waterslide ride. Then everything went black.

24

I stared up at the house, feeling groggy and disoriented. How had I landed here? I remembered climbing the stairs . . . the floor was wet, the door was swaying in the wind, and —

What was that noise? It sounded like my name. Or had I damaged my brain and now suffered from hallucinations?

No. I definitely heard a human voice coming from above me.

"Abby?"

"I'm in the bathtub," I croaked.

And I *was* in the bathtub. Well, half in the bathtub. One leg dangled over the mangled faucet, and my backside rested in three or four inches of muddy water. I rose up on my elbows.

Steven was standing above me where the bathroom used to be. "Are you okay?" he said.

"Yes, but we'll definitely start here with the redecorating." I attempted to extricate myself from the pile of jagged porcelain and shattered lumber. But moving wasn't as easy as it had been prior to my plunge into renovation hell. I hurt. Everywhere.

"How did you end up down there?" he called.

"Obviously I fell, idiot." But I was the one who felt like an idiot.

"Don't move. I'm coming down!"

At that point I became aware of the persistent and extremely annoying rain, which, despite the summer heat, was probably contributing to the chills threatening to shake me silly.

After bringing the ladder from the garage and propping it on the side of the house, Steven hoisted me carefully from the tangled pile of beams, fixtures, and broken ceramic tile, then helped me climb down.

"You're bleeding," he said quietly, wiping my forehead with the heel of his hand once we stood on the soggy lawn.

"That's probably mud," I argued, but then my knees buckled. He caught me, saying gently but firmly, "Shut up. I know blood when I see it."

My teeth started chattering and waves of tremors began in my shoulders, spreading to my arms and legs as he lifted me and carried me to his truck. After a few minutes passed, I noted with relief that all limbs remained attached to my body and I had all my teeth.

The drive back to Houston was a blur.

Thank goodness he didn't take me to the hospital. Injuries aside, I would have died of embarrassment. Most folks fall *in* the bathtub, not *into* it.

Kate paled when she opened the front door and saw Steven supporting me. I could imagine how I must have looked. Luckily I seemed to have sustained only a puncture wound to my butt from a nail and a gash on my forehead. Nothing seemed to be broken, but my hero insisted he had to help me upstairs, and I didn't have the energy for a dispute.

"Despite appearances, I'll survive," I reassured Kate as Steven walked me up the stairs. "To the bathroom. Okay?"

"Sure." He steered me left at the landing, with Kate following close behind.

"Let's be real careful before we go in, though. I discovered today that bathrooms have this strange way of disappearing."

"This is all my fault," Steven said. "I knew that section of the house was unstable. I should have blocked off the stairs so you wouldn't go up there." He helped me sit in front of the vanity.

Webster appeared, wagging his tail. Apparently he considered mud and blood a delightful combination and began licking my legs.

"I'll be picking up tarps to seal off the damage as best I can," said Steven. "Otherwise the rain will saturate the entire second floor. I'll tow your car back, Abby, but before I leave, are you sure you don't want to reconsider and visit a hospital?"

"Positive. Thanks for everything," I said. He left.

I gratefully took the towel Kate offered and wiped my face.

"Tell me what happened," she said. "Looks like a bomb exploded in your immediate vicinity." She stooped and pulled my shoes off.

"The bathroom succumbed to the fatal allure of gravity, requiring only my one hundred and twenty pounds to reach that decision." I took off my shirt, and thank goodness Webster enjoyed sniffing that filthy, tattered remnant better than running his snout over my body.

Kate turned on the bathwater.

"Bubbles. I need lots of bubbles." I stood on unsteady legs and finished undressing.

"Once I help you in, I'm calling the doctor."

"I don't need a doctor. I'll sit in this wonderful, fully appointed tub — a far cry from my previous experience in the bath — and recover immediately."

"Abby, for God's sake, you just fell off a house!"

"Don't remind me." I slowly descended into the hot, soapy water and knew what heaven was about.

"I'm calling. I don't care what you say." She stomped out, pulling a reluctant Webster, who bade a fond farewell with a longing look at the offensive shirt on the floor.

If calling the doctor would occupy Kate for a while, that was fine by me. I didn't want to slap her with the truth about Daddy. Not yet. I had a row or two to hoe with someone else first.

I had just settled into bed when Kate entered and handed me a snifter half-filled with amber liquid.

"What concoction is this, Dr. Kate?"

"Brandy," she said.

"Where's the chamomile tea? The feverfew? The valerian root?" I said, accepting the glass. I was thinking that all this attention for a few bumps and bruises was making me more uncomfortable than I already was.

"This occasion requires something more potent. And brandy is medicinal."

I sipped, and since I rarely drink alcohol

after my experience with Steven's problem, the brandy had an immediate effect, both soothing and warm. I set the half-empty snifter next to me and readjusted the quilt over my knees.

"When I explained to the doctor what happened," Kate said, "he thought you should go to the emergency room, but I told him you wouldn't cooperate. He insisted you come to his office tomorrow for a tetanus shot, though."

"He insisted? And will he have a medical tantrum if I don't obey? Or maybe send me to noncompliant-patient jail?"

"Humor me if not him, Abby. I'm guessing that was a very nasty, dirty nail that stabbed you in the patoot."

The doorbell saved me from pronouncements of the fate awaiting me if I refused medical care, although I had to admit a tetanus shot was probably a good idea.

"That's Terry," Kate said. "Mind if he comes up?"

"Invite the neighbors, if you want. But they may have to watch me sleep, because I'm damn tired."

As it turned out, Terry wasn't alone. Jeff Kline was with him, and he definitely looked irritated once I explained about my fall without grace.

Terry hadn't eaten, which was closer to an emergency than my own accident, so he and Kate went down to the kitchen, offering to bring me up something in a few minutes. They left Jeff and me alone, and he wasted no time getting to the point.

"Busy today?" he asked, propping his feet on the tapestry-covered footstool near my bed. His inquiring eyebrows, not to mention the snide slant to his tone, confirmed this would not be a pleasant conversation.

"Besides examining the plumbing on P Street?" I said, trying to sound innocent.

"Before that." Out came the gum.

I was beginning to understand about the gum — how the quantity and chewing speed increased proportionately with his level of agitation. I shifted off my aching rear end and said, "This sounds like an interrogation, Sergeant."

"Darn right, Abby. Or should I call you Police Consultant Abby? I had no idea we had an Unsolved Crime division. Very creative."

"Oops."

"I could have come here with a warrant for your arrest."

"How did you find out?"

"All you care about is how I found out?" he said. "You're not even sorry? Not even grateful you won't be arrested? You're just bothered by *getting caught?*"

"Arrest me if you think I've committed a crime," I said, surprised I had the energy to raise my voice. "But if you'd done your job, I wouldn't have been at Feldman's house in the first place." I snatched up the snifter and downed the rest of the brandy in one gulp. And choked.

Not content with my failed attempt at self-destruction earlier in the day, I now threatened to drown in my own secretions. What an attractive picture I must have presented — bruised and scraped practically beyond recognition, and now turning blue from lack of oxygen.

Jeff pounded my back, and when it was obvious I'd survive another brush with death, he switched to rubbing circles and massaging my neck. I relaxed against his strong, kneading fingers.

"Are you sure you're okay?" he asked. "Kate said you didn't break anything, but you look miserable."

"I'm okay. And I'm sorry for flying off the handle. I should never have taken Terry's business cards, and I probably deserved to fall off the house, and —"

"Quiet, Abby."

"But Jeff, you don't understand. I can't

drop this investigation until I find out —"

He reached down and took my face in his hands. "Hush."

I met his eyes and blinked hard, fighting tears.

"Slow down." He brushed my hair away from the cut on my forehead before pulling back — a withdrawal that came a tad soon for my liking. He said, "Feldman phoned the precinct and complained that an officer harassed him about Ben's murder investigation. Guess who they routed that call to?"

"Again, I'm sorry." A few deep breaths eliminated the threat of tears.

"If you suspect this man is a murderer, what's to keep him from hurting you?"

I didn't tell Jeff that I wasn't sure it mattered at this point whether Feldman hurt me or not. I didn't say anything.

He took my hand. "I'm stuck with an unacceptable emotional involvement in this case and —"

"What do you mean, unacceptable?"

"As the lead detective, I need . . . No, let me rephrase that. I must remain objective. Emotions block the truth. They cloud my instincts. Did it cross your mind that someone could have arranged your tumble today?"

"Arranged it? What makes you think that?"

"Paranoia goes with my job. Seriously, could Feldman have figured out you weren't a police officer? Could he have tampered with those boards that gave way?"

"He didn't know I was playacting. If you didn't tell him any different, he may still think I work for the police. And remember, he called you. Why draw attention to himself by phoning the police if he planned to kill me?"

"Okay. You've got a point."

"And besides, I overheard Feldman on the phone before I left his house, telling someone the police had visited."

"Okay, so he believed you, but he may have killed a man right here a couple weeks ago — a well-publicized crime, with you and your sister's pictures in the *Chronicle*. What's to say he didn't snap to who you were after he called us?"

"I suppose he could have, but that still wouldn't have given him time to mess with those boards. He would have had to follow me," I said. "But I never considered the publicity. His wife, Helen Hamilton, the woman who runs Parental Advocates, may have realized who Kate and I are because —" I stopped. I couldn't tell Jeff about Daddy's lies until I told Kate.

"Go on."

Damn. Now I had to tell him *something*. I decided on a watered-down version of the truth. "Kate visited Hamilton, pretending to be a prospective client. And, well . . . she gave Hamilton a check. We got it back, but Hamilton made a copy."

"This check had her real name on it?" he said.

I nodded.

"I can't believe this." He uttered a sarcastic half laugh and shook his head. "If Feldman and his wife are involved in Ben's death, they now know your sister was scrounging for information — probably know you were, too."

"Yes, but —"

He withdrew his hand from mine. "This check scam was your idea, right?"

"Please let me —"

"That first time I saw you, I told myself you were trouble. Pegged you as stubborn and driven from the beginning, despite your damn seductive eyes. But did I keep my distance? No, I had to go — Oh, forget it." He turned away, chewing ninety to nothing on his gum.

Seductive eyes? Wow. "Go on. I think I was going to like the next part."

He looked at me, unsmiling. "We'll deal with personal matters later. Stop messing in police business. You and Kate could be in danger."

I leaned against my pillow. I'd already figured that much out, so why did he have to remind me?

"No more meddling," he continued. "I'm still working this case and you'll have to be patient, understand?"

"I understand. Now . . . how about the personal stuff?" I nudged the fingers that rested tantalizingly close to my thigh.

He took a deep breath. "Later." He stood, emptying his wad of gum into a wrapper. "Patience, Abby. Lie here tonight in the dark and concentrate on becoming more patient."

But after he left I asked myself why would I think about patience when the memory of his fine blue eyes was the only thing capable of distracting me from the disturbing truths about the past?

25

The next morning I learned the term *rude awakening* held genuine meaning. I felt like a parakeet that got caught in a badminton game. Every atom hurt. After easing out of bed, I stood under the shower until my prunish fingers warned me to cease and desist. It seemed to take five full minutes to get down the stairs, and when I finally shuffled into the kitchen, Kate was preparing to leave for school.

She smiled. "Need a wheelchair?"

"Yeah, go ahead and smile. You can use your facial muscles without feeling like you've been pulled through a knothole backward." I slowly approached the coffeepot.

"It's a good day to stay home in bed anyway, because tropical storm Carl has stalled above us and we'll see nothing but rain." She opened the refrigerator and said, "Before you have coffee, drink this shake to soothe those achy muscles." She poured something thick from the blender into a glass and brought the concoction over to me.

It was green. My sister expected me to drink a green milkshake at ten o'clock in the morning. "Can I tackle this after my coffee?"

"I suppose. But don't go dumping it down the sink," she warned. "And I expect you to relax while I'm gone."

Webster barked at the door as she left, then turned to me, tail wagging, rear end wiggling.

"How'd you like a nice, big milkshake, fella?" I asked, holding the glass near his nose.

He sniffed briefly, then ambled to the back door, where he lay down and pretended to be asleep. If our canine garbage disposal wasn't tempted, I wasn't risking it either.

I spent the next two hours on-line researching Jane and Morris Mitchell, the people who were supposed to be my biological parents. The couple had indeed died in a plane crash, but the article from the El Paso newspaper archives reported that they were survived by a ten-year-old son. No twin infant girls. I then placed a call to Aunt Caroline, and told her I needed to see her immediately, saying I'd had an accident — which was true.

She arrived within thirty minutes and knocked at the back door. I'd made it halfway there when she let herself into the kitchen and propped her umbrella against the wall.

"What happened, Abigail?" she asked, squinting at my forehead. "Did you and Steven finally come to blows after all your years of off-again, on-again romance?"

"This has nothing to do with Steven and everything to do with you." I stared her straight in the eye.

She shifted her gaze, flicking at her sleeve before removing her raincoat and draping it over the back of the chair.

"I've uncovered some disturbing information," I said. "I learned yesterday that Kate and I were deceived for a very long time."

"Whatever are you talking about?"

But I could tell she knew. "I know about the adoption, so you can quit lying."

Her gaze slid away again.

I went on. "Kate and I were stolen from our mother. She was murdered because she tried to find us, and I want answers."

"You can't possibly know she was killed because of anything Charlie may have done."

"I want the truth!"

She gripped the back of the kitchen chair, then came around and lowered herself onto it. She suddenly looked old, the scars from her face-lifts, just visible where her jaw met her ears, standing out white despite her foundation makeup.

"Tell me," I said. "Tell me exactly how it happened. How he fooled us all those years. You can start with the pictures. The ones Daddy showed us of the people who were supposedly our parents."

Aunt Caroline stared at the table. "He got real pictures of the people that died in that plane crash. Went to El Paso for them. He knew you'd have . . . questions."

"Why did you go along with this hoax?" I said, proud of maintaining my even, rational tone despite the rage whirling like a small tornado inside me.

"I didn't have any choice. As I told you the other day, I had been less than discreet in my life."

"I see. Daddy had more on you than those letters in the attic, huh? Was it an entire dossier, Aunt Caroline?" I was repulsed at the thought of my father blackmailing his own sister.

"I warned him this would happen. I told him he should tell you the truth. But he insisted you'd never find out."

"And of course you never considered telling us yourself, because you've never had a clue about doing the right thing."

"You are being unreasonably vicious. You and Kate never wanted for anything," she said, her voice rising. "He gave you everything! He worshiped you. Oh, he threw money at me, that's true, but none of the love he showered on you and Kate after Elizabeth died. Every time I suggested he come clean, he'd say 'Keep your mouth shut, Caroline, and you'll be well cared for.'"

"He paid you to keep his secrets. You must be so proud."

She didn't reply, just looked at her hands, twisting one ring.

"Did he kill her?" I said quietly.

She jerked her head up. "Are you crazy? He'd never do anything like that. I know this is a shock, but —"

"You don't know the first thing about it."

"Please try to understand," she said. "I know we haven't agreed on much, but I do love and care for you. I will always consider you my family."

"If that's true, which I doubt, I want the rest." I sat down, every muscle tight with pain and rage.

"Okay. Where to start?" She hesitated,

then said, "Charlie and Elizabeth desperately wanted a family, but she couldn't have children, and because of her illness, because she wouldn't last more than a few years at most, no agency would allow them to adopt."

"But surely some reputable lawyer rather than a criminal like Feldman could have arranged an adoption? Daddy was a better judge of people than to do business with him."

"Desperation doesn't make for clear vision, Abigail. Charlie knew Feldman was . . . an unsavory person, but he wanted to make Elizabeth's dream of a family come true. He never anticipated that the woman would come looking for you years later."

"That *woman* was my mother," I said.

"Yes. I know. But Charlie didn't kill her. He made mistakes, granted, errors in judgment, but he wasn't a killer. Ask Willis. He'll tell you. He was the one who found Feldman to begin with."

Of course. Willis.

I pointed my finger at Aunt Caroline. "You can leave, but don't you dare talk to Kate. She doesn't know — and *I'll* be the one to tell her."

26

The rain had continued unabated for twenty-four hours and was threatening to send the bayous over their banks and flood the streets. But I had to see Willis before I told Kate the truth. She returned from school early — businesses and colleges were closing up shop because of possible flooding — so I borrowed her 4Runner to better maneuver through any high water, telling her I'd made an appointment for the much-needed tetanus shot. I didn't feel too guilty about omitting the other part of my itinerary, because I really was going to the doctor.

The nurse at the clinic gave me the shot and samples of an anti-inflammatory medicine after the doctor pronounced me remarkably fit, considering my circumstances. I swallowed a couple of pills before leaving the office, and by the time I reached the CompuCan building, I was almost pain-free.

I paced nervously in Willis's reception area while he finished with a client, and a few more pieces of the puzzle came together. Why hadn't I seen through Willis's attempts to stop me from investigating Ben's murder, especially after he followed me all the way to Shade the day after it happened?

But before I could answer my own question, Willis opened his office door.

"Why, Abby," he said, his client passing me on the way out. "I didn't expect you. Say, what have you done to yourself?"

He made a move to touch my face, but I jerked my head away.

"You put on quite the dog and pony show, don't you?" I brushed past him into his office and sat down in a client chair.

"What do you mean?" he asked, following at my heels and then perching on the desk.

"Tell me, Willis. How did you keep up this masquerade so long?" I crossed my legs, rotating my foot in agitated circles.

He straightened his tie. "Could you start again? Obviously you're upset, but I'm not sure why."

"I pegged Aunt Caroline as a liar and a cheat long ago. But you? No, you and Daddy had me buffaloed. Tell me . . . was he paying you to keep quiet, too, like he paid Aunt Caroline?"

I read sadness in his eyes and wondered if the emotion was for himself or for Kate and me.

His secretary poked her head in the door. "If you don't mind, Mr. Hatch, I'll head home. They say we're in for heavy flooding, and my subdivision entrance fills when the weatherman even mentions rain. Can I get you anything before I go?"

"No, Dolores. Go on."

I waited until she was gone, then said, "I want answers."

When he finally spoke, he sounded resigned. "You couldn't leave it alone, could you? I told you not to pursue this, Abby. Now you and Kate have been hurt."

"What about the ones already hurt? The ultimate hurt. As in dead. Tell me, Willis, did you help Daddy . . . or did he help you?"

"What are you talking about?" Willis looked tired and confused.

"I'm talking about you and Daddy murdering my mother. He wasn't around to help you with Ben, though. You handled that murder all by yourself, didn't you? Ben must have been ready to tell Kate and me the truth and so you killed him. Killed him for a stupid thirty-year-old secret."

He blinked several times. "That's ridiculous. Where did you ever get the idea that I, or your father, for that matter —"

"You knew Ben's real identity, didn't you?"

345

"Yes, I'll admit I did, but —"

"If you're so innocent, if you didn't kill him, why didn't you share what you knew with the police?"

"Because I —"

"Oh, I know why." I stood, leaned close to his face, and poked my finger in his chest. "You were covering up. You had a hand in an illegal adoption, and even if the statute of limitations had long passed, you'd be in serious trouble with the bar. Your reputation would be ruined."

"You think I'm a killer?"

"You had motive, and you sure as hell had the opportunity to fix up that cyanide trap."

"I certainly didn't want you and Kate to find out about the adoption from Ben, but I didn't kill him, and neither Charlie nor I murdered your mother."

"I've been lied to my whole life. Why should I believe anything you say?"

"Charlie didn't even know your mother's name when he adopted you two. He didn't want to know. I handled the deal with Feldman."

"Because what you were doing was illegal, right?"

"That, and he feared that if you knew your mother was alive, you'd want to find her one day." He reached out to touch me and I shrank from his outstretched hand. "You have every right to be angry, Abby, but —"

"Angry? Angry doesn't begin to cover it." I turned away, hugging my arms, trying to contain the pain his betrayal had caused.

"Charlie thought he had all the bases covered. Feldman assured us no one would know. Said the mother didn't want you. So when she showed up . . ." He shook his head. "Charlie was devastated. But I swear he had nothing to do with murder."

I turned back. "Quit lying, Willis."

"That's the God's truth."

"So how did you find out she was looking for us?"

"Feldman called. God, Charlie was furious. He blamed everything on me at first. Said I should have researched the mother. But I could tell he realized this was as much his fault as mine. And then he took off for Galveston to deal with Feldman himself."

"And not long after Cloris Grayson died. You're telling me that was all Feldman's doing? You still insist you and Daddy had nothing to do with her murder?"

"We didn't know the woman was dead until Ben showed up."

"Why don't you just tell the truth? Because I'm going to the police with what I know no matter what."

"Go ahead. But before you do that, get all the facts," he said. "I happen to know Ben and your father made some sort of agreement right before Charlie died."

The room was quiet, in stark contrast to the scene outside, where wind was hurling rain at the windows. Beyond, the sky was as dark as night.

"What kind of agreement?"

"I'm not sure, but I don't think Charlie would have contacted Feldman. He hated the man." He shook his head, looking puzzled.

"Did you know Daddy made Judge Hayes resign? Were you sweating bullets that night at the country club while I blabbed on about her?"

"I never knew how Charlie dealt with the, uh . . . problem, until you told us Judge Hayes resigned."

"Not plausible. You're a lawyer. You'd have heard about the resignation. And you also know Daddy could have permanently silenced my mother."

"He couldn't have killed her, Abby. He didn't have it in him."

Willis was good. If I didn't know the two of them had lied through their teeth for years, he might have pulled off this innocent act.

"Come on, Willis. It's over. I'm going straight to Jeff. He'll help me find the proof I need to put you and Feldman away."

"If you're hell-bent on proving this theory of yours, I'd take a closer look at the CD from the safe-deposit box. Charlie told me he had kept a record of everything that had transpired since the adoption, and I tried to get my hands on it, but you found it before I did."

"Are you saying Daddy confessed on that CD? That he imbedded information about the adoption in that program?"

"I'm not absolutely certain. Charlie said Ben Grayson was pressuring him, but had agreed to give Charlie time to tell you and Kate himself. I was surprised when Ben didn't come to you right after Charlie's heart attack. But maybe all this is explained on that CD."

And then I remembered the day of the murder, recalled Ben saying how he knew Kate and I were grieving for our father and so he'd been waiting for the right time to "say what needs saying."

Willis was speaking and I refocused on him. "After Ben died I knew I had to check the files at the Victorian," he said, "I realized Charlie could have hidden the information about your adoption there. So I went over, sure I'd find either a document or a disk."

I blinked. "Oh, my God. *You* were the intruder on P Street! And then you tore up the attic the day Aunt Caroline moved out half of our belongings."

He held up his hands as if to fend me off. "Okay. I did search the files in Galveston, but I never went near your attic. Caroline must have made that mess, despite her protests to the contrary."

It was all coming together, making me sicker by the minute. "*You* bashed Steven in the head!"

"I'm sorry about hurting him. All I could find was a wrench, and I tried not to hit him too hard. He took me by surprise and I had to search through —"

"You could have killed Steven!" The anger smoldering in my gut ignited again. "How could you come to our house, eat with us, give advice, act so damn moral and condescending when the whole time . . ." Tears stung behind my eyes. "Jeff Kline is going to get an earful, and so help me, Willis, if you call Kate, there'll be another murder. Yours. Do you understand?"

He couldn't even look me in the eye. He shook his head and said, "I'm sorry, Abby. I'm so sorry for everything."

350

I didn't want to hear his empty apology. I turned on my heel and left.

I called the police station from Kate's car, but Jeff was out of the building. I left a message for him to contact me, keeping one ear tuned to the radio broadcast announcing road closings. The freeways remained passable, so the weather hadn't gotten too serious yet, but if this horrendous rain kept up, it wouldn't take long for the entire Gulf Coast to flood.

I revisited my conversation with Willis, realizing it didn't all add up. Why would he admit some things and lie about others? Obviously I knew everything, so what was the point?

He confessed to hitting Steven, but he swore he didn't ransack the attic. But if not Willis, then who? Caroline? She had no reason to lie about messing things up, since she'd already 'fessed up to taking her letters.

It all came back to Willis. He had to be lying. But why did one of those lies include his insistence that my father was innocent? Why protect a dead man? It would be so simple to blame Cloris's murder on Daddy. Dead men can't deny anything.

I'd missed something somewhere.

I needed that CD.

Once I returned home, I tore past Kate, who was chopping up vegetables near the sink, and went straight to the study.

Where did I file the thing?

Kate followed me and stood in the doorway, knife in hand. "Abby, what's going on?"

"I'm hunting for the CD from the safe-deposit box. Have you seen it?"

"I lent it to Steven yesterday. He said he needed a better spreadsheet setup to document the renovation expenses."

"Great," I said in exasperation. "But why the CD? I have an updated copy of that program on disk. It's right here." I turned the disk carousel, then scratched my head, puzzled. It wasn't there. "Where is it?"

"Now do you see why I lent him the one from the bank? I couldn't find that one either. You said they were close to the same thing."

"They are, but I wanted another look. Steven probably took it to his office." I picked up the phone and speed-dialed his number.

"What's happening?" asked Kate. "You've got 'frantic' written all over you."

I listened to Steven's phone ring and his answering machine picked up. *Damn.* I held up my hand for Kate to wait while I spoke into the receiver. "Steven, this is Abby. Kate says you have the CD from the safe-deposit box. Call me. And take care of it. It's valuable."

"What have you found out?" she said after I hung up.

I took a deep breath. I couldn't put this off any longer. "We need to talk." I took her hand and led her to the kitchen.

I was trembling when we sat down, and stalled by turning over the quilted place mat in front of me several times. My anger had protected me when I spoke with Aunt Caroline and Willis, but this was different. Finally I looked up into Kate's soft brown eyes, mirrors of my own.

"What's wrong, Abby? You're scaring me."

"I met Feldman yesterday," I began.

"You did?" Her eyes widened, then lit with excitement. "What did he say? I'm sure he didn't confess or anything that simple. Is that why you're upset? Because he won't admit —"

"He didn't tell me anything directly, but I overheard him on the telephone. You'll have a hard time accepting this. I know I did." I put my hand over hers.

"Tell me," said Kate, her lips now ringed with white.

353

I swallowed, but the lump in my throat wouldn't budge. "It's Daddy. He lied. He . . . How do I say this?" I stared at my hand covering hers; then those blasted tears I'd been fighting all day escaped. I swiped them away angrily with the back of my hand.

Kate's eyes filled, too. "Abby, please. I can't stand seeing you like this."

"Our parents didn't die in a plane crash. Our mother was murdered when she tried to find the babies Feldman took from her. Twin girls born to Cloris thirty years ago."

She scooted her chair back, almost as if she believed that if she distanced herself from me, she wouldn't have to hear the truth.

She shook her head. "Don't be silly. I don't know what you overheard, but I think you misunderstood or —"

"Cloris was our mother," I said softly.

"No! Please, no!" She covered her mouth, eyes glistening.

"Lies, Kate. We were fed nothing but lies." I continued on, telling her everything I had learned from Sally Jean, Judge Hayes, Aunt Caroline, and Willis. It helped me detach from my emotions as I explained. When I was finished, Kate sat silently for what seemed an eternity.

Finally she said, "When you found Ben

murdered, I had this sense that somehow his murder was connected to us — in some personal way. But I didn't want it to be true. I thought maybe if we hurried and sold the house, we could escape the past. Funny how you know something before you really know it. That doesn't make sense, but —"

"We both knew. But I ran toward the truth instead of away from it," I said.

"Are you turning this information over to Jeff? Please say that's what you plan to do."

"Yes, but I want that CD, Kate. I want to hear Daddy's side. I don't want to believe he murdered our mother or cooperated with Feldman, even though I'm almost certain that's what I'll discover."

"What about Feldman's wife? She's one cold, calculating female. Couldn't she have murdered Ben?"

I nodded. "Maybe. But the killer knew the routine here, with the roses and all. That means Willis. Lord knows he had motive. His reputation and his law practice were at stake." I stood.

"Where are you going?" she asked.

"That CD is important. I'm heading for Steven's office. I can never count on him to pick up his messages."

"But the roads are terrible, and they'll be

in worse condition the farther south you travel."

"Can I use the 4Runner again?"

Kate stood. "I'll go with you."

"You need to stay in case Jeff or Steven calls. Give them my cell number. And if Steven does phone, tell him to bring me that CD."

"Please be careful. It's pouring bullfrogs and heifer yearlings, like Daddy used to . . ." Her voice trailed off and she bit her lower lip.

Steven's office, located about halfway between Houston and Galveston, occupied the far-west stall of a strip mall off the Gulf Freeway. The water on the feeder road leading into the parking lot sloshed halfway up my tires, and still the muddy skies poured rain.

The office was locked and Steven was nowhere in sight, but the cleaning crew hadn't left. They were jump-starting their van with cables attached to another vehicle. The same lady who always cleaned Steven's office recognized me and unlocked his door when I told her what I needed.

The place hadn't changed. Steven always marked the map on the wall showing his ongoing construction jobs with colored pushpins, but aside from the pin on P Street, he had only one other job going. *Can't make much of a living like that,* I thought, my eyes scanning the office.

I didn't see any CDs, maybe because papers were strewn all over, along with stacks of blueprints. I checked the drive on the computer. No luck there, either.

But when I moved aside a paper, I spied a floppy disk with a familiar label. My disk. The one I'd looked for in the carousel at home just a short time ago.

So why did Steven need to borrow the CD if he had a disk with an updated program?

Cold fingers of fear gripped my heart and squeezed.

"Shit," I whispered, tearing out the door.

27

I climbed back in the 4Runner and was back on the freeway heading toward Galveston seconds later. Why had Steven told Kate he needed the CD if the same program on disk had been here in his office all along? Unless he realized the CD contained important information.

Okay. So maybe Steven wanted to help me uncover the truth, and this was his latest attempt at inserting himself back into my life. Somehow he figured out before I did that the CD was the key.

My IQ through most of my so-called investigating had equaled my bra size: meager. But as blind as I'd been, believing for one nanosecond that Steven Bradley had borrowed the CD to help me find Ben's murderer took the cake, the ice cream, and the hired clown.

Despite his newfound temperance, Steven still took care of Steven. If he wanted that CD, he had a damn good reason, one that didn't involve helping anyone but himself.

Checking the rearview mirror, I watched

the wake of dirty water, knowing I shouldn't be speeding in this weather. I might pirouette straight into the hereafter on a highway so treacherously close to impassable.

But I didn't care about my safety. Not anymore. I was dealing with the realization that I had badly misread every person in my life besides Kate. But folks were finished pissing in my boots and telling me it was rainwater. Feldman wouldn't be tossing me out this time. Not before I had the truth.

An umbrella would have been useless with the wind commanding the rain every which way, so I settled for my purse, holding it over my head as I rushed to the Feldmans' front door. My hand rested on the bell, but I didn't press it. Why would Feldman or Hamilton ever invite *me* in? So I tried the knob.

The door opened.

"Anyone home?" I called into the chandelier-lit foyer.

No response.

I stepped inside, immediately creating a puddle at my feet. I looked around for a mat to wipe my sopping Keds and discovered that an unlocked door wasn't the only thing out of the ordinary at the Feldman home.

A trail of what looked like blood meandered from the left and stopped at the front door. Some blood had even rusted the small pond around my feet.

I announced my presence louder. "Is anybody here?"

"What are you doing in my house?" called Helen Hamilton from the landing. She clutched a wad of lingerie in one hand and a hair dryer in the other and sounded pretty pissed off, but then, so was I.

"The door was open," I said.

"It's *still* open. Find your way out the same way you came in."

"Do you know who I really am, Hamilton?"

She sneered down at me. "I know exactly who you are. Now get the hell out, and if you're smart, you'll get off this island."

She disappeared into a room off the landing.

"If you won't come to me, I'll come to you," I muttered, tackling the curving stairs. I hadn't had one of those lovely pain pills lately and my thighs started aching again, making it seem like a very long climb to the second floor.

Hamilton was packing, if that was what you wanted to call it. Actually, she was throwing things into a suitcase as fast as I'd seen anyone move in a long time.

I leaned on the door frame. "Did you know there's blood in your foyer?"

She ignored me and continued her frenzied raid of the dresser.

"Are you hurt? Did Feldman do something to you?" I asked.

She whirled. "You think that's *my* blood down there?" She shook her head. "Not yet, anyway."

"Then where did it come from?"

"I could make an educated guess, but I won't." She swiped the dresser top, clearing off hairbrushes and perfume bottles. After gathering them up, she stuffed them into the suitcase.

"Did you ask your husband what happened down there?"

"I don't have time for your questions," she said.

"Where's Feldman? I need to talk to him before the police get here and arrest him."

"He's not here. And that's the problem." She paused, a hand on her hip. "You see, he never leaves. And I mean *never*. Samuel has this phobia about outdoors. It's been three years since he's even seen the sun. But I came home and bingo — he's gone! No explanation except the blood."

She closed her suitcase, retucked her blouse into her skirt, and slid her long, skinny feet into shoes retrieved from under the bed.

Those shoes. I'd seen them before, hadn't I?

She glanced briefly into the mirror above the oak dresser and picked up the suitcase.

"Wait a minute. You're leaving without even trying to find your husband?"

She pushed past me and I followed her down the stairs.

"I'm not waiting around for the cops to arrive or for someone to add my blood to that." She nodded at the marble floor.

"Feldman was involved in murder, and I'm thinking you might know quite a lot about that involvement," I said.

"I'm not saying a word without a lawyer. But they have to find me first."

She hurried out before I could move, slamming the door after her.

Knowing I should call 911 and tell the police to follow her, I instead sat on the bottom stair, anger, fear, and confusion taking over. Maybe Jeff got my message. Maybe he was available.

I opened my purse to find my cell phone, but instead my fingers touched something at first unfamiliar. And then I remembered the small videotape from Hamilton's office. I'd forgotten all about it.

I imagined myself huddled behind the door that day at Parental Advocates, holding my breath as Hamilton came in for the copy of the check.

And then it clicked.

Hamilton had come back to her office with a man that afternoon. I'd heard his voice. Probably wasn't Feldman the Phobic, if what she said about him earlier was true. I had a sick feeling I knew who it was, though.

Hamilton's shoes, the ones I'd seen her put on upstairs, were the same Pappagallo shoes tucked under Steven's coffee table the night I went to his apartment about the canceled checks. Could the man who accompanied Hamilton to her office that afternoon have been Steven? Had I felt so guilty about rejecting him, been so worried he'd relapse into alcoholism, I chose to be blinded by his "I'm so in love with you" act? Hell, they write country songs more believable than the game he'd been playing with me.

The checks Daddy had written to Steven loomed large in this picture. My ex-husband had indeed changed in the last few months, but not in the direction I thought. When he stopped drinking, that conniving mind of his had kicked into high gear. And then the night Steven and Jeff had fought on my lawn returned like it happened yesterday. What if Steven had dismantled the attic looking for evidence connecting Ben and Daddy? What if he was *leaving* my house right after he'd done just that — and was not *arriving,* as I'd assumed? He probably spotted Jeff Kline's car across the street, and knowing the neighborhood, correctly assumed that a stranger parked there at one a.m. had to be either a cop or private security. That was when he came back in the house and fabricated the blueprint cover story — after making enough noise to ensure that I awoke and investigated. I nodded, my mouth settling into a frown. Another betrayal, one I should have expected.

I stared at the tape I held. Here was the proof. When I had hidden behind the door at Parental Advocates, the camera was recording everything. With the door wide-open, it would have taped the outer office — and whoever was in the outer office.

I turned the tape over and over, eyes closed, jaw tight. "Don't do this, Abby," I said. "You don't need to see this right now. Give the tape to Jeff."

I was feeling what Steven probably felt every time he thought about taking a drink. *I shouldn't. This will hurt me. Don't destroy what little hope you have left.*

And like Steven, I couldn't stop myself.

"There's got to be a VCR somewhere in this mausoleum," I said, rising.

After wandering through the lavish home, I found a room large enough to accommodate the Houston Rockets for pre-season practice. Beyond the pool table and bar sat a big-screen TV. I supposed that if you hadn't left your house for three years, it helped to have a few fancy toys to pass the time. Feldman had all the equipment I needed to confirm my suspicions about Steven, even an adapter for the smaller-size tape.

Not the greatest quality, I noted, once I got things working. The picture was huge, very grainy.

There I was, sneaking around in the hallway. And there I was hiding after I heard them arrive. The door opened and . . . yes! I could make out a man's figure framed in the front doorway. But the daylight behind him made it hard to make out his features. In the next few frames, Hamilton walked back out with the paper in her hand and picked something up — her purse — then shut the door. I rewound, stopped the tape, and advanced frame by frame, then paused and took in the man's poorly focused face. That hairline, the curve of those lips, God, I knew them almost as well as my own. Knew the face of a killer.

28

I called home once I was back on the road, and Kate answered, sounding breathless and anxious.

"It's me," I said. "Did Steven call?" I swerved to avoid a patch of high water on the right.

"No. I'm relieved to hear your voice. Where are you, Abby?"

"Galveston. What about Jeff?"

"He phoned. I gave him your cell phone number. After I told him you were looking for that CD, he sounded pretty irritated, and I'm feeling the same way. You took a bad fall yesterday, and the roads aren't fit to travel. You should have been home long ago."

"With this weather, it'll take me an hour to get back to Houston. Expect me about nine."

"Wait a minute. Don't you have your radio on? An eighteen-wheeler overturned on the causeway and it's taking an hour to get from Broadway off the island."

"Damn. I'll wait on P Street, if it's not flooded over there already."

"That street sometimes fills with water, Abby. Why not wait it out in a restaurant or —"

"I need a quiet place, somewhere to think things through."

"Are you okay?" Kate said.

"I'm fine. Call me when the causeway is clear. The digital networks jam up in emergencies, so phone me at the Victorian."

She didn't know the number, so I gave it to her; then she said, "If Steven calls, I'll tell him where he can reach you and —"

"No!" I practically shouted. "Tell him nothing."

"There *is* something wrong," said Kate.

I steered around more gigantic puddles. "You've had enough revelations for one day. Besides, you're starting to break up. 'Bye." I clicked off the phone and, seeing that the battery was low, plugged it into the cigarette lighter.

I turned onto Seawall Boulevard and found the street practically deserted. Usually the tourists hung in like a hair in a biscuit no matter what the weather, but not tonight. A jagged flash lit the murky gulf to my left, and a tremendous clap of thunder followed.

My neck ached and my rear throbbed where that nail had punctured me. I wanted to be home sleeping, free from the truth now invading my life like Attila stomping across Europe.

When I turned onto P Street, the water was almost to the curb. I'd have to pay attention, be ready to leave if real flooding was imminent.

The house next to the Victorian was vacant and sat on higher ground than ours, so I took the precaution of parking the 4Runner in that driveway. I used the back entrance leading to the kitchen, anxious to swallow more pain medicine. I ached all over.

Steven had cleared a path through the mudroom and patched the damage done by the fallen bathroom, but he hadn't tidied up. I found empty Gatorade containers, bug spray, crumpled brown bags from McDonald's . . . but not a glass amid the clutter. I gave up and cupped my hand under the faucet, gulping the pills down.

I wandered back into the front parlor, knowing I should go upstairs and make sure the whole second floor wasn't soaked because of that gigantic hole in the wall. But the pain in my legs reminded me of the challenge stairs presented.

I limped to the window and opened the wood shades, checking on the street flooding. Just then I noticed a truck turn the corner and deaden its lights.

I quickly narrowed the shades, recognizing that pickup. I turned out the light and slipped into the closet, not wanting to confront Steven alone. Not stranded here. I huddled in the far corner, praying he'd come and go quickly.

The back door opened and I heard Steven grunting and groaning, then dragging noises.

He must have turned on the hall light, because a sliver of brightness appeared. Almost simultaneously the closet door flew open.

I tried making myself invisible in the corner, some mean feat in an empty cubicle.

But he was so concerned with shoving his tarpaulin-wrapped load into the closet, he didn't see me.

29

Steven dropped his heavy bundle, and I flinched at the lifeless thud. He leaned on the door frame, catching his breath and wiping rain and sweat off his forehead with his forearm.

And then he saw me.

His eyes flickered, but I didn't read surprise in his face. I stood, putting my hands flat against the wall behind me, knowing I was trapped in this closet and in this house — and in my own living nightmare.

He said, "Your gears are turning full speed, aren't they, Abby?" He blocked the door with his spread arms, and the smell of his perspiration fueled a wave of nausea.

I had to get past him somehow.

"Sorry I missed you over at my office," he said. "Seems I remember you telling me more than once to not leave the CD drive open. Too easy for dust to get inside the computer. Very careless of you, babe." He smiled.

I felt my breath coming faster and kept looking down at the tarp. At the body. I wished I'd hear a moan, or see some small movement, but nothing came, and I feared nothing would.

"After I took care of my friend here, I planned on telling you how I damaged the CD by accident."

"Could we discuss this somewhere else?" I glanced again at the black plastic shroud. Wisps of silver hair protruded from the end nearest me.

Steven took my arm as I stepped over Feldman's body — it had to be Feldman — then pulled me toward the parlor.

"I needed a place to park Sammy's weary bones until the weather lets up," he said. "The argument which led to his little accident concerned you, so you've only got yourself to blame for his death."

I halted, his fingers tightening on my arm.

"You killed him, and it's my fault?" I said, incredulous.

"An accident, Abby. Don't take it so hard." He reached over and flipped the lights on, then rubbed his chin with his free hand. "You showing up here complicates things." He stared at me, his green eyes narrow. They caught the light and seemed almost yellow, like a snake's.

"But you know something, babe? I think it's time you had the truth. I owe you that before we say good-bye."

A permanent good-bye, of course. "What happened? How could —"

"What happened?" He yanked me toward him. "Once upon a time I married a princess. A beautiful princess, with the softest skin I ever touched. But she wanted someone exactly like beloved King Charlie. Did anyone ever tell you to be careful what you wish for, Abby, because you might just get it?" He squeezed my upper arm.

I pulled away and a day's worth of grief, fear, and rage exploded. "I can't believe how you manipulated me! And now you've got the gall to say I'm to blame for the mess you've made?"

He shoved me hard. "You're not getting the last word this time!"

I hit the wall hard, my head bouncing off the plaster. I went down, my palms sliding against the textured paint, scraping the skin on my hands.

I was too stunned to move for several seconds.

He sat cross-legged opposite me, his spread knees close enough to keep me pinned, his eyes tired and wild at the same time, his whiskey breath hot in my face.

I swallowed, trying to rid myself of the tightness in my throat. "Go ahead," I said softly. "Tell me how we got to this corner of hell." I willed back my tears, vowing I'd never reveal how afraid I was to him. *Never.*

"Guess you figured out your daddy wasn't so perfect, huh? Pure dumb luck when I stumbled on the truth. The day I found out about Feldman, I bet I could have pitched pennies down the neck of a swinging beer bottle and made every one. Charlie had a regular gold mine of well-kept secrets and would have spent every last dime to keep the truth from you and Kate."

"I know Daddy paid you, but those canceled checks he wrote to you were dated *before* Ben came to work for us. How do those connect to the murder?"

"Those checks were first payments on a special insurance policy. How should I put it? Charlie was paying me for services *not* rendered."

"What are you talking about?"

"I had these pesky gambling debts. Jerks in suits breathing down my neck, wanting their money plus interest. So Charlie said he'd help me out. But only as long as I kept my hand out of the cookie jar — you being the cookie jar, babe."

"He paid you to stay away from me?"

"That's right. Your brain's firing like one of your damn computers. No matter what happened between us, I never doubted your smarts for a minute."

I was aware of my chest rising and falling way too fast. I closed my eyes. Squeezed them shut. I couldn't focus on Daddy's betrayal. I had to stay calm, watch for any chance to escape, even though I felt like a knife was slashing at my heart. "But you didn't stay away, Steven. You were always hanging around."

"But I didn't make any moves on you, either. I could have had you back in bed in a New York minute. Too risky, though. Charlie might have caught us, or you might have blabbed to him about us getting back together."

Okay. He's drifting into fantasyland. And he wants to gloat. So let him. "Did Daddy come to you, or was that arrangement your idea?" I asked.

"Let's say we came to a mutual understanding. I picked up the checks at his office downtown, so you wouldn't see me. But one weekend I ran out of cash and stopped by your house to see if Charlie would front me a little extra. By then we were better buddies than when you and I were married. I went around to the back after no one answered the door, and heard Charlie and Ben out in the greenhouse. I got quite an earful about this little illegal adoption."

"So you started blackmailing Daddy," I said, scanning the room. Had to escape through the back. The front door was locked.

"You could say I got quite a raise in my take-home pay," he said. "The last thing Charlie wanted was you and Kate learning the ugly truth from the likes of me."

He drew out a leather-covered flask from his back pocket and took a swig. "Join me?"

The more he drank, the more he'd talk. He'd get meaner, too, but I'd take that risk. I accepted the bottle, and the whiskey burned all the way down after I swallowed.

"Not your favorite chardonnay, but then I didn't invite you to this party." He capped the flask and propped it against his thigh.

"So when Daddy died, you took a salary cut, huh?" I said.

"Give me a little credit, babe. I'm not stupid. I had more than one iron in the fire."

"Feldman?"

"Boy, it's been hard staying a step ahead of you." He laughed and shook his head. "Did you know Ben built houses up in Shade? We had some long talks when Charlie wasn't around."

"So you befriended Ben, and he told you about Feldman?"

"Ben wanted to find the guy and put him

away for killing his wife," he said.

Ben believed Feldman killed my mother. Feldman and not my father. He was probably right, but this was cold comfort. "So Ben trusted you," I said. "Did he mention how he found Daddy in the first place?"

"Ben never said. Charlie agreed to help him find Feldman, and in return, Ben would wait to tell you and Kate the truth about the adoption. But then Charlie up and died from that heart attack."

"Daddy had already found Feldman, though, right?" I said.

"Not quite. Charlie knew Feldman was still in Galveston. Nothing more. Ben told me as much at Charlie's funeral."

"So you'd lost one source of income, but saw another possibility. And you found Feldman first."

"Yup." Steven grinned and patted my cheek. "Such a smart girl. And guess what? Feldman had as much money as Charlie. When I told the old man Ben Grayson was about to show up with a uniformed cop on his elbow, Feldman realized he needed my help. I took care of the Ben problem. Got a nice down payment on what was supposed to be Feldman's lifetime commitment to me."

"Who will pay your bills now, Steven?" I

said, and realized immediately I'd taken the questions a step too far.

"That's none of your goddamned business."

"I'm sorry," I said quickly. "You're right, of course."

"Damn straight, I'm right," he said, sounding calmer. He began to trace small circles on the top of my hand.

His touch, once familiar and welcome, now felt like a rattler's tongue before the strike. "So Feldman killed Cloris himself?" I said.

He nodded. "Sounds like you're a lot like her, babe. She was making waves. Digging around where she had no business."

"Had no business? We were her flesh and blood."

"She made a deal with the devil. You do that, you end up skewered on a pitchfork." His hand moved to my knee.

I tensed. *Keep him talking; then find a way out.* I had to focus on those two things, or my rage and disgust might make me do something stupid.

"My mother never made any deal," I said. "Feldman tricked her. But after years of searching she finally tracked him down, didn't she?"

He uncorked the flask and drank, then

wiped his mouth with the side of his hand. "Yeah. He told me about her. Seems she had proof Feldman forged the adoption papers and threatened to file suit. And then there'd be criminal charges. So he followed her back to Shade. Watched her house . . . her routine . . . and when he saw her pick up that cold medicine at the drugstore, the rest was easy. Her door wasn't even locked, he said. He just walked in when she was gone, put the cyanide into the capsules, and left."

He swigged again and continued. "After the ambulance and cops left her house, he got inside and removed the evidence. Seems they weren't all that particular about their crime scene up in Shade."

"Evidence? What evidence?"

"Some handwriting expert's written opinion that the papers were forgeries. But don't you think I bettered Feldman with my acid-cyanide deal when I doctored your roses? Ben never knew what hit him."

"You played us all like a fifty-dollar fiddle, didn't you?" I said.

"Aren't you proud of me, Abby?" His eyes were red-rimmed and liquid. "But you know what's funny about all this?"

"What, Steven?" I asked. Had to keep him talking. As long as he kept bragging, I stayed alive.

"When Ben started sniffing around, Feldman didn't care as much about the whole world knowing he was a baby thief and a murderer as he did about having to leave his house. Geezer was a fucking nutcase." He offered me the bottle again, almost like we were sitting at some bar, having a good old time drinking and bullshitting.

I took a tiny sip and handed it back.

"You had to snoop around, babe, didn't you? Ruin everything. Why did you have to do that?" He took my hands between his own.

I felt like springs were uncoiling in my stomach. I didn't like the change in his tone. "I don't know why, Steven."

"Every time you filled me in on your little detecting game, I had to stop and think how to stay ahead of you." He turned my hand over, wet his finger, and rubbed at the dried blood on my palm.

It required every ounce of willpower not to pull away.

"I kept Helen and Feldman in the dark about you as long as I could," he said. "See, Sammy didn't know about you and me. He thought I worked for Charlie, thought that's how I found out about the adoption. But when Kate brought that check over to Helen

. . ." He waved his finger in my face. "Big mistake, Abby."

"Your girlfriend Helen knew who I was?" *Keep talking, Steven. Please keep talking.*

"Ah, so you know about us. She came on to me first, if you're wondering. Anyway, seems you got Sam all riled up. He blabbed everything to Helen — the old adoption, how I had killed Ben, the blackmail." He brought my hand to his cheek. "Another mistake pretending to be Terry, sweetheart. Feldman panicked, called me over there today. 'Do this,' he said. 'You have to do that.' And he got in my face. So I pushed him. He cracked his skull. And all thanks to you."

Thunder rumbled above. "What about your girlfriend? What will you do about her now that she knows everything?"

He smiled, and how I wished this mellow mood would last. "Helen's a smart woman. Almost as smart as you. She won't talk."

"You couldn't keep your hands off her, could you?" I said. I was running out of ways to stall him and thought maybe he'd like to brag about her for a while.

"She was married to an old man," he said. "And you know how I can't stand seeing a woman in need."

"I know way more than I ever wanted to

about that, Steven."

He cupped my face in both his hands. "Jealous, babe?"

I stared into his eyes. "Yes," I said. "I think I am."

His thumbs pulled my mouth into a tight, painful smile. "You should smile when you lie, babe. It's much more convincing."

He pulled my face to his and crushed his mouth against mine, forcing his tongue between my lips. He tasted sour — foul. When I couldn't even fake a response, he put his hand on my breast — and shoved me away.

I hit the wall again, the pain slicing through me as if I'd been shot.

"Lost that lovin' feelin', huh, babe?" he said, his words slurring ever so slightly.

The fear inside me seemed to be shrinking to something hard and strong, like a fist, ready to strike. *Fear could help you,* I thought. Fear was a powerful thing. I stood. "I'm leaving. This is over."

He grabbed my arm, his grip like steel. "Time to finish this."

Finish this? How? How would he kill me? As he started to drag me toward the stairs, more thunder sounded, and a vicious squall began to hammer the roof and side of the house.

"You can't, Steven," I said. "I know you can't."

His voice was cold. "You don't know the first thing about me. You walked out of my life and nothing ever hurt so bad. I tried scaring you off the case. I loosened that board upstairs, hoping to put you out of commission, but twenty-four hours later you're digging deeper than ever. Why couldn't you wait until I had Feldman under control? Why?" He shook me, then pushed me, and I stumbled backward.

The phone rang.

His head jerked in that direction.

Then everything went black. The electricity had gone out.

I took off, brushing against a wall, the phone still shrieking behind me.

I heard a thud and Steven cursed.

I rushed through the empty dining room into the kitchen. Felt my way to the counter and swept with my hand, searching, sending twisted paper bags flying and plastic liter bottles clattering to the floor.

Where is it? I saw it thirty minutes ago! I saw it!

I was trembling all over as I groped for what I needed, wishing my eyes would adjust quicker.

There!

Steven found me, took hold of my shoulders, and spun me around.

I drew back as his breath blew warm and menacing near my forehead.

"Got you!" he said.

I felt for his face. For a landmark. And sprayed him with the roach killer.

He yelled and let go of me.

I ran for the back door, slamming my hip on the counter along the way. I nearly tripped over the rubble still littering the mudroom floor, but stayed close to the intact inner wall. I made it out the door.

And realized that the water had risen to knee-deep, and was all roaring motion.

A flash flood. God, no!

But I walked out anyway, pushing through the current with one leg, then the other. I stayed clear of the trees, knowing how water moccasins slithered up the trunks to avoid being swept away. I didn't want to cross paths with one of them.

Even though I couldn't run, my canvas shoes gave me an advantage. Steven's cowboy boots would be far more cumbersome.

I moved toward the car, fighting for every step, digging in my pocket for the keys.

Then I heard Steven splashing and sloshing behind me.

I trudged on, and finally tugged the keys out. I pointed the remote at the outline of the 4Runner in the distance, but couldn't hear if the locks released. I struggled on, panting and gasping, and when I finally reached the door handle, my legs buckled. I leaned against the vehicle for support.

Hurry, Abby. He's coming.

I lifted the handle. The remote key hadn't worked. *Damn!*

I took a deep breath and fit the key in the lock.

Don't look back. Don't look back.

I heard the blessed sound of the locks releasing and climbed into the 4Runner, pressing the auto lock to keep Steven out. I closed my eyes, fighting for air, my head resting on the steering wheel.

A voice inside was screaming for me to drive, to get moving! But my hands were shaking and I had trouble finding the ignition.

It seemed like forever before I started the engine . . . turned on the headlights. I licked my dry lips and shifted into reverse.

In the side mirror I saw the raging waters surging through the street, carrying trash cans, lawn chairs, and tree limbs. I maneuvered out, praying I'd find the road — otherwise I might get caught in the ditch. As the 4Runner swung out, the headlights panned the yard between the two houses.

I spotted Steven flailing in the rising waters, not moving in any purposeful direction. He must be stuck in the soft ground or tangled in debris. I shifted gears and slowly edged forward in the river that used to be P Street, guessing at the position of the driveway. Using the mailbox as a guide, I pulled in as close as I could.

Steven fell, probably to his knees, because the water was up to his chest.

No matter what he'd done, or threatened to do, I couldn't leave knowing a human being would surely die if I did so. I could never live with that.

I picked up the phone and called 911.

And listened to the ring . . . six times . . . seven.

We weren't the only ones who needed help tonight.

I rolled down my window.

"Can you get up?" I yelled.

But he was drunk, not to mention incapacitated by water that had probably risen six inches since my escape to the car.

I heard a muffled "What is your emergency?" coming from the phone in my lap. I gave the address, but I knew by the time help arrived it would be too late for him. I clicked the phone off and squinted out into the darkness. If I waded out to him, he'd pull me down in his panic or his rage.

So I needed a rope.

I climbed over the front seat searching for one, but of course found nothing but Kate's usual folders and library books. And laundry for the dry cleaners.

It might work. I could make it work.

I hurriedly knotted several pairs of linen pants, silk shirts, and a black crepe dress together, twisting them as I tied. I only hoped the line would be long enough as I got out of the 4Runner and attached one end to the front bumper.

With the headlights to guide me, I started toward Steven, but fear nearly overwhelmed me then. Nearly took over every muscle. I was a quivering bundle of undirected energy. Steven might finish me off if I got to him. Drown me.

Don't be a fool, Abby. Leave him!

But though this storm was not a hurricane, I knew its power. I knew who my real enemy was — the enemy who would prevent anyone else from getting here in time to save a man who didn't deserve to be saved. The whirling winds and stinging rains demanded I give in, flattening me against the 4Runner and threatening to toss me into the current.

My defeat, if it came, would be at Storm Carl's hands, and for some strange reason, I found that thought comforting.

Clinging to my homemade lifeline, I set out again toward a floundering Steven.

But the makeshift rope wouldn't reach.

"Come closer, Steven!" I hollered over the thundering water.

But fighting the flood had exhausted him. Only his head was visible now, his eyes glazed with fear. With each passing second the water kept up its punishing pursuit of us both. Carl would have his way.

I needed more line. Maybe twenty-four measly inches. I slipped out of my saturated T-shirt and added it to the other clothes.

I leaned forward, holding out my T-shirt so he could grab on. Once he did, I planned to follow the chain back to the 4Runner, hoping he had the sense to hang on for his life.

"Steven! Take this!" I screamed over the howl of rushing wind and water.

His head moved in the direction of my voice, but I didn't think he saw me. The bug spray must have played havoc with his contacts.

"Here! I'm right here!" I shouted.

Finally I managed to find his hand, but

his slick fingers slipped away, and I reached toward him again, straining. I was so focused, I didn't even notice the pontoon boat making its way toward us.

But then I heard Jeff's voice through the darkness. "Don't tell me you're rescuing murderers in your underwear?" he yelled above the motor's drone.

As relief displaced terror, the feeling lifted my soul within a whisper of being tangible. Surely this was the most blessed emotion I had ever experienced.

A few minutes later, on our way to the Galveston police station, I promised Jeff I'd discuss my lingerie with him anytime, anywhere . . . which brought an amused guffaw from the man driving the rescue boat.

But I didn't recall much else on that ride. I concentrated on pretending the quivering form in handcuffs at the other end of the boat was invisible.

30

Several hours later, I was huddled in the passenger seat of Jeff's car. Sometime earlier, an officer at the Galveston police station had wrapped me in a blanket, and I still had the scratchy green wool cloaked around me. I wasn't certain whether the car's air-conditioning or my brush with death had caused the shakes, but I couldn't seem to stop trembling.

The rain had stopped, permitting the streets to drain, and the causeway was open to traffic. The threat of more flash floods was subsiding now that Carl had taken his nasty disposition north.

Before we had left to return to Houston, Jeff spent an hour negotiating with the Galveston police over the prisoner once known to me as my ex-husband. I had decided all possessive pronouns connecting Steven and me would be forever banished from my conversation. Even *ex* was too good for him.

The cops in Galveston wanted to hold Steven for Feldman's murder, and Jeff wanted him transferred to Houston so he could be charged in Ben's death. They worked it out, and I didn't even care to know the resolution. As far as I was concerned, he no longer existed.

Now that we were safely on our way back home, I was suddenly exhausted. But there were still so many unanswered questions. Stifling a yawn, I asked, "How did you get here? Wasn't the causeway backed up halfway to Houston?"

"Not southbound," he said. "No one with any sense wanted on the island."

"I heard you tell someone back there at the police station that you followed Steven. How did that happen?"

"Actually, I went looking for you after I called your cell phone. I couldn't get through. Lots of emergency calls were being made on cell phones tonight. But when I arrived at Mr. Steven Bradley's office, he was there. I tailed him."

"But you started out looking for me?"

"When I called your house, Kate told me about the CD, and I knew that meant trouble, so —"

"What do you mean, you knew that meant trouble?"

"Despite what you think, I have been working this case, Abby. I'd already researched the financial status of all the suspects and —"

"All the suspects? Who are you talking about, besides Feldman?"

"If you keep interrupting, I'll never finish. I distinctly remember telling you I'd handle this. You didn't trust me." He glanced my way, his face reflecting the green glow of the dashlights.

"I'm sorry. You did say that. I feel so stupid . . . so used."

"You're not stupid. Not by a long shot."

"Minor consolation. Go on. You followed Steven. Then what?"

"Talk about feeling stupid. He had Feldman's body in the truck bed the whole time I was tailing him. Course, I had enough to do to keep his taillights in sight in that storm, much less recognize that load in the rear was a corpse."

"Why didn't you follow him straight to P Street?" This time I couldn't stop the yawn. I clutched the blanket closer.

"Steven had no problem with high water, since he was in a truck. But I needed a rudder and a sail, the way the streets were filling. I detoured to the police station, figuring since I knew where Steven was probably headed, I could catch up with him later. No one — including him — was leaving the island anytime soon."

"Yeah," I said. "And some of us really wanted to."

"Be thankful for that sister of yours, is all I can say."

"Thank goodness for Kate," I said, smiling. Then I turned my head and leaned against the headrest. I couldn't keep my eyes open.

Later, with Jeff helping me up the stairs, I told Kate, who was following behind, that I felt as cold as a brass commode in the shade of a glacier.

I remember stripping off my wet clothes and falling on the bed. Then sleep took over.

The next morning, Diva was rubbing against my ankles as I sat at the kitchen table holding a mug of coffee in both hands. Sun splashed through the windows and promised I wouldn't have to look at another raindrop for a while.

I had awakened sometime in the night to find Kate and the cat curled together at the foot of my bed, with Webster stretched out on the floor next to us all.

I had considered getting up and showering, but the next time I opened my eyes it was morning, and all my visitors had deserted me.

Kate and Terry were currently arguing over the pancake recipe, and I was waiting for those fat pain pills to work their magic. Their main dispute was apparently whether whole-wheat flour would produce light enough results.

"You'll never win, Terry," I said. "If you marry Kate, reconcile yourself to brown rice at the wedding ceremony, too."

There was a loud knock at the back door, and Webster growled in response.

"Aren't you brave when the person has so clearly announced their presence?" I attempted to stand, but discovered my muscles had another idea. If I thought I was hurting yesterday before slamming a softball-size bruise onto my hip and wading through that monsoon, I had no idea what pain was about.

Kate took pity on me and answered the door.

It was Jeff.

Kate greeted him with a hug, saying, "We owe you so much."

"I just mopped up. Abby did most of the dirty work." He pulled out the chair next to mine. "You almost look human this morning."

"Almost?" I said.

"Hey, that's a compliment," he said.

Kate and Terry, meanwhile, had resumed their squabble.

"Could we pass on the difficult decisions?" I asked. "Unless you'd like semi-whole-wheat griddle cakes, Jeff?"

"Those two doughnuts I ate an hour ago will carry me until dinner," he said.

Kate said, "Do you realize the calorie count of one doughnut equals —"

"Six pieces of toast with jelly," I finished.

"Ask me if I care," he said.

"A man after my own heart," I replied.

"I will have coffee, though," said Jeff.

Terry poured two cups and joined us at the table, followed by Kate, who carried the compromise plate of melon slices.

She said, "Abby's been mum, saying she wanted to wait until you arrived, Jeff. So don't keep us in the dark any longer. We want details."

I said, "As I recall from our conversation last night, Jeff, you were saying how you followed Steven to Galveston. And that's the last thing I remember."

"Right," said Jeff, "I'd been investigating the finances of anyone potentially involved in Ben's death. Trouble was, I made an incorrect assumption that set me back a few days."

"You mean your assumption that Ben

had killed Cloris?" said Terry.

"No. I agreed with Abby that Ben probably didn't kill his wife. I'd turned my focus to Willis and Caroline, figuring they had the opportunity to tamper with the roses. And then there was Steven, who hung around here even in the middle of the night."

"So you suspected Steven from the first?" asked Kate.

"Along with the aunt and the lawyer. You see, banks won't talk about their customers unless they're persuaded by a federal judge that it's in their best interest to cooperate, so I wasted a fair amount of time obtaining Caroline's bank records first. Your father paid her regularly. So regularly, for so long, she probably lost out when your father died. Willis's finances seemed straightforward enough, but Steven? Active accounts. Very active. He made so many deposits and withdrawals I had to take a closer look." He sipped at his coffee, then took out his Big Red and offered it around, without takers.

Terry said, "So what put you onto Steven, Abby?"

"When Kate said she lent Steven the CD, I went looking for it." I explained what happened after I left Steven's office.

"So that's when you pegged him as the killer?" asked Kate.

"Of course not. Like the fool I've been since the moment I laid eyes on that man, I didn't want to believe the worst about Steven, only the semiworst. So I went to Feldman's house, still thinking Feldman did both killings. Once I arrived at his place, I found Helen Hamilton frantically gathering her belongings and Feldman missing. Hamilton told me his disappearance was a pretty darn ominous development, since he had this weird complex. She said he never left the house — that he hadn't been outside in years."

"It's called agoraphobia," said Terry.

"State trooper picked her up, by the way," said Jeff. "She confessed to pocketing more money than Texas allows for these adoptions."

"She may not have known everything about Feldman and Steven," I said, "but she knew enough to run. Something's been bugging me, Jeff. Why did Steven go to his office instead of coming straight to P Street with the body?"

"You know those miniwarehouses by his office?" he said.

"Sure," I said.

"He rents a space there. He loaded a couple bags of cement and headed back to P Street. Cement. Now that concerned me, so I followed him."

"Cement?" said Kate, looking puzzled.

I shuddered. "You know, that handy body-sinking stuff."

"But if he planned on killing Feldman, why not bring the cement with him when he went to Feldman's house in the first place?" asked Terry.

"He swore to the Galveston cops that Feldman's death was accidental," said Jeff. "Which may be true. We found evidence Feldman hit his head on a coffee table. Anyway, Steven needed to dispose of the body and went back for the cement."

"He mentioned it was an accident," I said. "But don't count on me testifying on his behalf. I have another question, Jeff. What made you take a boat ride down to P Street during a flash flood?"

"I told you in the car last night, but I guess you were already asleep. Kate called you at the Victorian and got no answer."

"That's right! The phone rang right before the lights went out," I said.

"When you didn't answer, I called the Galveston police," Kate said.

"And I was at the station waiting out the storm," said Jeff. "I planned on picking up Steven's tail after the rain let up, since that cement had me real agitated. When Kate's call came in, an islander offered his pontoon boat. He already had it gassed up, ready to rescue anyone stranded by the storm. The rest is history."

But my memories of last night wouldn't fade into history anytime soon. "Do you have enough evidence to convict?"

Jeff smiled. "More than enough, since he's confessed. I think it's safe to give you this." He removed a CD from his inside sports-coat pocket and slid it across the table.

"Where did you find this?"

"In Steven's truck," he answered.

"Thank you," I said quietly.

Jeff stood. "I'm headed back to work, if that wraps this up." He focused on me. "Rest up, Abby. I'm off tomorrow and we've got plans."

"We do?"

He nodded.

"Okay. Maybe then I can properly thank you for putting up with my behavior." I turned to Terry and Kate. "And I'm glad the two of you are still speaking to me after all I've put you through." At least there were a few people left in the world I could still count on.

Later that morning, I sat in front of the

computer monitor with Kate behind me. Daddy's version of what had happened in the last thirty years resided in a Word file listed right in the help index — a place I'd failed to search the first time. The title? *Adoption.* Simple enough.

I printed out the file and we began to read his "Adoption Diary." Kate looked over my shoulder as we turned the pages. Most of what Daddy had recorded we now knew, but the CD did offer proof that Daddy, Elizabeth, and Willis all believed the adoption had been legal, until Cloris Grayson showed up years later.

His version supported much of what I had already learned, but did tie up one loose end. Feldman had apparently lied and told Daddy that when Cloris showed up looking for us, she only wanted money. He claimed she didn't want her children back. So Daddy gave Feldman a huge hunk of cash, supposedly to pay Cloris off. Only when Ben arrived three months ago did Daddy learn the truth. Feldman, of course, had kept the cash and silenced Cloris. The final page documented Steven's blackmail and how much this had angered Daddy.

He wrote, *Another problem has surfaced since I started combing creation for this reptile Feldman. Me and that lying, cheating ex-*

husband of Abby's are now connected at the hip — as in wallet — but only until I come clean with the girls. Then I'll cut Steven Bradley loose as quick as a roadrunner on a rattler.

I'm making sure this is in writing because the good Lord might decide all this will happen differently. So Abby and Kate, if you don't hear this directly from me, I have left this earth without finishing my job as your father and surely stand in hell with my hat in my hand.

That was all.

I put the last page facedown on the desk, and neither Kate nor I spoke for a moment.

I wanted to say I could forgive him. Maybe then this bitterness inside would find a way out. But instead I said, "He should have told us right away."

"He was afraid," said Kate.

"But we missed out on knowing our mother, and she ached her whole life for us . . . died young because of Daddy."

"But he didn't know she wanted us. How can we blame him if he didn't know?"

"Maybe you've got a point," I said, not sounding convinced.

"I know you're angry, but I'm not sorry I spent a good part of my life with Charlie Rose. I only wish he were here right now," she said.

I looked back over my shoulder at her and

saw tears had welled.

"Because you miss him?" I said, putting my hand over the one of hers resting on the chair back.

"No, so I could forgive him. Then maybe he could rest in peace."

31

"No one ever got bit by a dog's shadow," I said to Jeff as we headed to Galveston. "But that doesn't mean I want to visit that house again. Ever. Can't we just stop at Landry's and eat crab and shrimp until we pop?"

"Nope. Not yet." And that was all Jeff said until we pulled up in front of the Victorian.

He started to get out of the car, but I didn't move. "I see no reason to revisit this crime, literally or figuratively. I'd rather have a realtor assess what the place needs, and hire someone to fix the damage. I want this house out of my life."

"That's why I brought you here. Don't you see that Steven has control, even from his jail cell? This place is worth saving, Abby, and you had plans to make it something special."

"Every time I come here I'll remember tumbling from the second floor, sharing space with a wrapped-up corpse in a closet, and —"

"We're going in."

He got out of the car and was up on the

porch before I could argue further, so I followed.

Crime-scene tape tied to the doorknob fluttered in the breeze.

I unlocked the door and stepped back, still reluctant. Jeff, however, had no qualms, and disappeared inside.

"Come on in here and tell me about this room," he called from the parlor. "How would you fix it up?"

I trudged in after him, knowing he was right. This was nothing more than an old house. Feldman's corpse was long gone. And Steven's betrayal wasn't written on the wall. Daddy's deceit wasn't hiding in the corner, either. Willis's and Aunt Caroline's lies weren't lurking behind a closed door. Those painful reminders were still inside my head, where they would always be. Maybe someday they could be filtered by a more reasonable voice, but for now the pain was as fresh as it needed to be. Running from the truth, avoiding this house because I didn't want to deal with the pain, wouldn't change anything.

So after I showed Jeff around downstairs, I said, "Want to see the upstairs mess?"

"Sure," he said.

His hand rested protectively on my back as we climbed, and his touch felt strong and right. Once on the landing, he pulled back the plastic sheet covering the destroyed bathroom.

Nothing had changed. Nothing except my whole life.

"I'm still selling the place," I said, "but I'm glad you made me come here. I need to stop feeling sorry for myself. I've been roaming through life without knowing what trail to follow. But I have a good idea the direction I should take now."

"Am I supposed to guess?"

"You may think this sounds stupid, but I want to help people find their pasts. Adopted people like Kate and me, people who have twists and turns in their childhoods they may know little about."

"An adoption detective?"

"Yeah," I said, smiling. "And I've got relatives I know nothing about. My inquiry to the adoption registry came back today, and no one ever registered looking for Kate and me. But we may have a father who's still alive and one day I plan to find him."

"Good. Investigating is well suited to your whirling-dervish personality," he said.

"Whirling dervish?" I replied. "Is that sort of like a tropical storm?"

"You could say that."

I peered past the plastic covering the door

and saw pecan trees in the backyard, their lush green leaves bright against an unclouded azure sky.

"Let's talk about other things now," I said. "For instance, how much I like you, Sergeant Kline. I even liked you before you saved my life." I smiled and outlined his lips with the tip of my finger, then traced the angle of his jaw.

"You know damn well I didn't save your life." He pulled me to him. "You had things under control before I arrived in that boat."

I grinned up at him. "Remember how you promised we could get to the personal stuff?" I leaned into him, draping my arms over his shoulders.

"You're a piece of work, you know that?" he said softly. He took a wrapper from his pocket and emptied his gum into it, then took my face in his strong hands.

His mouth met mine, and I remember thinking how I had always favored cinnamon, but never more than at that moment.

About the Author

Leann Sweeney was born and raised in Niagara Falls and educated at St. Joseph's Hospital and Lemoyne College in Syracuse, New York. She also has a degree in behavioral science from the University of Houston and worked in psychiatry. Currently a school nurse, she has been writing in the mystery genre for many years. Leann is married with two grown children and has lived in Texas for most of her adult life. She resides in Friendswood with husband, Mike, three cats, and a geriatric dog.

The employees of Thorndike Press hope you have enjoyed this Large Print book. All our Thorndike and Wheeler Large Print titles are designed for easy reading, and all our books are made to last. Other Thorndike Press Large Print books are available at your library, through selected bookstores, or directly from us.

For information about titles, please call:

(800) 223-1244

or visit our Web site at:

www.gale.com/thorndike
www.gale.com/wheeler

To share your comments, please write:

Publisher
Thorndike Press
295 Kennedy Memorial Drive
Waterville, ME   04901